SECOND TIME'S THE CHARM

SECOND TIME'S THE CHARM

STEPHANIE ROSE

That's What She Said Publishing, Inc.

Cover Design: Najla Qamber Designs

Cover Photo: © Shutterstock

Editing: Lisa Hollett—Silently Correcting Your Grammar

Proofreading: Jodi Duggan

ISBN: 979-8-88643-945-8 (ebook)

ISBN: 979-8-88643-946-5 (paperback)

042224

For MaryAnn,

You always said that your "beautiful Elizabeth could do anything," and I never leaned into that harder than while I was writing this book. Your belief in me, even if I can't see you anymore, helped me create something I'm very proud of.

I could see your beautiful smile and hear you say, "Like there was ever any doubt."
(Oh, Mare, there was...)

We love and miss you more than you could ever know.

When the sun shines its brightest, I know it's because of your light from the other side.

PROLOGUE
EMILY

Twenty years ago

"A WHOLE HOUSE TO YOURSELF AND YOU WANT TO GO OUT? What a waste," Sabrina sighed in my ear as I tried to balance the phone in the crook of my neck as I dressed.

"My mother reminded me a million times that if I needed anything while she was at Aunt Mary's until tomorrow, she asked the neighbors to keep an eye on me. The sight of Jesse's car in my driveway overnight would be reported back to her before we even woke up." I plopped onto my bed after buttoning my jean shorts. "*You're* the one who likes to take risks."

"Caden's parents don't care. They wave at us when we head upstairs to his bedroom and never give us shit for closing the door."

"You know you guys are playing with fire, right?"

"No, we're not. We're friends who, when we're unattached, become extra friends. No harm, no foul."

"*Extra* friends. Is that what you're calling it now?"

When our best friends would hook up with each other

1

at random, Jesse and I tried to mind our own business, even when an ex-girlfriend of Caden's would wait for Sabrina after school to call her a whore, or when the last guy Sabrina dated had to be held back in the cafeteria from shoving his fist into Caden's face.

I'd hoped they'd become a little smarter about their dangerous arrangement now that we'd graduated. Either they'd stop this and get together for real or, at the very least, stay under the radar from angry exes now as they would be attending colleges in different states.

"How are you and Jesse going to function this fall? After four years of being attached at the hip, you'll be six hours away from each other."

"I'm trying not to think about it. And Jesse doesn't seem worried, so I'm following his lead for now."

Graduation had only been two weeks ago, and I was giving myself until July to stay in denial and not freak out. *We'll be okay* is all I'd kept repeating to myself since I'd accepted my full soccer scholarship to a university in Maine. I'd tried to get into schools that were closer, but no other school had given me a full ride.

I'd be loan-free, as my mother kept insisting, and she'd barely had the money for my Catholic high school tuition. There was no way she could finance a four-year college, even with a partial scholarship and financial aid.

After my parents divorced when I was three, we'd moved in with my grandparents to save on rent and for a free, round-the-clock babysitter when my mother had to work late. My father was nothing but a fuzzy memory, never sending a birthday card, much less a child support check. Soccer was the only treat my single mother could afford. And once it became apparent it was something I could excel in, my mother had pushed me to make it my path into college.

Once all the acceptances had come in, there'd been only one choice. Plus, this school was known for its soccer team and boasted of students who'd gone on to play professionally. I'd been working up to this all through high school, maybe even most of my life, as I'd played soccer since I was seven years old.

I couldn't say no, even if the act of enrolling didn't give way to even the tiniest bit of excitement. Dread hung low in my stomach like a growing brick, weighing on me every time I allowed myself to think of what would happen to Jesse and me this fall.

"And this is why I told you not to date the same guy for all four years of high school. A little variety and distance maybe would have prevented you from being such a sad sack this summer."

"I'm not a sad sack," I fired back, straightening as I sat on the edge of my bed.

"No," she said, a little sympathy in her audible sigh. "But I know you. You're heading there."

I let out a long exhale through my nostrils as Sabrina's words heated my blood. No one understood why I'd been with no one but Jesse, but they didn't have to.

My soccer coach in elementary school had told my mother and me that if I wanted to get a sports scholarship, St. Kate's had the top-ranked high school soccer team in the league and would be my best chance. Once my mother had sorted out what bus I could take to school, it was settled.

I'd arrived that first day of freshman year after getting up at the crack of dawn to travel forty minutes and get to school on time. I'd crouched at my desk after I'd walked into class, not knowing one single soul and feeling more alone in that crowded classroom than I'd felt in my entire life. My friend Penny from my elementary school soccer team had enrolled at St. Kate's too, but we had no classes together that first semester.

I remembered watching all the classmates I didn't know and wondering what it was like to have choices and options.

That hadn't changed much in four years, if at all.

Then a beautiful boy had come down the tight aisle next to my desk. He was tall and lanky, his blue-plaid tie swinging back and forth as he'd maneuvered his gigantic backpack. With one quick turn, he'd knocked my pencils and books off my desk, meeting my gaze with a horrified look before he fell to his knees to pick everything up.

For the first time that morning, I'd crawled out of my own pity party and had felt terrible for this poor kid who had only been trying to find a seat. After panicking over almost missing my stop for the last twenty minutes of my bus ride and still shaking off the nerves, I'd related more than I could have expressed.

"I'm so sorry," he'd said in a surprisingly deep voice, a much lower octave than I'd expected from his baby face and lips. His eyes were a light chocolate, warm and bottomless at the same time, as he'd given me an apologetic wince.

"It's all good. The aisles are so narrow, I almost fell over trying to sit." I'd tried to joke as I'd grabbed at the pencils along the carpet. Our fingertips had brushed reaching for the same one, sending an unfamiliar zing of electricity up my arm.

"I'm Jesse," he'd said after his jaw had relaxed enough to give me a genuine smile.

"I'm Emily." My reply was gravelly as I tried to will the air back into my lungs.

From that day on, no other boy had given me a reason

for even a second glance. Friends never understood, all of our parents were concerned, but we'd never cared.

He was the bright spot of my every day from that moment on. He came to every soccer game, cheering so loudly, I'd hear him from wherever I was on the field, listened for hours when my mother's pushing would frustrate me to the point of tears, and starred in all my dreams about now and the future.

The only ones who needed to get us were us.

"I worry about you. All those romance novels warp your mind."

"They don't warp my mind. They keep me optimistic. All books are good like that. You should give one a try."

"You're a bookworm too adorable for this world, Em. Hey, I'm rooting for you both, but I'm just a little scared for you, if I'm being honest."

That made two of us.

"Maybe I don't have to go so far. Nothing wrong with community college until I figure things out, right?" A nervous laugh escaped me as I admitted out loud for the first time what I'd been contemplating for weeks.

My eyes clenched shut when Sabrina gasped.

"You *cannot* be serious. You busted your ass getting straight As and practicing every damn day, to give up a full scholarship and go to community college? That is fucking ridiculous. As your best friend, I won't let you do that."

"What are you going to do?" I taunted. "Come over and shake me?"

"No, I'll call your mother and tell her what you're planning to do."

I winced, picturing how my mother would totally lose it if she had any idea what I was considering.

"You're going to state college. What's the big deal?"

She groaned in my ear. "I was a B student and still have no clue what my major will be. You've had it all figured out since before I even met you. Maybe you're the smarter one of us, but I won't let you be stupid and throw your future away for a guy. Even if it is Jesse."

My eyes fell on the large acceptance packet at the edge of my desk, detailing the terms of my full scholarship, including room and board. If I called the admissions office and said that I wasn't coming after all, they'd immediately give my scholarship to the next female soccer player on the long list. Maybe it was a crazy decision, but shouldn't at least one decision about my life be up to me, regardless of what my reasons were?

"It was just a thought," I lied as I headed downstairs, just as Jesse pulled up in front of my house. "Let me go. Jesse is here."

"Fine. But promise me you aren't going to do anything dumb."

"Aren't you heading to Caden's later after he breaks up with Corinne?"

"Look, fuck his brains out all summer if you want. I have no issue with that and even encourage it. Just don't give up your scholarship. At least think about it before you—"

"I'll think. I promise."

"Fine. I know I'm being a bitch to you right now, but it's because I love you."

I stared out my window as I waited for Jesse to get out of his father's old Corolla. As I peeked out the glass, a bad feeling settled into my gut. Jesse had shut off the engine but stayed in the driver's seat, tapping on the steering wheel as if he was either agitated or nervous.

"I know that. And I love you too. Let me go, I'll talk to you later."

I hung up and opened my door to head to where Jesse was parked. His head jerked to mine when he noticed me, but he didn't flash me that slow, dirty smile. Instead, he stepped out of the car and slammed the door as if he was bracing for a fight.

"Is everything okay? Why do you look so tense?"

His features were tight, his brown brows knit together when I clasped the back of his clammy neck. He bored his eyes into mine for a long minute but jerked away when I tried to kiss him.

"Okay, what the hell is going on? Tell me what happened. Are you all right?"

"I'm fine," he snapped back. "We need to talk."

"Well, come inside—"

"We need to end this. Now."

"Wait, what?" I said, my voice quivering as panic filtered through me. I had just spoken to Jesse two hours ago, and he'd been fine—teasing me about what kind of panties I was wearing tonight and telling me to wear shorts loose enough for him to slip his hand inside.

We'd only been having sex for the past month, after about a year of doing everything but, and he loved exploring my body with his hands and mouth every chance he got. I'd get choked up whenever he'd say he wanted to "savor me" for the summer with a wistful gleam in his eyes, but he'd never given me any indication of wanting to break up.

Something was off.

What could have happened in the past few hours that now he couldn't even stand to be next to me?

"A clean break. Now. It's for the best. You live your life, and I'll live mine. We've already dragged this out long enough."

His jaw was tight as his eyes darted everywhere. He'd

look at me for a second before turning away, as if it caused him pain to look me in the eye.

"Dragged this out?" I felt my eyes widen as I stepped directly in front of him, so he'd have nowhere else to look. "What is this about? Where is this coming from?"

"Where is this coming from? You can't be that naive, Em."

He raked a hand through his dark hair, disheveled enough to look like he'd been sifting through it for hours.

"You're going to school six hours away. We'll never see each other. That's not a relationship. We need a clean break."

"So you've said," I spat out, crossing my arms over my chest. "But you can't mean that."

"I do! Go to Maine, play soccer, and have a nice life, while I figure out what the hell to do with mine."

Jesse was going to major in IT at a school on Long Island. He didn't know exactly what he wanted to do, but he'd been a computer geek from the day I'd met him. I knew he'd do something with technology and be great.

I also knew he loved me, but now I wasn't sure—about him or anything else.

"Just come inside, and we can talk about this."

"No. Even that's too much," he muttered, more to himself than to me. "I need to go." His eyes were glossy when he lifted his head. "I *have* to go."

I swore his voice cracked as something I couldn't identify flitted across his face. Anger, resentment, devastation, or maybe that was just the swirl of emotions racing through *me*.

"No, you don't," I whispered, wanting to bring him into my arms but afraid to touch him at the same time. He stuffed his hands into his jean pockets, his biceps shaking as tension radiated off him in waves.

He backed away, slowly for the first few steps, and then almost sprinted to his car, jumping in and peeling away from the curb. The screech of the tires ripped through me, shock the only thing keeping me upright.

How stupid was I? How stupid had I almost been?

I shook my head as tears dripped down my cheeks.

I had been planning my life around someone who'd just thrown me and us away without even a kiss goodbye. Ten minutes ago, I would have given up everything just to stay close, but now, six hours away wasn't nearly far enough.

1

EMILY
PRESENT

"This is the saddest thing. Why did we come here again?"

I turned my head at Sabrina's huff as we headed into the catering hall.

"Because when we got the invitations, you said, 'What the hell, let's go and see what everyone looks like.'"

She huffed at me as we navigated through the long hallways, past all the gowns and suits from the different parties that were being held here tonight, and followed the signs to the St. Kate's twentieth high school reunion.

"You couldn't have pointed out what a bad idea it was?"

"I believe I said, 'Really, you want to go?'" I tapped my chin. "And you said, 'Sure, it's just one night.'"

"As my best friend, you're supposed to shut me down when I suggest stupid things like this. This sad night is all your fault."

"Well, we're here now. May as well make the best of it," I said, studying the men in front of us. From a quick glimpse of their profiles, I had no clue who they were. Granted, I hadn't seen anyone from high school in a long time, but I'd figured whoever we'd run into tonight would at least look a little familiar.

"Maybe if they didn't have it in the same place as our prom. There's such a thing as too much nostalgia. And who the hell are they?" she whispered and jutted her chin to the men now signing in. "Did they even go here?"

"Why would you sneak into someone else's high school reunion?" I told her while still scrutinizing their faces.

Yep, no clue who they were—then or now.

"Easy hookup. Make up memories and then have a one-nighter for fake old times' sake," Sabrina said as she watched the tallest one stride into the reunion room. "I could pretend I knew him from high school if he wanted me to."

"That sounded like a very thought-out answer."

"It has to be better than swiping on the app, and hooking up now with someone from high school means no pesky aftermath. No rumors at school on Monday about what we did or didn't do. Could be fun." Sabrina tapped my arm as her gaze followed our possibly fake former classmates.

"Having the same boyfriend for all four years limited my high school experience, I guess," I mused as I scanned the registration table for our place cards.

"I told you that a million times, but you never listened to me. It was all Jesse, all the time." She pressed a dramatic hand to her chest.

"I was young and stupid and in love. I didn't listen to anyone else either."

"Now, wait a minute," Sabrina said, leaning over me to snatch one of the table cards. "This boring night may have just gotten interesting." She turned it around to show me the name. "Speaking of, check this out."

Jesse Evans. The name of the boy I'd loved for four straight years. The one who'd taken all my firsts and thrown them back at me when he'd ripped my heart to shreds only two weeks after graduation.

I slipped it out of her fingers, staring at the smeared blue cursive for a long minute before putting it back on the table.

"He's here. So what? He graduated with us, so this isn't a plot twist."

"But the last time we snooped for old classmates on Facebook, he was living in Seattle, remember? I can't see anyone flying in for this thing—" she grimaced as her eyes darted around the room "—so he must be back. Or within drivable distance anyway."

"I flew in for my college reunion, mostly because I didn't want to make the long drive, but a lot of my friends came in from all over the country. I'm sure people do that for high school reunions too."

Like Sabrina, I'd thought—and hoped—Jesse wouldn't be here since he'd lived across the country. I'd managed to forget about him possibly showing up until my stomach plummeted at the sight of his name.

"And if he's here, he's here. It's not like we're anything to each other anymore."

Even though I'd fought hard to push him out of my consciousness back then, his memory now crystallized all too easily and quickly in my brain. The big, dark eyes against his olive skin, the long lashes a boy shouldn't have had the right to have, and the broad shoulders that always made my heart kick up when I'd noticed him from the back in the hallways.

"But you're still pissed at him."

I finally spotted our names and scooped up our place cards.

"Why would I be pissed? It was twenty years ago." I stuffed Sabrina's card into her palm. "We're at table seven. Let's get settled and find the open bar."

I scanned the room, spotting the number 7 at the table right in front of the bar.

"Now, this is good placement," Sabrina said, tossing her purse onto the table and shrugging off her light jacket. "And broken hearts don't have time limits. It's understandable to be nervous about seeing him again."

"I'm not nervous. I'm...uneasy." I lifted a shoulder and took the seat next to Sabrina. "And it's stupid to be *uneasy* about seeing my high school boyfriend."

"Not stupid. You guys were close, closer than I ever got to a guy in high school." She snickered and reached for the bottle of wine in the middle of the table. "Maybe if you were in love and happily committed to someone, seeing the boy who broke your heart in high school wouldn't bother you as much."

"It doesn't bother me." I peeked at the entrance, trailing the new crowd coming into the room.

"But you're looking for him, aren't you?"

"You know, having fun at your best friend's expense is mean," I teased.

"I'm not having fun at your expense, but it does make the night slightly more exciting. And honestly, in your line of work, you should know that time means nothing to a broken heart," she said, raising her brow as she sipped from her glass. "Wow, this tastes like shit."

"Most table wines at catering halls do." I twisted the glass stem back and forth between my fingers. "And I'm an editor. I don't write love stories, at least not that often. I fix them to make sure they make sense."

"You need to know what makes a good story in order to

fix them, and you were always a hopeless romantic. Another reason why all the first-love memories may be throwing you a little."

"I edit all genres, not just romance."

With the travel back and forth to grueling games all over the country during college, I'd lost whatever interest I'd once had in pursuing a lifelong career in sports, but books had remained my solace whenever life became stressful or upsetting.

It was a cheap and convenient defense mechanism I'd learned as a kid with a working single mother who could only afford the bare minimum.

My full sports scholarship ended up financing a degree in communications and English, and now, I read for a living.

While, yes, I still enjoyed reading romance and allowed myself to get lost in a story, after my engagement had imploded a few years ago when we were just months away from the wedding, I'd filed true love under fiction, just like the dragons in the paranormal novel I'd edited last week.

The irony of helping to craft perfect happily ever afters when I couldn't figure out one for myself was not lost on me.

"Again, he was your first love. It's hard to forget that magic, you know?" Her smile was wistful as she lifted a shoulder. "All that sloppy passion mixed in with raging hormones. It warps your mind."

I ignored Sabrina and picked up the program on the table, flipping through until I found my soccer team championship photo. In it, I beamed at the camera, my rosy cheeks obvious even in the black-and-white image. I could still feel the clueless and pure happiness radiating from me.

"What's that? A yearbook?" Sabrina's brows drew together as she glanced over my shoulder.

"Sort of. It looks like someone just pieced together photos from senior year."

"Oh good, a refresher." Sabrina snatched the program from my hand. "Maybe if these shots have captions, we can figure out who some of these people are." She turned the program around, pointing to my soccer team picture. "Damn, girl, look at those quads."

I cracked up at Sabrina's whistle. "It was all those drills." I rubbed my thigh, remembering the pain accompanied by the bile rising in my throat when daily practice became torturous enough to want to throw up.

"Yeah. That's why I always told you to roll up your skirt more. I was jealous of your legs in high school. Not jealous enough to run back and forth after dismissal kicking a soccer ball, but still."

"They aren't bad now, though." I uncrossed my legs and stretched one out, circling my wedge-heeled foot.

"Yep. You still got it, my friend." She patted my knee and scrunched her nose at the cluster of men settling across the table. "I wonder how many weirdos are here that we forgot about in high school," she whispered.

"Nice to see you ladies," one of the men called out to us, raising a beer bottle in our direction.

I nodded back, sneaking a look at Sabrina. She closed her eyes and gave me a quick shake of her head.

"You played soccer, right?" The taller one leaned back in his chair, scrutinizing me as he ran his thumb along his bearded jaw. "Ellie?"

"Emily," I corrected. No, they weren't crashers, but I still couldn't place them.

"I'm sorry for being rude, but I can't place you."

He regarded me as if I'd just lapsed into a different language.

"Gage Sheridan. I guess you were so busy with soccer, you didn't go to any football games." He chuckled as his two sidekicks snickered next to him.

"No shit," Sabrina said, her jaw slack. "Sorry, but I didn't recognize you either."

Gage had been the high school quarterback, with the ego to match his massive shoulders. While I worked out to be healthy and liked to think I still looked good, I was nowhere near the stellar athletic shape I'd been in back in high school and college. Judging by the two-sizes-too-small suit he was sporting like a peacock, he lacked the awareness of who he was now, post-athlete life. I felt bad for the guy as the waistband of his pants appeared to be cutting off his circulation.

"I was busy with soccer and knew who you were then, but I would never have recognized you now." I shrugged, pursing my lips for effect. "Sorry."

"Maybe we can all get reacquainted?" The friend on his left quirked a brow at us. Once I pictured his shiny head with hair, I realized who he was. All three had been on the football team and wouldn't give the girls soccer team the time of day, even though we were the ones with the championship banners hanging in the gym.

I didn't hide my eye roll as I turned to Sabrina.

"Cocktail?"

"God, yes," Sabrina breathed out before popping out of her seat. "And we give this an hour before we get out of here," she whispered behind me.

"I'd like to eat the plate I paid for." I glowered back at Gage and his crew when I spotted them gawking at us. "We'll give it at least two hours."

"I can't believe this shitty turnout," Sabrina said after she ordered our drinks.

"They tried. I guess. Graduates move away or aren't interested. It's probably hard to get people to come."

"Or get people to care to come."

I shrugged. "Maybe reunions just suck in general."

"But the cocktails don't," Sabrina sputtered, setting the glass on the bar after her first sip. "Now that's a drink."

I eyed her over the rim as I sipped my gin and tonic, wincing after the initial burn rolled down my throat.

"It sure is. We're here, so let's make the best of it." I clinked my glass with Sabrina's. "To old times. May we push past them so we can have good ones."

Sabrina's smile was sad as she nodded.

"I will one thousand percent drink to that."

"Sabrina? I thought that was you!"

Our heads whipped around to a—finally—familiar voice.

"Caden! Holy shit, how are you?"

I stuffed a single in the bartender's tip jar as they embraced in a long hug. It took me back to the days I used to warn Sabrina about the weird friends-with-sometimes-benefits relationship they'd had, but watching them simply enjoy seeing each other again made me smile, despite the twinge of envy at their unburdened history.

I reached back to the bar for a napkin as they got reacquainted, but I didn't realize someone was standing right behind me and lost my footing. I tried to grab on to something for purchase but tripped, almost dropping my drink as I fell back into a hard, broad chest.

"I'm so sorry—"

I gazed into familiar chocolate eyes, now with a few more crinkles in the corners, as a slow grin split his full lips.

"Hey, Em."

2

JESSE

"Sorry about that," Emily said, breathless as she clutched my biceps. "I should have looked behind me before I backed up."

When I'd come here tonight, hoping to see Emily again and maybe finally getting to apologize for what I'd done all those years ago, the already beautiful girl I remembered paled in comparison to the gorgeous woman who'd fallen into my arms.

"No worries at all. I should have... I should have watched where I was going. You look...amazing," I breathed out, still regaining my balance from almost falling over and coming face-to-face with the first girl I'd ever loved. "Wow. I mean..." I let go of Emily's arm to press my palm against my forehead, my stupid attempt to maybe push something coherent out of my mouth.

"Thank you," Emily said. "And you don't look so bad yourself. Of course," she muttered as the corner of her red lips twitched. Her eyes fell to where I still gripped her arm. "I think I'm totally upright now, so you could let go."

"Right," I said, dropping my hand. Emily's beauty had

left me speechless and stupid from the moment we'd met, and I guessed that hadn't changed.

"Just like old times," Caden said, smirking at me over Emily's shoulder. "Give me a hug, J—Emily." He held out his arms, grimacing for a second. He'd always busted my chops by singing "Jessie's Girl" to Emily, so often that it had become his nickname for her.

The last time we were all together, she *was* my girl. It was a long time ago, but being here with Emily now, even though we'd broken up years ago, somehow made it feel like it had all just happened.

If I hadn't literally run into her tonight, I would have been clueless as to how to approach her. It was almost as if I'd been catapulted back to our freshman year of high school when we'd first met. I'd spotted her from the hallway, my eyes lingering on this beautiful girl and not where I was going when I'd knocked everything on her desk onto the floor.

She'd set me at ease with a kind and gorgeous smile, draining the air from my lungs because she was fucking breathtaking. I'd decided at that moment that she was mine, and she had been for all four years, until the thought of losing her had scared me shitless.

Maybe the initial devastation I'd felt as a stupid eighteen-year-old running on hormones and emotion had evolved over time to regret, but the burning need to apologize and confess that regret was palpable, even if it was pointless two decades later.

I'd always joked she was the jock in our relationship. All those hours playing soccer had given her a gorgeous body of lean muscle. I shook off the random memory of her strong legs wrapped around my waist, rocking me into her as we'd explored each other.

Her curves were softer now, but as she adjusted her purse on her arm, I noticed the cut of muscle in her bicep and the same sexy shoulders when she tucked a lock of chestnut hair behind her ear. When I allowed my eyes to drop lower, the hem of her black dress teased just enough of her toned thighs.

Fuck, she was gorgeous.

I'd known she would be, but I hadn't expected to get so goddamn tongue-tied in her presence.

"Nice to see you, Jesse," Sabrina said with a little wave. "We noticed your name on one of the cards."

I bit back a smile when Emily narrowed her eyes at Sabrina.

"Yeah, we got here a little late. Jesse's fault." Caden motioned to me. I nodded, not wanting to go into why I had to settle things at home before I went anywhere now. It was almost a relief to feel and think like a teenager tonight, as juggling grief and guilt on a daily basis as an adult was exhausting.

"You didn't miss much so far." Sabrina chuckled before taking another sip of her drink. "That's our table. Remember Gage Sheridan and his crew? The years haven't been too kind."

"Shit, for real," Caden said, craning his neck toward their table.

"And even though they wouldn't even make eye contact with us in school, they've been leering at us since we sat down," Emily said, her nose scrunched as she glanced behind her. "They asked us to get *reacquainted*."

"And that's a hard no," Sabrina said, her face twisted in disgust.

"How the mighty have fallen," Caden said, shaking his

head. "Our table seems to be empty. Why don't you sit with us?"

"I wouldn't mind that. Would make the night less awkward," Sabrina said.

"As long as you don't mind," Emily said. I searched her gaze for any reluctance, but she appeared not to care one way or the other.

"Not at all," I said, stepping in front of Emily on instinct to block their view when I caught the tools at their table still staring at them.

Hope bloomed inside my chest that maybe Emily didn't hate me as much as I'd always suspected she did. Or maybe everything that had happened between us was so long ago, it didn't matter to her anymore.

Instead of nervousness and guilt, embarrassment settled into a sour pit in my stomach. I'd carried what had happened between us with me for so long, when she might not have even cared anymore. And if she didn't, why did that make me feel even worse?

"Sabrina originally thought they snuck in here," Emily said as she took a seat at the end of the table next to Sabrina. "I didn't think so, because what is the allure of someone else's twenty-year high school reunion?"

"Seriously. I barely wanted to come." Sabrina shook her head and grimaced when she glanced back.

"Don't ask me." I held up my hands. "Caden was the one all excited to be here tonight." I settled into the chair next to Emily, ignoring Caden's smug grin in my periphery.

"Why not? I'm shallow enough to want to show all the jerk-offs we went to high school with that I, in fact, amounted to something. And I liked a few people enough to be curious about them now." He nudged Sabrina's shoulder.

"You always said the sweetest things," Sabrina said, clasping her hands under her chin.

"Will you look at this? The whole gang is still together."

Sharon Foster flashed us a saccharine smile, pulling out the empty chair next to me as if we were all old friends.

Our first familiar face of the night, other than Emily and Sabrina, but just like when I'd run into her back in high school, I wasn't all that happy to see her.

Sharon had been a big hit with the teachers because she'd known how to sell it. She came from money, and she had always been the first to volunteer or donate anything for the less fortunate. But when no one was watching, she'd pick who she'd felt was worth being nice to and made life as hard as she could for everyone else. I could never figure out how she had all the faculty snowed, or how Caden had tolerated dating her for a couple of months in senior year.

"It is so great to see all of you." She scooted closer to the table and hooked her purse over the back of her chair.

We all shared a look when she turned her head.

"You look great, Emily. Time was wonderful to you. I was very excited and proud to spot your name in the last book I read."

"Oh, thank you," Emily stammered, furrowing her brow. Sharon had ignored both of us throughout high school, but when she'd dated Caden, I'd been worthy of a hello once or twice. I'd never known what to do with her fake kindness back then either.

"Wait a minute," I said, my head snapping up as what Sharon said sank in. "You're a writer now? That's fantastic. I knew it."

"You knew it?" She narrowed her eyes at me. "How?"

"Well, I figured writer or soccer star—or maybe both?"

I caught a blush run up her cheeks.

23

"I'm an editor, not a writer. I loved playing soccer in college, but that's as far as I wanted to take it. I earned a communications degree while I played, and I worked at a big publishing house before I went on my own. I have ghost-written in the past, but not for a long time. Editing is where I like to live."

"That's pretty fantastic too," I said, my smile growing when her gaze slid back to mine. "Congratulations."

"I've spotted your name in a few books now," Sharon gushed, breaking what I thought was almost a nice moment between Emily and me. "It's so awesome to point out to friends and say how I knew you back when."

"Excuse me," Sabrina said, choking out an exaggerated cough as she set down her water glass. "Must have gone down the wrong way. Too bad you don't have any pictures with *your friend Emily* from high school to show the people who attend your seminars."

"Right," Sharon said with a tight smile, turning back to Emily. "I love seeing professional women start working for themselves. Such an empowering accomplishment."

"Thank you. I like to think so. Being able to work from anywhere makes everything much easier."

"Very true," I agreed. In my case, the ability to work from home wasn't only easier, it was a godsend. Being so afraid to leave my condo these days was part of the reason Caden had pushed me into this reunion, and my mother had been so quick to offer to spend the night.

"Oh, I'm so sorry," Sharon said as she popped up from the chair. "I need to go take my seat at the sponsors' table. Emily, I'll message you on Facebook." She scurried across the room, not addressing, or even looking back at, the rest of us.

"Was it something I said?" Sabrina pressed her hand to her chest. "Of course she's one of the sponsors."

Caden laughed as his gaze followed her departure. "She didn't even say hi."

"She barely looked at any of us. Other than calling us a *gang*, Emily was the only one lucky enough to get a direct acknowledgment." Sabrina smirked at Emily.

"And here I'd thought we'd had a thing," Caden said on an exaggerated sigh.

"What did you mean by seminars?" I asked Sabrina.

"You didn't hear about that?" Emily squinted at me. "Sharon is a motivational speaker. I think for the past ten years or so."

"Motivational speaker?" I chuckled. "Sharon? Motivation for what?"

"Living your best life, overcoming obstacles, loving yourself. She is *all* over YouTube. Emily and I trade video links all the time for sport," Sabrina said. "I actually wondered if she'd be nicer and if she really practices all that toxic positivity crap she preaches."

"Not me," Emily scoffed. "The idea of everyone deserving self-actualization is her platform rather than her belief, at least from what I can tell. But I guess if she's really helping some people live their best lives, no matter what her agenda is, it ends up for the greater good, right?"

Emily's smile was warm and genuine, showing none of the trepidation I had been called out for before I'd left my house tonight.

I was an odd mix of relieved and disappointed. Yes, it was great that she didn't seem to hate me. But it would be a big blow to my ego if I carried all this guilt over how we'd ended for a couple of decades and she hadn't even thought twice about it. Maybe she was married or attached and didn't have time to think of her jerk ex-boyfriend from high school.

"So, what do you do for a living? Now that we've talked about my *fame*," Emily joked and reached for one of the rolls in the bread basket. I inched closer to the table, trying not to be so obvious about checking out her ring finger as she picked up her butter knife.

"I'm a systems director for a company in Farmingdale. I can do most things from home, but I have to show my face in the office a couple times a month and take the train into Manhattan for quarterly meetings."

"Ah, of course." She nodded before taking a bite. "I figured it would be something like that."

"Well, I was the computer nerd, and you were the jock, remember?"

Her smile shrank as she chewed, darting her eyes away from mine for a moment. Maybe she did care a little. Whatever I'd just seen flash across her face made me feel better—or at least like less of a sad jerk.

Emily had always been so far out of my league, she was in another stratosphere. It still shocked me how, for a brief moment in time, she had belonged to me. Then adult complications got in the way of a simple love, and the frightened kid in me had panicked and run.

I finally had my chance to tell her why I'd run that night —and how I'd regretted it ever since.

3

EMILY

WHY COULDN'T JESSE JUST BE THE SAME JERK HE'D BEEN THE night he'd broken up with me? No, he had to show up as the sweet, adorable guy I'd fallen in love with as a teen. Except the boy had grown up into a man so gorgeous, the fight to stop looking at him gave me a headache from the eye strain.

While I didn't actively think about it, I remembered the night he'd broken up with me in too much detail. And because this was the first time I'd seen Jesse since then, it seemed like a million years ago and yesterday at the same time.

I couldn't find it in me to blame a lifetime of failed attempts at love on a high school breakup, but I'd wondered on and off over the years. We had been kids—ruled by feelings and hormones, as Sabrina had said—so to connect all my hang-ups to Jesse and still be mad at him for it was ridiculous.

Yet every time a smile would spread across that perfect mouth and light up his stupidly handsome face tonight, ridiculous or not, it pissed me off.

I'd always expected to run into him someday, but I'd

never seen him again. There had been no reason to be in each other's towns if we weren't together anymore, which had given me a much-needed buffer. Not worrying about running into Jesse made it easier to leave my house, not that I'd wanted to those first few weeks.

Sabrina had lived in the same town as Jesse, almost walking distance to St. Kate's, but she'd come to see me during holiday breaks from school and summers, or we'd meet halfway somewhere.

She'd never called me out for being the coward I was back then, and I still adored her for it.

Jesse had moved away, or so I'd seen on Facebook when I'd let weakness win and had looked him up a few years ago. The second I'd spotted that damn table card with Jesse's name on it, despite my best attempts to deny it to Sabrina, all I'd been able to think about was what it would be like to finally see each other again.

Now that I had, it wasn't so bad. Nice, even. That both relieved and annoyed me. Asking him why he'd run out of my life after all this time was pointless, yet the longer I sat at the table, making small talk with Jesse and Caden as I tried to ignore Sabrina's side-eye and smirk, the more the question burned in my brain.

"I swear, I still don't recognize half these people," Caden mused as his gaze swept over the dance floor.

"Maybe some are just plus-ones," I offered. It was nice to hear music that I knew most of the words to for a change, aside from in my car and at the grocery store. Sabrina had dragged me to the dance floor a couple of times, and while things weren't as tense between Jesse and me tonight as I'd expected they would be, a break from the table was welcome.

"Not that I have anyone to bring, but I couldn't see

bringing anyone here." Caden shook his head before he tipped back his beer bottle.

"Again, you're the one who suggested we come here," Jesse said as he narrowed his eyes at Caden.

"Because I was nosy, not excited to come. Two very different levels of motivation."

"And this is why we always got along." Sabrina tapped his arm. "So, what's your story for being without a plus-one?"

"Divorced." Caden shrugged. "It's been a couple of years. She got the house, so I'm living in town again. How about you?" He tipped his chin to Sabrina.

"Same. We never worked up to a house, so I guess that's a good thing." Sabrina's smile was always muted whenever she mentioned her divorce. It had been about a year since it was finalized, but the hurt would still flicker across her face whenever anyone would bring it up.

"It sucks. I'm sorry. Whoever he was, he was an asshole."

Sabrina laughed and bumped her shoulder against his.

"So was she."

"How about you, Emily?" Caden asked me. "Where is your plus-one tonight?"

Jesse's head whipped to mine in my periphery. The question, along with his eyes on me, triggered tension across my shoulder blades.

"Chronically single, so no plus-one. Although, I agree with you. I wouldn't bring anyone to a reunion I wasn't thrilled about attending myself."

"But you're successful enough for Sharon to want to have lunch with you. That's high school reunion glory right there," Caden joked as he pointed a finger at me.

"I suppose so," I said, a nervous chuckle slipping from my lips as I anticipated Jesse's answer. After a few long seconds, he didn't offer anything, and I wasn't about to ask.

"A few people are supposed to head to a bar after this," Caden said, lifting a shoulder. "Would you guys want to go? I figured we're all out anyway." He grimaced as he pushed his plate away. "And you're good for the night, right, Jess?"

Good for the night? When Jesse replied with a reluctant nod, my curiosity was piqued. What was going on at Jesse's home? Whatever it was, it was none of my business, and while I wanted to know, I didn't want to know at the same time. Keeping tonight superficial between us was fine and preferable.

"That sounds more fun than this," Sabrina said, craning her neck.

"You guys go. I think I've had enough reunion for the night." I stuffed my phone into my purse and stood to peel my jacket off the back of the chair.

"Then I'll take you home," Sabrina said, pushing away from the table. "I'm not letting you take a cab."

"Don't be silly." I waved a hand. "Go enjoy."

Tonight was the first time in a while that I'd heard a laugh from Sabrina that didn't seem forced. I didn't want her to put an end to a fun night with an old friend because of me, but I'd also had enough reminiscing and wanted to be alone to process it all.

"I can take you home," Jesse said, wrapping his hand around my arm. "I don't want you taking a cab either."

"I appreciate the offer, but no. It's out of your way."

"No, it's not."

My head snapped up to Jesse as his brown eyes bored into mine with a determination I didn't know what to do with.

"You don't know where I live. How do you know it's not out of your way?"

"How do you know it is?" Jesse lifted a brow, a smirk tipping his lips. "You don't mind getting a ride with Sabrina, do you?" he asked Caden.

"As long as she doesn't." Caden nodded to Sabrina. "I live not too far from where the bar is. I can walk home from there."

"That's fine. I'll take you and drive you home. I think this all sounds like a great idea."

I narrowed my eyes at her wry grin.

"Okay," I conceded. "It's silly, but yes, thank you for the ride."

Another smile split Jesse's perfect mouth, and the victory spreading over his features annoyed me as much as the warmth spreading through my chest.

"After you," Jesse said, extending his arm in front of me.

"Thanks." I gave him a tight smile as I strode past him, my skin prickling from his presence behind me. What the hell was wrong with me? I'd sat next to him for the night and managed to hold it together, but now that we were alone, I was antsy. Our history had been easier to ignore with Caden and Sabrina running interference.

"Would you mind if I made a quick phone call first? I'll just be a minute."

"Not at all. Do what you have to do."

I leaned my shoulder against the wall when Jesse stepped away, too curious about who he might have been speaking to with that big of a smile plastered to his face, when I was clobbered from behind with a hug.

"Sneaking out?"

I smiled at Penny's voice behind me. She'd spotted me on the dance floor, and I'd had every intention of seeking her out to catch up. Trying to appear aloof in front of Jesse had taken all my effort and brain cells for most of the night.

"Are you heading to the bar too?"

I shook my head while my gaze veered to Jesse. His smile deepened, happy to hear the voice of whoever was on the other end. That smile used to be mine once upon a time, but it had belonged to the boy, not the man.

"No. But now that I live back on Long Island, how about a nice download over dinner one night?" I suggested, trying to will my eyes to focus on her and not watch the one-sided conversation behind me.

"That sounds fantastic. Yes, lots to catch up on."

She brought me in for another quick, tight hug.

"I'll let you get back to..." She glanced over my shoulder, scurrying away before I could set her straight that Jesse was just my ride home.

"I promise I'm okay."

I pretended to pick an imaginary piece of lint off my dress as I fought hard to ignore Jesse's deep chuckle. "You don't have to worry about me. I'm fine. And I think it's a little past your bedtime, young lady, even if it is the summer. I'm surprised you conned Grams into letting you stay up this late."

Jesse had a kid. A little girl. I'd bet he was a great dad too. Judging by the love written all over his face, he adored his daughter. I was happy for him, if a little sad for me. I'd always wanted kids, but nothing had ever worked out. I'd been looking into other ways to go about it, but as I was nearing my thirty-ninth birthday, I needed to figure out what I wanted to do soon.

The pang in my chest from eavesdropping on Jesse and his daughter was enough to tip the scales for the moment.

I turned, fighting to keep my eyes straight ahead and not intrude on a conversation that was none of my business.

"I'm parked on the side street," Jesse said, coming up behind me and almost making me jump. "We can just get right in and not wait around for valet." He pointed to the already long line by the entrance as we headed out.

"They tried, I guess," Jesse said, smiling as he clicked the key fob in his hand. A midsize SUV parked on the corner chirped in response.

"They did. I remember us saying the same thing when they had the prom here."

Jesse rushed in front of me to open the passenger side door.

"Well, prom was more fun. For a lot of reasons."

The only light on the street was the lamp on the corner, but I saw something in his eyes as they held mine. I spied equal parts heat and regret. Could nostalgia be kicking his ass a little bit tonight too?

"I suppose," I said. It was a wimpy reply, but it was all I could muster as I shifted to climb into his truck.

"We could stop at the diner on the way home if you're up for it."

I stilled at his invitation. I didn't want to be rude, but at the same time, I wasn't sure how much one-on-one time I wanted with Jesse tonight if the simple notion of a car ride home had me this jittery.

"Maybe they still have that carrot cake you used to like?"

I examined Jesse's face, annoyed at his easy grin.

"I think I heard that the Starlight Diner was under new management. I doubt the carrot cake is the same."

"Wouldn't hurt to try, would it?"

"That depends." I lifted my foot out of the car and

leaned against the back door. "How far down memory lane are you expecting to go?"

"I don't know." He shrugged, again with that damn smile. "A cup of coffee, a piece of cake, talking without our friends eyeballing our every move. Would that be so bad?"

"Maybe not," I said, crossing my arms as I darted my eyes away from Jesse and toward the street.

"Maybe not," he repeated, his deep chuckle so maddening and yet sexy at the same time. "I'll take that."

I should've told him just to take me straight home, but hadn't I wondered about Jesse enough over the years? Maybe I didn't owe him a cup of coffee and a talk, but I owed it to myself—even if the answer I'd always wondered about would hurt me all over again.

4

————

JESSE

"Your truck is really nice," Emily said as I pulled into the diner parking lot.

Every time I'd glanced her direction on the ride to the diner, she'd been focused on the back seat as if she was searching for something.

"Thank you. It's new, so I'm still getting used to all the features. The seats have their own heating and cooling if you want to try it out. One of the few things I've mastered," I joked, hoping I'd get at least a smile out of her, but her face was unreadable when I looked her way.

"Um, no. I'm fine," she said, her eyes once again wandering toward the back.

"Are you sure?"

"Why wouldn't I be sure?"

"Because for most of the drive here, you've been staring into the back seat, like you're looking for something or want to escape." I chuckled, but still nothing from Emily but a quick nod.

It hadn't exactly been comfortable sitting at the same table for the night, but we'd managed easy small talk. Now, her body was rigid with tension as her eyes darted every-where but in my direction.

Maybe being alone with me kicked up the awkwardness between us. God knew I was nervous. I'd imagined seeing Emily again a million times in a hundred different ways, but I'd never known what I'd say to her.

Tonight, now that she was finally here, I was going with the truth, however it came out of my mouth.

Emily stayed silent as we headed toward the diner entrance, only speaking to the hostess to ask for a table for two.

We slid into opposite sides of one of the vinyl booths, exactly as we had when we were kids. Emily and I had spent hours in this diner, talking about everything and nothing.

It was a big contrast to now, as she looked like she wanted to bolt, but since I was her ride home, I had her cornered—or cornered enough to hear what I had to say.

"So, do you still want just coffee and cake, or something else?"

"Did you really ask me here for just coffee and a piece of cake?" she asked, flinging the laminated menu onto the table.

"No," I said, setting the menu down. "I asked you here because I wanted a chance to explain how we..." I groaned, once again losing any coherent words when it came to Emily. "Why I did what I did that night."

"Explain," Emily said, narrowing her eyes. "Now?"

"I know it's been a really long time, but I've thought about that night—and about you—a lot over the years."

"You did?" She huffed out a laugh. "That's funny because I *never* heard from you again after that."

So, she did care—at least, enough to glower at me from across the table.

"Okay, fine." She crossed her arms and leaned back. "Explain or say whatever you brought me here to say."

I nodded, sucking in a deep breath before resting my elbows on the table.

"That night, before I got to your house, I was out with some of the guys, and they were talking about you."

"Talking about me?" Emily's brows drew together.

"Yes, talking about you. They *always* talked about you."

"They did? You never told me that. What did they say?"

I rolled my eyes. "A couple of them used to make stupid jokes about you being a star athlete, if you were that *limber* when we were alone."

Her brows popped up.

"Ew," she said, her face twisting with disgust. "That's gross."

"Tell me about it. I'd ignore it for the most part—or try to. But they'd always bring you up, like they couldn't believe how lucky I was to have you. I didn't disagree."

I caught an eye roll from her but kept going.

"We were talking about college, and they kept asking me what I was going to do when you became a big soccer star all those hours away, and did I really expect to stay together when every guy on your campus would want you?"

I waited for her reaction, any reaction. Her eyes were still thinned to slits and focused on me, but she said nothing.

"And I knew that. You were so goddamn beautiful and talented." I exhaled with a slow shake of my head. "But I guess I never really thought about what would happen to us until that night. Or I didn't let myself consider it, not really, until then."

I stretched my arm along the back of the seat, my eyes still on Emily's.

"One of them told a story about their older brother trying to have a long-distance relationship with his girl when she went away to school, and when he went up to visit her, he caught her with another guy. All I kept thinking was, how was I going to function with you all the way up there, wondering what you were doing?"

"So, you didn't trust me. Just because of what may or may not have happened to your friend's older brother?"

"Wasn't that I didn't trust you. Well, I guess maybe it was. You were the first girl I ever loved, and thinking of other guys leering at you or you finding someone else made me crazy. I was young, stupid, and scared. I was aware that I was losing you a little already, but that was when it really sank in."

The clench in Emily's jaw loosened a little as her eyes went glossy.

"I didn't know what was more awful, losing you there or losing you here. But I couldn't keep you. I figured that much. You worked your ass off for that scholarship. What could I do? Tell you to give it all up for me, your high school boyfriend who still didn't know for sure what his major was going to be?"

"You were more than just a high school boyfriend to me. How could you not know that?" Emily's voice was soft and small.

"I did, but I was too nuts over it all at that point to remember. I actually didn't drive to your house intending to break up with you. I wanted to talk and for you to tell me that it would all be fine, so we could forget about it for the rest of the summer. But then the more I drove, the angrier I became, until I decided to just do it. Get it all over with before it really hurt."

Emily's eyes bored into mine so hard I didn't catch her blink.

"Did you really think that night didn't hurt? Going from being happy and in love one day, to you telling me... What were your words?" She tapped her chin. "Right. That we should just end it now and move on with our lives. Then before I could figure out what to even say, you peeled out of my driveway and my life. You really thought that was the easier way?"

"Like I said, I was a kid. A stupid, stupid kid who loved a girl who was too good for him and it made him crazy."

"Jesse," Emily breathed out. "Come on."

"It's true. I still stand by that." I gave her a sad smile. "You were a straight A student who would have ended up with a scholarship, with or without soccer. You were smart. Beautiful. Fucking exceptional."

A smile ghosted my lips as I watched the now-stranger sitting across from me. I didn't know the woman she was, but I'd known the girl she used to be, as much as I could have known anyone.

What we'd had could have been dismissed as puppy love, but whenever I allowed myself to think back to that time, the love between us was real enough to be searing. I just hadn't known the extent of it until I saw her again—and too many years had passed to do anything about it.

I'd doubted myself on and off for how I'd ended it. And at the time, I'd wanted it to go on forever. Wanted *us* forever.

But it wasn't meant to be. No matter how old I became or how many reunions we'd run into each other at, that would always sting.

"You were destined for great things, and I didn't want to be the one to hold you back. Well, I did, but I couldn't."

"I don't understand. How would you have held me back?"

"You were already mapping out dates you could come home, an almost twelve-hour round trip, to see me. If you didn't have me to think about, you could, eventually, I hoped, relax and maybe enjoy it. You never had a second to relax and never really enjoyed high school."

"Who does?" she scoffed. "I only enjoyed high school with you."

"I know you did." That lost look in her eyes made me want to leap across the seat and draw her into my arms, however inappropriate now. "I enjoyed every second with you. But I thought breaking it off quickly would mean I wouldn't have to worry about who you were with every minute of the day and be dreading the moment you'd realize you could do so much better than me."

"And you didn't think I had the same feelings about leaving you? My biggest worry was that you'd forget me, and that night, you basically told me you wanted to forget me *and* us as soon as possible."

"Only because I felt like I had no choice. But regardless of the selfish and childish reasons why, or how much I hated it, looking back, I believe it was the right thing."

"Because I became a big soccer star?" She scoffed.

"So, you didn't make soccer your career. But I'm sure you loved playing in college."

She bobbed her head in a reluctant nod.

"If you'd had me at home to worry about, it wouldn't have been the same. Your focus wouldn't have been where it was supposed to be."

"Maybe not. But you took that choice away from me." She lifted her head, her jaw clenched again. "I loved you too. We could have figured something out."

"I really don't know if we could have. Not in the state of mind I was in anyway. I think what would have ended up happening was a lot of tears and a shit-ton of heartbreak. And even though I was an asshole about it, I still believe dragging it out would have been worse."

I searched her face for clues that maybe I was getting through before I continued.

"And look at you. You're successful. Whether or not you made it a career, you had the chance to play and travel all over the country. I've only been to, like, ten states. Maybe."

My joke fell flat as she averted her gaze from mine.

"But you wouldn't have held me back," she said in a soft whisper.

I shook my head. "You don't know that."

"*You* don't know that."

"I guess I don't," I conceded. "But I can't change what I did."

"But you didn't have to do it...like *that*." Her jaw tightened when her gaze came back to mine.

There was the fire I remembered. Emily would have fought for me. I knew that even back then, and it was a big reason why I hadn't stuck around to hear what she had to say. Running away like a scared little prick had been my way of being brave. I would have folded like a sad deck of cards had I allowed myself to stay and see how much I'd hurt her.

"No, I did," I coughed out a laugh. "I had to be a jerk about it. I needed it to stick and give you no room to talk me out of it because I loved you too much. It's as simple and as complex as that."

Emily chewed on her bottom lip but didn't try to argue with me. I hoped maybe that meant I was getting through, or at least making her understand a little.

"I loved you. And I never, ever wanted to hurt you." I

scooted closer to the edge of the booth. "I hate that I did. If it's any consolation, I was a wreck after I left and basically the rest of the summer. I broke my heart that night as much as I broke yours."

Her expression softened but still seemed pained. She swallowed, her eyes shining as they held mine.

"I hope someday you can believe me. But today, that's all I have."

"I'm sorry for the holdup."

We didn't break eye contact when the waitress came to our table.

"What can I get the both of you?"

"I'll have a cup of coffee, please," I muttered, still staring at Emily.

"I'll have a cup of coffee and a very big chunk of the carrot cake that I saw on the way over here." She pointed a finger at the glass case of desserts behind the counter.

"Sure," the waitress said, scribbling on her pad.

"Make that two," I said before the waitress walked off.

Our eyes locked for a long minute. Now that I wasn't afraid to be caught staring at her for too long, I had the chance to really appreciate how beautiful she was. Sitting across from her, I still felt like that lanky kid who only needed a minute to fall for the girl of his dreams.

Too bad he hadn't been able to keep her.

"So that's what I wanted to talk to you about. It was easier to do that without Caden and Sabrina and everyone we ran into tonight leering at us like we were zoo animals."

A little weight lifted off my chest when a tiny chuckle shook her shoulders.

"I don't expect you to forgive me. But whether you wanted to hear it or not, I needed to explain and at least try to make you understand. Even just a little." I pinched the air between my thumb and index finger.

"You know," Emily started as she unwrapped the paper napkin from around her knife and fork. "That day, I almost gave up my scholarship."

I fell back against the seat, my eyes wide.

"You're kidding me," I whispered.

"Oh yes," she said with a slow nod. "I had been researching how to apply to one of the local community colleges until I could get into a four-year school maybe the next semester. I hadn't filled out any applications for any schools other than the ones that I was trying to get a scholarship to."

She nodded a thank-you to the waitress after she set our cups of coffee on the table.

"Before you came to my house and told me that we were over and needed to move on with our lives, I was planning to call the admissions office and rescind my acceptance."

"Wow," I breathed out. "Your mother would have killed me. I escaped certain death that night."

A laugh bubbled out of her as she stirred cream into her coffee.

"Honestly, what you just told me? That *really* confirms that I did the right thing."

"Jesse," she said on a long sigh. "Again, I could have gotten a communications degree anywhere. I didn't pursue soccer—"

"But *again*, you had the option to. You went to a great school on a full ride. I ran because I was a jealous asshole, but I'd like to think staying out of your way helped give you a great future. I never wanted you to hate me, but I understand if you did."

"Here you go," the waitress sang as she set our cake

plates down in front of us. "This is my favorite, so it was a good choice. Enjoy," she said before leaving the table.

"Well, I don't know about you," Emily said as she picked up her fork. "But I have never needed a big slab of cake more than I do right now."

She sliced into the icing along the side and slid her fork into her mouth, my dick twitching when she let out a moan.

"I didn't hate you. Trust me, I tried." She bit into another mouthful of cake. "I would have given up everything to stay with you."

"So, maybe I was right?"

She glared at me and lifted a shoulder.

"Maybe you were a little right."

A tiny smile twitched at the corner of her mouth.

"I just wish you would have talked to me instead of yelling at me and driving away."

"I had to make it stick." I shrugged and picked up my fork.

"So you've said. We at least could have had one more night. Or a couple of weeks." She set down her fork and picked up her coffee.

"And what would a couple of weeks have done? I almost caved when you'd asked me to come inside. I wouldn't have been strong enough to resist more time with you if I had. I thought doing it early in the summer would give us a chance to...get used to it."

"Get used to it?" She arched a brow.

"I still missed you. I missed you for longer than I should probably tell you. But at least when you left, it wasn't so raw."

"Maybe for you. Did you think I just stopped thinking about you? That everything was erased about us after one night?"

"No, I didn't. At least, I hoped not. I was a little worried when you were too nice to me tonight."

"You're serious?" Emily squinted at me.

"While, like I said, I didn't want you to hate me, I wanted to think you missed me enough to be pissed at me. At least a little."

"So, what did you want me to do? Try to stab you with my butter knife when I saw you?"

"Maybe," I said, bunching my shoulders in an exaggerated shrug. "Would have been nice."

She dropped her fork onto the table and glared at me before she laughed.

"Yes," she said, an easy smile spreading her mouth as she tilted her head. "I missed you. A little."

For the first time tonight, the silence between us was comfortable and familiar as a deep relief washed over me.

"So now that that's sort of straightened out, tell me about yourself." I poured cream into my coffee. "What have you been doing since high school, other than becoming an editor successful enough that Sharon wants to have lunch with you?"

"Right?" Emily chuckled. "That's a big claim to fame, you know."

"For sure," I said, lost in her pretty gaze for a long minute before I tore my eyes away. I wanted to be friendly tonight, not flirty. I couldn't afford flirty, even if her beauty still distracted the shit out of me.

"I've been good. I lived in Manhattan for a long time when I worked for the publishing house, but then I went out on my own and did most of my work at home. I moved back when I couldn't justify the rent for the sake of a commute I didn't make anymore. Plus, I wanted to be closer to my mother."

"Is she okay?"

"She is. Slowed down with age, which is kind of hard to see, but she's holding her own. She found an apartment in an over-fifty community not too far from St. Kate's. It's just her and me, so I wanted to be closer and be able to visit more. But she's still exactly the same as you remember her."

"I am very glad to hear it."

"You are?" She laughed as she poured sugar into her coffee. "After all the shit she used to give you?"

"I liked that about her. She made me work for it, and I appreciated that. She knew that her daughter was special—and never *ever* let me forget it."

Another easy laugh slipped out of her. I hadn't needed any reminders to know how special Emily was, then or now.

"She probably really would have killed you had I given up my scholarship," Emily said around a mouthful of cake.

"And don't I know it," I said, the relief filtering through my veins relaxing me enough for an easy smile to coast across my mouth. The regret still clung to me like a shadow, but for additional reasons now.

Emily was halfway through her cake, and I'd hardly touched mine. After years of wondering about Emily, I wanted to take in every detail. The auburn highlights in her chestnut hair, her long lashes, her eyes that were even more beautiful when they crinkled at the corners.

She'd said *I* not *we* when she'd mentioned moving, and she'd said she was single when Caden pressed earlier tonight. But I couldn't help trying to clarify.

"And no boyfriend for a while, or husband or whatever?"

"Smooth, Jesse," she said, wiping her mouth with a napkin. "And no, none of those for a while. I might get a cat, though. Embrace that over-thirty single life."

I wanted to know everything about her now, and I didn't

want to stop at just tonight. And if things turned out differently, maybe I wouldn't have to. Feelings long buried had bubbled up, thanks to the memories that had bombarded me the second my eyes had landed on Emily again.

Memories screwed with you. They made you think that the past still lingered in the present.

I had enough to worry about in the present.

Her gaze landed on my phone, focusing on Maddie's picture on the screen. I had a feeling Emily had heard enough of my conversation before we'd left the reunion to assume whom I may have been speaking to. But she'd be wrong, and I didn't have the energy to correct her and explain.

Tonight had been filled with enough emotions and old heartbreak. It wasn't that I didn't want to tell her. In fact, in a weak moment during the worst of it all, I'd almost called her. She knew more than anyone how much Tessa had meant to me and would have understood how broken I'd been after losing her.

But after hurting Emily the way I had, no matter why I'd done it, I hadn't deserved her comfort then and felt wrong about seeking it now.

I'd done what I'd come here to do, and it was amazing to have Emily with me tonight for a little while, even though I still couldn't keep her.

———

"This was nice," Emily said as I pulled up in front of her house. "I'm glad you ambushed me on the way out."

"I wouldn't say ambush. That's a strong word. I more took advantage of an opportunity." I turned to her after I parked and unlocked the doors.

"You don't have to walk me to my door. I'm fine."

"Yes, I do. What kind of guy just drops a girl off to walk inside alone?"

"Um, you all through senior year."

"That was different. Thanks to all those long goodbyes, I couldn't get out for—" I flicked my eyes to my belt buckle "—reasons."

She swatted my arm before digging into her purse for her keys.

"But I always watched you to make sure you were safe."

Because I could never take my eyes off her. Not that first day we met, not when she was running up and down the soccer field, not all those times she was in my arms and I'd revel in how fucking lucky I was to have her. Maybe I had been memorizing her without realizing it, knowing she'd become my most painful and beautiful memory.

It was why I hadn't been able to look her in the eyes on the night I'd broken up with her. My resolve had been dangling by a thread, and all these years later, I could still feel how close I'd been to falling at her feet instead of speeding away from her as fast as I could.

Teasing my beautiful ex-girlfriend wasn't the worst offense.

As long as it stopped there.

"I wouldn't mind a cup of coffee once in a while. That cake was pretty good."

Her expectant gaze triggered that same inner turmoil demanding me to bring her closer, when stepping away was the only thing to do.

I stuffed my hands into my pockets and nodded.

"That could be nice," I said, not wanting to promise or commit, but I didn't have it in me to tell Emily no. I never had.

She shifted toward me after unlocking her door, pressing her hand to my chest and brushing her lips against my cheek.

Just like that, I was fourteen again and flexing my fingers into a fist to ward off the tingles down my arm.

She lingered for one glorious second before pulling back.

"Goodnight, Emily," I whispered as I pressed my lips to her temple. "Thank you."

She nodded and stepped inside. I waited until the lock clicked before heading to my truck, this time taking a moment to give her door one last look before I drove away.

5

JESSE

"DID YOU SEE A LOT OF YOUR FRIENDS LAST NIGHT?"

I smiled at Maddie's reflection in my rearview mirror. She looked so much like her mother. Sometimes it was a comfort and momentary balm to all the grief, and sometimes it was a gut punch, especially as the resemblance to my sister seemed to deepen each day.

She was only eight years old, but because she was so tall, she was often mistaken for ten or twelve. Despite her height, she was a young eight—affectionate and clingy—and we were all too happy to indulge her. Her legs would drag on the floor whenever she'd climb into my lap, but I'd never deny her the reassurance that we both needed.

"I did. Not as many as I thought I would, but it was fun to see how everyone changed."

"Kind of like when you go back to school after summer, and everyone looks different."

"Exactly. But this is after twenty summers, so everyone looked *really* different."

I reached back and squeezed her legging-covered knee until I pulled a giggle out of her.

"I thought maybe you were going on a date."

My eyes met hers in the rearview mirror.

"You did?" I said, recalling how she'd eyed me with suspicion as I'd slipped my feet into the black loafers I'd kept for special occasions—or any other time I couldn't show up in jeans and boots. "What made you jump to that conclusion?"

"You were dressed up." Maddie peered at me with the same big brown eyes as her mother had had and scrutinized me the same way. "And Grams said I couldn't stay up to wait for you."

"And all those clues told you that I had a date?" I asked, smiling until I spotted a frown pulling at her lips.

"Could've been a funeral too. You wore those shoes to church." Her voice was a quiet whisper as she dropped her chin to her chest.

As usual, my niece was an observant little girl. I'd worn those shoes the day we'd said goodbye to her mother and she'd officially come to live with me. She had always been on the shy and quiet side but took in every single thing around her. She'd even picked up on the tension in my embrace when she'd hugged me goodbye as I'd stressed over possibly seeing Emily later that night.

"No funerals or dates, kiddo. Just a long, boring night in a dining hall and dessert with an old friend after."

"Was dessert fun?" She perked up and leaned forward. "Where did you go?"

Her innocent question jabbed me in the chest. Dessert with my friend had been the most important part of the entire night, because it was the one part of the evening I couldn't stop thinking about.

"It was. We went to the diner for coffee and a piece of cake." I tried to sound flippant and casual, mostly for my own denial. My ex-girlfriend living rent-free in my brain, along with the feel of her lips on my cheek, had at least distracted me from the usual knots in my stomach today.

"I love diner cake." Her brown eyes lit up as a smile bloomed on her face. "And diner pancakes."

"Yes, I know you're a big diner fan," I said, forcing an easy smile as I pulled into the medical office's parking lot for Maddie's therapist. "Maybe we can stop there on the way back?"

I both dreaded and looked forward to this appointment. Her pediatrician had suggested therapy to help her grieve and adjust to all the changes in her life, and I'd gladly agreed, grabbing all the assistance we could get.

We'd done the best we could to prepare her, but we were all going through our own stages of denial and, later, mourning. Losing someone so important and upending life as we all knew it was a huge struggle for our entire family.

Maddie had been opening up more and more, but it would come in short spurts, like recognizing the shoes I wore to her mother's funeral or one heartbreaking night a couple of weeks ago when she'd asked how long I was going to let her stay with me. I'd told her that I wanted her to stay forever, but I had no way of knowing if that was the reassurance she'd needed or if it had made her feel worse.

My sister becoming a single mother at twenty had been a shock to all of us, but we'd all fallen hard and fast for her daughter. I'd had the easiest relationship with this kid from the day she was born, with nothing but love and fun between us.

All the love was still there, but the fun wasn't so easy now that the dynamic had changed. With Maddie's father out of the picture before she had even been born, Tessa had asked me to be Maddie's guardian "just in case." When just in case became a reality rather than an unlikely possibility, my sister had still insisted she wanted her daughter with me.

We were ten years apart, and while we'd argued at times, we had never been at each other's throats like my friends and their siblings. My parents used to joke that Tessa thought I'd hung the moon and would fight anyone who said otherwise, and my favorite part of coming home after school was hearing her squeal my name before she'd rush toward me.

I'd never refused my sister anything, in life or...now. But I'd never been so terrified of letting her down.

Going from uncle to full-time parent was the biggest adjustment of my life, but I did everything I could to make our new condo a home for Maddie. As comfortable as I tried to make her feel, I knew there were things she couldn't talk to me about—at least not yet.

"Who is this lady I have to talk to?" Maddie asked as I pulled my truck into a spot.

"She's a doctor." I unbuckled my seat belt and shifted to face her.

"Yeah, that's what Grams said. But I'm not sick." She rested her head against the inside of the car door.

I was very lucky that this therapist saw patients on Saturday mornings. I wouldn't have to worry about taking off from work or pulling her out of school if we made this a regular thing. Therapy would simply be another part of our weekend routine of holding it together—or doing our best to act like it.

"No, she's not that kind of a doctor. She's a doctor for feelings. All you have to do is tell her anything that pops into your head."

She tapped her lips with her finger as if she was mulling it over. A smile broke out across my lips when she nodded.

Anytime I thought I'd gotten through to my niece, even a little bit, equal parts of exhilaration and relief would course through me. My parents kept stressing to take baby steps, but I'd take the slightest pull in the right direction as a tiny victory.

"Okay. I'll talk to the doctor."

I stepped out of the car and made my way to the back seat to open her door. She wrapped her arms around my waist after she climbed out and peered up at me, her brown eyes fixed on mine as she gave me a hopeful smile. "I'll try to do a good job, Uncle Jesse."

I shook my head, forcing out a laugh to hold in the sob in the back of my throat that wanted to break free.

"Don't worry about doing a good job. Just tell her the truth, whatever it is. I'm already proud of you for being brave enough to speak to someone new." I bent to press a kiss to the top of her head. "Okay?"

She whispered an *okay* back and grabbed my hand. We ambled through the parking lot toward the entrance in silence.

I'm trying here, Tessa. I'm really, really trying.

"This must be Maddie," Dr. Asher said as she greeted us in the waiting room, crouching in front of Maddie. "I'm Dr. Asher."

"Hi," Maddie said in an almost inaudible whisper.

"Did your uncle tell you anything about me?"

"My uncle Jesse told me that I can talk to you about whatever I want."

Dr. Asher snuck me a smile. "That's right. For the next hour, we can discuss whatever you'd like to talk about. I'm excited to get to know you." She motioned to her open office door.

"I'll be right here when you're done." I pointed to the chair behind me.

I had come to meet Dr. Asher last week to feel her out before I introduced her to Maddie. I'd liked her instantly after she'd managed to put me at ease in the first fifteen minutes. She was an older woman, but not as old as my mother. Her hair was platinum and fell slightly past her shoulders, but she had a grandmotherly way about her. I figured Maddie needed all the women in her life that she could get at the moment.

I settled into a chair and tried to exhale a calming breath after Dr. Asher closed the door behind them.

Right now, her sessions were just one-on-one, but I would be able to speak to Dr. Asher for a few minutes after.

After I dug my phone out of my pocket, I noticed a text from Caden once I swiped up.

Caden: *You should have come out last night. It was fun. A lot more fun than that stupid reunion.*

Me: *I'm glad you had fun, but I wasn't feeling like hanging out at a bar with people I hardly remember.*

Caden: *And you were in a rush to take Emily home after you dumped me. Really took me back to high school.*

Me: *Emily and I stopped at the diner on the way home.*

I watched the texting buttons pop up then stop, then pop up again for a long minute and go away.

Caden: *So, did she, like, throw coffee at you or smash a slice of pie in your face?*

A chuckle slipped out, as I'd almost expected her to at one point.

Me: *No. We talked. It was good. I think she might understand why I was such an asshole back then.*

Caden: *And I heard she's single. Sabrina told me she's been mostly unattached since she broke up with her fiancé a while ago.*

Fiancé? It was further than I'd ever gotten with a woman, and I wasn't sure why the thought of Emily engaged to someone stung.

Or I *was* sure, but I didn't want to acknowledge it.

Caden: *Maybe this is your chance. Second time's the charm and all that.*

Me: *That's not how the saying goes.*

Caden: *Whatever. That girl has been under your skin since day one, and now you finally have another shot.*

Me: *It was a ride to the diner to clear the air. I wouldn't call it a chance.*

Caden: *But you could.*

I dropped my chin to my chest and groaned. Caden was

the only one who could be just as big of an exasperating jackass in text as in person.

> **Me:** *You know as well as I do that I can't. I am not available for her or anyone. No charms, no chances. I'm very glad she doesn't hate me, and it was a nice end to the night. That's it. Please drop it.*

> **Caden:** *Your sister would hate this. She'd roll her eyes at you just as much as I am now. Just because you have a kid to take care of doesn't mean you have to be a monk.*

> **Me:** *Right now, only one woman has my attention. And she needs all of it.*

> **Caden:** *Did you tell Emily about Maddie?*

> **Me:** *No. I think she assumed I had a kid, and I didn't bring it up or correct her.*

> **Caden:** *That's your call. A stroll down the good part of memory lane for a night or two wouldn't hurt, but I'll drop it.*

> **Me:** *You hooked up with Sabrina again, didn't you?*

> **Caden:** *No, I didn't hook up with her, but I'm thinking about it. What's the big deal? She's still hot. She's single. I'm single. We both had shitty divorces we'd like to forget.*

> **Me:** *You always used each other to forget.*

> **Caden:** *And it always worked. With no hard feelings.*

Me: *Just fistfights after school with whoever you'd both piss off.*

Caden: *Don't be jealous of our system. We could even double-date if you wanted to.*

Me: *Did you not hear anything I just said?*

Caden: *I did, but I'm trying to ignore it. Seriously, Tessa wouldn't want this, and you know it.*

I let my head fall back as I clenched my eyes shut. Tessa *would* hate this, especially if I ever had the chance to reconnect with Emily again.

And while I couldn't argue how annoyed she'd be at my missed chance, charm, or whatever, she'd appreciate me making her daughter my priority, especially now.

Maybe I could think of dating in the distant future, but not in the present, regardless of who I was interested in—or trying not to be interested in, as was the case now.

Me: *Be that as it may, I need to figure out how to be a father first, and that means no distractions.*

Caden: *I get that. I just wanted you to give yourself a break, but I'll lay off for the moment. Good luck with the therapy session.*

I shoved the phone back into my pocket and scrubbed a hand down my face. In another time and place, would I consider starting something up with Emily again?

Absofuckinglutely.

Seeing her again for the first time in twenty years rattled me, and all the old feelings I'd never given either of us a chance to deal with bubbled right to the surface. Considering how I couldn't shake the imprint of her soft lips on my cheek or how my head spun too fast when I got close to her, distance was the only option I could handle.

Even if her offer to meet up again registered like a siren song.

I was lonely, uncertain, and usually just this side of terrified since I'd become a full-time parent. Emily had always been the one to soothe me when we were younger, and I was probably subconsciously seeking out that old comfort. Whatever it was that drew me to her so much, I didn't have time for, and I had to find a way to stop dwelling on it.

I flipped through an old magazine, not reading any of the words, until I heard the door squeak open.

My inclination was to rush over and flood both Maddie and Dr. Asher with questions about how it went, but I held myself back. Maddie's smile was small but bashful, piquing my curiosity even more as to what she'd said during the session. But I had to calm the fuck down and let them both tell me what I needed to know and when.

"Now, sit right here while I talk to your uncle Jesse. There's some loose LEGO in that bin in the corner if you'd like to build."

"She loves to build. She's the proud owner of three LEGO princess castles." I smoothed a lock of hair behind her ear, my chest pinching at her smile widening by a couple of inches as she lifted her head with pride.

I couldn't expect all our problems to be solved in one session, but the almost contentment on my niece's face shot my hopes up. Again.

"I'll only be a minute. Okay, Mad?"

"Okay," she said, heading for the box of LEGO but

keeping her eyes on me. I gave her a tiny nod as I followed Dr. Asher.

"I know you probably can't tell me much, but it looks like it went well, maybe."

Dr. Asher's lips curved into a warm smile.

"It did. Took a few minutes to get her to talk, but we had a nice chat. She misses her mother, but she loves staying with you. And she's afraid she's making you feel badly because she's sad her mother isn't here anymore."

"We *all* hate that her mother isn't here anymore for a million reasons, but the last thing I want is for her to worry about me." I propped my elbow on the arm of the couch and rubbed my temple.

"Kids are perceptive. She sees a family in grief who now has to take care of her like her mother used to. It's a natural reaction."

"I need a better poker face. She shouldn't see me like this," I muttered and rubbed the back of my neck.

"She shouldn't see how much her uncle misses his sister? I disagree. I think working through it together is how you'll all start to heal. And bringing her here is a step in the right direction. Give yourself a break, Jesse."

I got what she was saying, but I still felt too guilty to agree. "Did she mention anything else?"

"She mentioned it felt different starting school next week in her new house without her mother, but she was looking forward to seeing her friends. An extracurricular activity may help distract her a little."

"Like sports?"

Tessa had tried to put her in dance last year, and it hadn't worked out. By the time she'd enrolled her, all the other girls her age had already been in dance for a few years, and they'd made fun of her for being so behind them.

Then my sister got sick, and she couldn't look into anything else.

"Well, maybe you could talk to the school and see if there's a sport she can get involved with or some kind of club. It's not that we want her to avoid dealing with her feelings, but we don't want that to be the only thing she deals with. Make sense?"

"It does. I just... I just need to think." I dropped my gaze to the carpet.

"Don't stress about that. I'm sure if you ask her teacher, she can direct you to something Maddie may like. I think it's important to keep her a kid as much as you can. Children who lose parents grow up very fast, but some fun with friends could go a long way."

"That makes sense," I said, trying to figure out what Maddie could be interested in. Since I worked from home, I could take her back and forth from whatever she chose, but new shame hit me as I had no clue about what she'd want to do.

"I'm trying to get her to pick out things for our new condo. I told her she could choose any decorations she wanted, and she's told me no every time. I understand that she's still adjusting to living with me, but I want her to feel at home, and I don't know how to do that without rushing her."

"That'll come in time. Until then, she seems fine, considering her situation, and it's very obvious that she loves her uncle."

"I love her too. So much. I just... I'm trying to figure out how to be what she needs. Which is why we're here." I motioned around her office and to all the different puzzles and games.

"I could see that." Dr. Asher's mouth curved into a kind

smile. "What you have to do is understand that both of you need time to adjust. This is a new situation. Nothing is going to be seamless from the beginning. Let yourself make mistakes along the way. Mistakes are how all parents learn. You just happened to be coming into it beyond the diaper stage."

"Well, I was around for the diaper stage but admittedly not that hands on. I mean, I held her all the time when I'd see her, but..."

We shared a chuckle.

"Be there for her just like you're doing now. And for the condo, maybe buy things you think she'd like and get her opinion that way."

"I'll do that. There's something else I wanted to ask you."

Caden's voice was in my head, and although I knew the answer, having Dr. Asher agree with me would at least give my decision some validation—to whoever was nosy enough to pry, and to myself when I had a weak moment.

"While I have her, especially for these first few months or maybe even years, it's a good idea if I don't date anyone, right?"

Her brows pulled together as she sat back in the chair.

"Are you looking for me to give you permission, or for me to give you an out?"

"I really don't know," I admitted as a nervous chuckle escaped me. "I feel like my attention should be on her and her alone. Some people are telling me that I'm overreacting about it."

"Well, only you could say if you're overreacting. The one thing I would suggest is that you don't introduce somebody new to her right away, unless you are pretty sure that they're going to be a permanent part of your life. But if you want to go out and have a good time sometimes until then, that's allowed." She shrugged. "All parents deserve some self-care and a little time to themselves."

"I suppose," I said, resting my elbows on my knees. Maybe I was looking for an out. The thought of getting lost in Emily again when I knew I wasn't enough for her felt like the worst kind of déjà vu. While I still believed my focus belonged on my niece without any distractions, if I was honest with myself, I didn't mind the barrier and excuse not to try to bring Emily back into my life.

I both wanted her and was terrified at the prospect of being consumed by her all over again and hurting us both.

The only thing I was certain of, leaving this office today, was that I needed my own therapist.

"I'm sorry if that's not what you wanted to hear," Dr. Asher said, her smile full of sympathy.

"No... I mean, that's fine. I understand what you're saying. Thank you."

"Of course. And, listen, you're already doing a great job as a new guardian," she said as she stood and headed toward the door. "My advice to you today is to give yourself some grace as you learn."

"I'll try," I said, meeting her gaze with a chuckle. I did feel a little lighter. At least now, I had sort of a plan and didn't seem to be screwing it all up yet. Try was all I could do.

I found Maddie building a LEGO tower near one of the end tables.

"Come on, kiddo." I reached out my hand. "Diner cake isn't going to eat itself."

Her eyes lit up when her gaze snapped to mine. She grabbed my hand and popped off the floor.

"We will see you next Saturday," I told Dr. Asher as I

brushed the hair off Maddie's shoulder when she leaned into my hip.

"That sounds like a plan. It was very nice to meet you, Maddie," Dr. Asher said. "I look forward to hearing about your first week at school."

"Nice to meet you too," Maddie said, still burrowing into my side as I led her out of the waiting room. She was silent as she took hold of my hand and followed me to the parking lot.

"Did you like Dr. Asher?" I asked Maddie as she climbed into my back seat.

"Yeah, she's really nice," she murmured as she buckled her seat belt and looked up at me with wary eyes. "Did she tell you if anything I said was wrong?"

"You didn't say anything wrong. You couldn't. I told you, this is just letting out how you feel. There is no right or wrong when it comes to feelings."

"Yeah, I guess so," she said in a low whisper.

"So, I was thinking that the living room needs new curtains," I said as I pulled out of the parking lot. "What do you think? What's your favorite color?"

"Purple."

"Okay, how about purple curtains?"

"You don't want purple curtains." She shook her head. "You're a boy."

"Hey, purple isn't only a girls' color. Everybody wears purple. And it's not only a boy's place. It's your place too. So how about after the diner, we stop at Target and get some purple curtains?"

I craned my neck toward her at a red light. The smile breaking out on her face scratched at the back of my throat.

"Could I get purple sheets and a blanket for my bed?"

I pulled into a spot in front of the diner and shut off the engine, turning my head to meet her hopeful gaze.

"Mad, you can cover the whole house in purple if you want."

"You wouldn't hate that?" She squinted at me, her adorable nose scrunched up in confusion.

"Nope, and seeing you happy would make me happy, so I couldn't care less what color you'd want everything to be. And I love living with you. Don't ever think I don't, okay?" I squeezed her knee until she lifted her head.

"Okay. I miss Mom, but I really like seeing you every day."

"Same, kiddo." I tapped her leg and climbed out of the car.

Maybe I could do this. I could be the person she could depend on every day, not just somebody to take her to water parks during the summer and hand over her Christmas list to once a year.

I loved seeing her every day too, and I should have moved back a long time ago—for her and for all of them. I wished I could have had both Maddie and my sister, but at least with my niece, I got to keep a piece of Tessa.

I couldn't and wouldn't fail either of them.

6

JESSE

"DO WE HAVE EVERYTHING?" MADDIE ASKED AS SHE LEANED forward in the back seat of my truck, her eyes darting around the cab as she bobbed her knee.

"You have everything that paper said that you needed," I told her in my rearview mirror. "You have cleats, shin guards, and long socks."

She drew her brows together and nodded, appeased for the moment or, I hoped, for the remaining fifteen minutes we had to get to the field.

Before I'd had the chance to contact her teacher about what activities she would recommend, Maddie had come home from school last week waving the flyer for local soccer league sign-ups, asking if it was okay to join.

After I called the number and verified that it was an open sign-up and not tryouts, I piled her into my truck the next day to head to the mall and get everything the coach on the phone had told me she needed.

I prayed this was a sign that, just maybe, the tides were turning a little. But as excited as I was to see her excited about something, I worked to keep my expectations in check.

I glanced back at my back seat, a grin splitting my mouth when I spotted Maddie's. "I never knew you wanted to play soccer."

"My friend Jeffrey plays. He said it's fun and mostly you just run and kick the ball," she said, lifting her shoulder in a shrug. "And I like playing kickball at recess. It's better than dancing," she mumbled.

"From what they told me when I called the number on the flyer, a lot of kids join the league at your age. So don't worry about that, okay?" I caught the hint of a smile when she lifted her head. "And if any kids do get stupid, I'll be right there with you."

"You don't mind driving to games?"

I opened her car door and shook my head.

"I told you, Mad. I work from home and will take you to anything you want to do whenever you want."

And I meant that with my total heart and soul. I'd chauffeur her all over the damn place, not only to give her the distraction, as Dr. Asher had suggested, but to help her grab any kind of joy she wanted to chase.

"I think we have everything." I took her hand and the purple duffel bag she'd picked out and headed to the entrance to the indoor sports facility.

"Maddie!"

A blond-haired little boy, who I guessed was Maddie's age, charged us as we stepped inside toward the fake grass.

"Hi," Maddie said as she surveyed the long line along the edge of the field.

"Don't worry about that," he said, turning his head to follow her gaze. "That's just check-in. I told you there aren't any tryouts. You can just sign up."

"I told her that too," I said, squeezing the tense little muscle in her shoulder.

Maddie hadn't talked about too many friends in school, but I'd heard the name of one boy a lot. I hadn't officially met Jeffrey before, but I already liked him for looking out for her and getting her here in the first place.

"I bet you're Jeffrey. Nice to meet you," I said, dipping my head to meet his gaze. He was an inch or two shorter than my niece.

"Yeah, how did you know?" Jeffrey said, his brow furrowed as he peered up at me.

"Maddie said you're the one who told her about today."

"Oh yeah. Hi," he said.

"This is my uncle Jesse. I guess, Mr. Evans to you." She squinted up at me.

"Let's get you signed up, Mad." I reached for her hand but stopped myself, tipping my chin forward instead. "We'll let you lead the way, Jeffrey."

"Okay, come on," he said before taking off. Maddie followed and I lingered behind. I hadn't been to a soccer game since high school, when I used to sit in the stands and cheer my superstar girlfriend on to victory.

The same superstar girlfriend I'd been trying to stop thinking about for the past couple of weeks, but the universe wasn't making it easy.

Watching the kids kick the soccer ball back and forth reminded me of the afternoons when Emily would come over after school and ask me to practice with her. I'd had no idea what I was doing but would exaggerate hovering and blocking just to get close to her.

Memories of that were both sweet and dirty since the back-and-forth was a high school version of foreplay, and I'd end up dragging her somewhere to attack her lips and run my hands all over that toned ass and up those gorgeous thighs.

I clenched my eyes shut and shook my head, trying to shake the images out of my horny brain like an Etch A Sketch.

Spotting the table full of forms attached to clipboards, I grabbed one and began to fill it out while Maddie spoke to Jeffrey, still scanning the space and taking it all in. I smiled at her excitement and clicked the pen to start writing when someone tapped my shoulder from behind.

"Jesse? I thought that was you."

"Penny? I didn't expect to see you here. I mean, I probably should have." We shared a laugh when I arched a brow. I'd caught a glimpse of her at the reunion, but I had been too preoccupied with Emily at the time to approach her or anyone else.

"This is what happens. You move back to town and realize how small it is. The whole damn island only looks big on a map but, in reality, it's pretty tiny." She was in full athletic gear, just as I'd always remembered her, only this time with a cap on and a whistle around her neck.

"I guess you're one of the coaches. I'm here to sign up my niece."

"I am, but I also run the league and manage the other coaches." I swore I saw her smile shrink by an inch for a second, as if she was bracing herself for something. "You said you're signing up your niece?"

"Yes, my niece is…mine. Long story, but she's excited to be here."

"I love hearing that. How old is she?"

"She's eight." I stepped closer, glancing over my shoulder to whisper. "Is there any way that she and Jeffrey could be on the same team? He's the friend who made her

69

want to come in the first place, so that may make it easier for her."

"Jeffrey Johnson?" She nodded when her eyes met mine, as she probably spotted my confusion. "The blond kid with the freckles." She pointed to where he was still in deep conversation with my niece. "There are a few openings on his team. Give me the form after you're done, and I'll make sure to add her to the list before I hand it off to the coach."

"Thank you," I breathed out. "I really appreciate it."

"Of course. In fact, that team would probably be better for her overall since you already know the coach."

"Jesse?"

The familiar voice behind me didn't hit me as hard as when I'd heard it for the first time in twenty years, but it almost knocked me on my ass just the same.

Emily was still just as beautiful as when I'd seen her at the reunion, this time in a snug tracksuit instead of a dress, when I found her standing next to me. Her long hair was pulled back in a ponytail, just like on all those game days when it would bob behind her as she raced back and forth on the field. I couldn't help but laugh when I spotted the whistle around her neck too.

Emily was Maddie's coach. I didn't have to ask to confirm because it would just figure.

"I'm a new coach. Penny talked me into joining when we met up after the reunion. I've never coached anyone before, but I have to admit being here has me all sentimental. Are you here to sign up your daughter?"

My stomach twisted as she examined me. I'd thought my lie of omission was harmless and the most stress I'd have today would be to get Maddie to mingle with other kids. I'd expected to have to explain that, while I wasn't Maddie's actual father, she was my kid. But explaining it to Emily was very different—different enough for me to have avoided the conversation altogether, even though I'd asked her to the diner to talk.

"Maybe I should put on my cleats," Maddie said, now at my side, peering up at me with her brown eyes full of worry. I had been too distracted by her new coach and what I was about to say to notice she'd come back over to me. "Some of the kids are practicing, and I don't want to get hurt."

"You won't need the cleats today, I promise," Emily said, grinning at Maddie as she bent to meet her gaze. "Today is more of a meet-and-greet, I think. Right?" she asked Penny.

"Yes. No worries about cleats." Penny said from where I'd forgotten she was behind us. "Jeffrey Johnson is her friend," she told Emily. "He's been in this league since he was four and I already had him signed up with you, so I thought we could add..." Penny trailed off as she turned back to my niece.

"Maddie," I answered, swiping my palm across the sweaty nape of my neck. Shit, I really didn't want to break this to Emily here—or at all. But I wasn't going to have a choice.

Penny eased closer and looked between Emily and me. "Unless that's a problem."

"No."

Emily and I both answered at the same time with the same gusto...or denial.

"Again. A tiny town on a tiny island," Penny murmured. "Well, at any rate, I'm happy to have friends in the league. You know, Emily and I used to play together when we were kids on a league like this. It's where I had the most fun and learned to love soccer."

"Me too," Emily said, her sweet smile running through me like an electric charge. I might have bought all the supplies that Maddie needed for soccer, but I felt unprepared and exposed all the same.

"Well then. Hi, Maddie. I'm Emily." She flicked her eyes to me and smiled. "It is great to meet you. I've known this guy for a long time—" Emily jerked her chin in my direction "—so it's nice to meet his little girl."

My chest tightened at Emily's comment. This was another problem I hadn't anticipated. I'd hoped to stop people with an explanation before they'd mistake us for actual father and daughter and make my niece feel even worse.

"You did? You were friends?" Maddie asked, a deep crease in her forehead as she looked between us.

"Yes," Emily answered before I could figure out what the hell to say to that. What Emily and I had been was a lot more than I could ever explain to myself, let alone an eight-year-old.

"We were friends a long time ago," I added, the hurt flashing across Emily's face mimicking the sour pang in my gut. I wasn't sure if it was dread, nerves, sadness, or a debilitating concoction of the three.

Jeffrey rushed over to us in my periphery, grabbing Maddie's arm.

"Hey, Maddie! Want to see me kick a goal? I can make the net jump!"

"Go ahead," I said, waving my hand and wanting to hug the kid for offering to show off to my niece and distract her for a few minutes. I hoped he'd kick the ball enough times to give me a chance to get through the short version for Emily.

"Wow," she whispered when the kids were out of earshot. "She looks just like Tessa. Right down to the butterfly earrings."

For a moment, I forgot the turmoil in my gut as a chuckle escaped me. Jeffrey took Maddie by the shoulders to place her in the perfect spot as he set up the ball and ran up to kick it.

"How is Tessa? I missed your sister." She said, still focused on the kids. "Maybe even more than you since I wasn't mad at her."

I pushed a weak smile across my mouth at her smirk.

Jeffrey screamed a "Yes!" as Maddie's expression lit up with wonder. Emily's comment about Maddie's resemblance to her mother hit hard as I remembered Tessa making that same face when she was excited.

"It's unbelievable," Emily said, shaking her head. "Tessa could be her twin."

"She was," I finally said as Emily's face twisted with confusion.

"She *was*? I don't understand—" My stomach bottomed out when her jaw went slack. "Is Tessa oka—"

"She's gone," I whispered, keeping an eye on the kids over her shoulder as I inched closer. "Passed away. Tessa was Maddie's mother, and now...I'm her guardian."

Turned out, I could sum up a short version of the story, but it didn't make it hurt any less.

"Jesse, I'm so..." Emily's eyes filled with tears as her jaw trembled. She sank her teeth into her bottom lip and reached for my hand, sliding her palm against mine. "I am so sorry. So incredibly sorry. I'd thought at the reunion you were talking to your daughter and that's who the little girl on your phone screen was. I assumed, and I shouldn't have and..." She trailed off, pressing her hand to her chest.

"You weren't wrong. For all intents and purposes, she *is* my daughter. The transition is a little tough from uncle to father, but we're putting in the work." I smiled, squeezing her hand before I dropped it. I was too tempted to pull her to me and bring her into my arms for my own selfish comfort, so I took a half step away from her instead.

"It's all still new. We're adjusting. It's why Caden and my mother pushed me out of the house a couple of weeks ago, even if it was to go to my high school reunion."

"I'm glad they did," Emily whispered, sniffling as she held my gaze.

"I'm glad they did too. Tessa loved you. She didn't speak to me that whole summer after we broke up. I'm sure she's getting a big kick out of this right now."

Emily sputtered out a watery laugh. "I loved her too," she said, wiping her cheek with the back of her hand.

Someday I would be able to talk about our situation without wanting to bawl like a baby, but something as simple as holding Emily's hand had quelled that constant storm tearing through me, at least for the moment.

"Maddie. Her full name is Madison, right?" Emily asked.

"Most people assume Madeline, but yes. How did you guess that?"

Her face crumpled as if she was about to sob.

"All of Tessa's dolls were named Madison. I gave her Madison Three, remember?"

"Wow," I breathed out as the wind was knocked out of me. "I can't believe I forgot that."

"For her birthday, I always bought two pairs of earrings, one for her and one for Madison Three." She brought her hand to her mouth when her voice cracked.

"I remember the earrings." I reached out to grab her hand back. "You were always great with her. That meant a lot to me."

"She was easy to love." She inhaled a long breath

through her nostrils and straightened. "It would be a privilege to be Maddie's coach. I'm glad you're both here."

Not thinking about Emily had just become a million times harder as I'd be seeing her all season, but I could figure out a way to do this for Maddie.

"Uncle Jesse, is Emily the friend you had the good dessert with?"

I shared a chuckle with Emily before I turned to where Maddie stood behind me. I had been so caught up in the swell of emotion between Emily and me, I'd forgotten to make sure Maddie wouldn't hear us.

More evidence that I'd made the right choice to keep my distance from Emily. She'd consumed me from the beginning, and I couldn't afford that now.

And somehow, I'd have to figure out a way to avoid it for the entire soccer season.

"Yes," Emily said, her voice steadier even though her eyes were glassy. "Diner cake is the best cake."

"It is! I love diner cake." Maddie's eyes lit up as she looked between us. Now that it was all out in the open, my shoulders sagged with relief, even if my heart rate still kicked up at Emily's wide smile.

Regardless if I'd resolved not to date anyone for a while and ignore whatever I was feeling for her, now that Emily was Maddie's coach, she was *very* off-limits, no matter what my intentions had been.

"I better get with the other coaches," she said, straightening her long chestnut ponytail, her old tell when she was nervous. "I am so excited you're on my team. It's going to be an awesome season." She looked between us with a wide smile and jogged behind the registration table.

"She seems really nice. And pretty," Maddie whispered

as she leaned against me. "Were you good friends in school? Why did you stop?"

I exhaled with a soft groan, my eyes still drifting toward Emily until I forced them away. I didn't know what to tell my niece and didn't have the energy to lie.

"Because sometimes, Mad," I sighed, letting my gaze linger on Emily's departure for one more minute before I dragged it away, "some things are too good to keep."

7

EMILY

"Hey, are you okay?"

Penny put a hand on my shoulder as I shoved the file folder with all the coach and league materials into my bag.

When I spotted the sympathy pulling at her features, I nodded back even though I had no idea how to answer.

After the parents and the kids had filtered out of the space, we'd had a little meeting to discuss rules and regulations and what we had to do before the first practice.

It was nothing unexpected, as I'd played in a league exactly like this as a kid, and I had a lot of great memories on the field and hanging out with my friends at Pizza Hut after a game.

After Penny had convinced me to be a coach, I'd gotten excited to plan those fun little events for my team and relive a little of the great experience I'd had.

Any ideas or plans I'd been thinking about had been forgotten as I'd fixated on one parent and child for the rest of the afternoon.

Seeing Jesse here signing up his daughter, much less

signing her up to be on my team, had been unexpected, but I'd been confident I'd find a way to manage.

Finding out his daughter really wasn't his daughter, and that he was taking care of his deceased sister's child was jarring and heartbreaking enough to rattle me for the rest of the day.

I'd forced myself to make small talk with parents and kids and half listened to Penny's coach instructions. Memories of Tessa floated around in my head, each one deepening the dull ache in my chest.

She had been the cutest little thing. Maybe not *little*, as she'd always been tall for her age, but she'd been the girliest girl I'd ever known. Every time I'd stepped foot into Jesse's house, she'd dragged me by the hand to her bedroom to show me her new dolls or a cool pair of earrings from the little store at the mall that I just had to see.

I'd remembered her as a sweet bubble of love and light and the pride and joy of her entire family—especially her big brother.

They'd never had that naturally combative relationship that my other friends with siblings closer in age had because he'd looked out for her like a parent rather than a brother most of the time. Despite how they'd squabble when she'd knock on his bedroom door at all the wrong moments when I was there, he could never hide how much he loved having her around.

I still couldn't imagine the pain he and his parents had gone through when they'd lost her.

I'd noticed after a quick scan of my team's roster that Maddie's last name was Evans. I'd taken that to mean her biological father wasn't in the picture, and that Tessa had been a single mother. Even though we'd lived with my grandparents, my own single mother was my entire world, and imagining what it would have been like to grow up without her was so unfathomable, I couldn't even think of it in hypothetical terms.

My heart broke—for Maddie, for Jesse and his parents, and for Tessa, who'd died so young and would miss out on most of her daughter's life.

"It's both strange and great to be back on a field." I tried for an easy smile, but the effort to push it across my lips was taxing.

When Penny laughed, I was hopeful that I might've been convincing.

"Listen, I'm sorry if I put you on the spot with Jesse's niece. He'd asked if she could be on the same team as Jeffrey, and since I'd already put him with you and I was still adding players to your team, I thought it made the most sense. But I should have pulled you aside and asked you first."

"You didn't put me on the spot. It's fine, really." I looped my bag strap over my shoulder. "We're all adults, and like I told you, Jesse and I hashed everything out, so there's no bad blood between us. I can absolutely handle it, so please don't worry."

"Okay, good. What a shame, right?" Penny clicked her tongue against her teeth and shook her head. "He didn't go into it, but it feels like there's a tragic story there. Wasn't his sister young?"

"She was," I said, clearing my throat around the lump I hadn't been able to swallow away for most of the afternoon.

In my mind, Tessa was exactly as I'd left her, about eight years old—her daughter's age.

When Maddie spoke, I couldn't get over how much she both looked and sounded like her mother. It was a double gut punch to both find out she was gone and to meet this eerily accurate replica of her.

Where was all this grief coming from?

When I'd run into Jesse at the reunion, because we hadn't seen each other for so long, the events of the past had been fresh and raw. I was taking the news of Tessa's passing as if it had just happened after the last time we'd played with her Barbies—the week before Jesse and I had broken up.

The sympathy or empathy or whatever I was feeling for the Evans family overwhelmed me, settling into my chest, and had made it hard to take in a full breath since I'd watched them leave the field. Jesse had kept hold of Maddie's hand as he'd led her outside, the silhouette of them reminding me so much of him and his sister I had almost sobbed.

"You should have everything," Penny said, motioning to my bag. "A list of cell phone numbers and emails for the parents and a list of rules from the league, which are pretty self-explanatory and haven't changed much since we were kids—other than the social media stuff." She bumped my shoulder with hers. "I'm glad I convinced you to sign on this year. It's like old times."

"I'm glad you twisted my arm too. Thanks for asking me." I tapped her arm and headed to the parking lot, where I could obsess over Jesse and his family in private on the drive back to my apartment.

While what had happened to Tessa was none of my business, I needed to know. I wanted to help, even if I didn't have a clue where to begin.

I sorted out all the coaching materials and tacked up the list of parent cell phone numbers to my kitchen whiteboard, my eyes lingering on Jesse's name and number.

Was contacting Jesse the right or even appropriate thing to do? I wasn't sure, but right or wrong, I wouldn't be able to sit still tonight until I reached out.

I pulled out my phone and cued up a text message, staring at the blank screen while I pondered what the hell to say. I couldn't think of any excuse to contact him other than the truth.

Me: *Hey, it's Emily. Apologies for the random message, but I can't stop thinking about all of you. I'm so, so sorry, Jesse. I wish there was something I could do.*

Three dots popped on the screen almost immediately. My heart seized each time they'd stop and start again.

Jesse: *Thanks, Em. I appreciate that. I wish there was something anyone could do too, but we're getting by. Or trying to anyway.*

Me: *Would you maybe like to get another cup of coffee or another piece of cake sometime? Cake can't solve everything, but it may help a little in the moment.*

I cringed at my attempt at a dopey joke.

Me: *I'm here if you need to talk. I just wanted you to know that.*

I put my phone down and pressed the heels of my hands into my eyes.

What was I doing? I truly had no idea, and yet I couldn't turn back.

Jesse: *Instead of dessert, how does dinner sound? My mother took Maddie for a sleepover tonight, and I was thinking of heading to the new bar and grill on 110 since everyone tells me I should leave the house more often. I know it's short notice, but would you want to join me?*

I hadn't expected him to agree to meet so fast or so soon. I was hurt that he hadn't trusted me enough to tell me who the child was on his phone screen. Hell, he hadn't even acknowledged her.

We'd kept everything superficial, which had been fine with me at the time. I never would have known about Maddie if fate's fucked-up sense of humor hadn't made me her new soccer coach. I understood why he'd kept Tessa's death and his new role as a father to himself since we'd already gotten through enough emotional truths and reveals for one night. While it hurt that he hadn't confided in me, imagining what he and his entire family had gone through upset me more. He'd never asked for my help once I knew, but I had a burning need to offer it anyway.

Why the need bordered on obsession was something I'd worry about later.

Me: *Sure. Is 7 okay?*

This time, I was the one pushing for us to talk things out, at least to prevent any awkward moments between Jesse and me that could make Maddie uncomfortable if she picked up on anything. But more than that, regardless of if it was my business, or who Jesse was or wasn't to me anymore, I needed to know what had happened to his sister.

I pulled into the parking lot of the restaurant Jesse had suggested, taking everything in on my way inside. I scanned the dining space next to the bar with various large-screen TVs hanging along the walls playing different games without sound, and I stilled when I spotted Jesse.

No man had a right to be that stunning in a simple T-shirt and jeans, and for the reasons we were meeting tonight, it shouldn't have been the first thing I noticed. He leaned his elbows onto the table and was about to take a pull from a tall glass of what looked like beer when his gaze snagged on mine.

He set down the glass, a smile curving his lips as he popped off the high seat and came over to me.

"Hey, Em."

I felt more than heard his raspy greeting over the din of the small crowd, yelling at something happening on one of the screens.

"Hey. Thanks for inviting me."

I'd noticed the extra layer of stubble covering his cheeks earlier today, and had tried to ignore how it'd made him even more attractive, if that was possible. I held back a laugh, remembering how he and Caden had tried and failed to grow goatees in high school.

But he'd been a boy then. Now, he was a man with a life and struggles that I had no idea about. I'd come here tonight to learn more and not just tell him how sorry I was about a thousand more times, although, at the moment, that was all I had.

"Have a seat." He gestured to the chair across the table. "I waited for you to order. I've only been here once, but the burgers are good, unless you're on a soccer diet."

I laughed at the smirk tipping up the side of his mouth and climbed into the seat.

"I'm only coaching, not playing. I won't put the kids through the same drills I had to suffer through in high school and college. It's less about building muscle than making sure my team doesn't destroy the field."

My smile deepened despite myself as Jesse chuckled.

"I can enjoy a burger tonight with no worries."

"I told the waitress a high table was fine, but if you'd rather a booth—"

"No, I'm good here." I set my purse down at the end of the table. "Thanks for inviting me."

"Thanks for reaching out. I was surprised that you still had my cell phone number."

I laughed as I picked up a menu.

"Full disclosure, I deleted your number during my first semester of college." I sent him a sheepish grin. "I read your number off the team roster. I shouldn't have used a parent's cell phone for personal reasons, but..." I stilled, not sure how to explain the burning need I'd had to talk again. "I was concerned about you. All of you."

Jesse shut his eyes and nodded. "I know you probably have a lot of questions."

"I do, and most of them are none of my business, I'm sure, so feel free to tell me that. But what I'm not understanding the most is why you didn't just tell me about Maddie when we went to the diner, especially since you asked me for the purpose of talking things out."

He propped his elbow on the table and rubbed at his temple.

"You're absolutely right. I didn't bring up Maddie or Tessa because I felt that we had enough emotions to get through for one night. After I dropped you off, I was relieved, yet exhausted."

"Same," I agreed. "I didn't know if you were married or a

single dad or what. And, honestly, I didn't have the guts to ask."

"I sweated it out a little when it looked like you were going to." He let out a nervous laugh. "We ended up in a nice place," he said with a shrug. "At least, I thought so. I wanted to take you home and hold on to the good from that night. And if I'm being honest..." he started, darting his eyes away from mine.

"Please do."

"That is why when you asked if I could go out sometime for another cup of coffee, I really didn't answer you. I'm not sure how to be...this yet or how to compartmentalize it enough to still have any kind of life for myself."

I narrowed my eyes.

"I just asked you for coffee at some random point in the future. I didn't propose," I joked.

"No," he said with a chuckle. "Since...Maddie...I don't even see Caden that much. Even having a drink with my oldest friend at the bar feels weird. I can't explain it."

I nodded, trying to process all he'd said.

"And, if I could be honest about another thing. Even though the conversation was tense at times, I liked being with you again. I didn't want to upset you or ruin a nice night, but I'm sure telling you then would have been better than finding out today."

I opened my mouth to say something, but the words caught in my throat. I would have been blindsided either way, but at the diner, I would have been able to be shocked and upset without anyone but Jesse watching.

Which, I agreed, would have ruined the nice end of our night, but now it didn't seem as genuine.

"Hi, what can I get you?" the waitress asked us during our long lull of silence.

He nodded at me.

"I'm sure you need a drink too."

"Yeah, it would be nice." I nodded and turned to the waitress. "I'd like a hard cider. And I guess a cheeseburger deluxe. Medium."

"I'll have the same," Jesse said and handed her our menus.

"So," he said, scooting closer to the table. "What do you want to know?"

He searched my gaze with an expression I couldn't decipher.

He was wary yet hopeful, as if he wanted to unload on me, but he didn't know if he could.

I leaned back, resting my elbows on the table. "How old was Tessa when she had Maddie? I was trying to do the math, but I think she was a teenager."

"Not quite. She was twenty, in college for nursing. She had a steady boyfriend whom I wasn't crazy about, but my parents told me to back off because I was being a little too big brother."

"I can see that," I said, nodding a thank-you to the waitress as she set down my drink. I took a long sip from the glass as I waited for him to continue. "I always pitied Tessa for when she'd start dating because I knew you'd be relentless."

A quick smile curved his mouth.

"I tried to stay cordial and cautious when I'd see him on long weekends and holidays I'd come home."

I had to laugh at the tic in Jesse's jaw.

"Despite what you may think, I did try to keep an open mind."

"I know you did." I tilted my head. "Mostly."

I grinned when I pulled a tiny smile out of him.

"You mean when you'd come home from Seattle?"

"Yes. I tried to come home whenever I could, a weekend or so a month, or whenever I had a long break. One Thanksgiving, they were all waiting for me at the kitchen table like someone had just died. Tessa had just told them she was pregnant, and other than offering her money for an abortion that she didn't want to have, her boyfriend didn't want to have anything to do with her or the baby. I flipped out, as you can imagine, but managed to stop myself when Tessa started crying."

"Because you wanted to kill him?"

"Wanted?" He scoffed. "That will never be past tense. Anyway, she still lived with my parents, so they all agreed she'd finish school while my parents took care of the baby." Jesse shrugged. "We were disappointed, not in Tessa but at this turn her life had taken. Everything was going to be a lot harder for her than we wanted it to be."

He took a long sip from his beer glass and lifted his head, a slow grin splitting his mouth.

"And then Maddie was born, and we all fell too much in love with her to think of her as anything other than a blessing."

My heart broke all over again when Jesse's eyes glossed over.

"For most of Maddie's life, I was the uncle with all the presents and fun trips. She loved to FaceTime me about everything at school and cool things she did with her mother and—" his smile faded as he shook his head "—I'll never forgive myself for not moving back sooner. At least I could have spent more time with them both in person rather than on a screen."

I shook my head and reached out for his hand because I couldn't help myself. "You had no idea what would happen, so you can't blame yourself for that. We always think we have more time than we do."

He took a long sip of beer and lifted a shoulder.

"Tessa always looked exhausted whenever we talked. She said it was because she was getting used to night shifts at the hospital and blew me off. Maddie had just turned six, and Tessa was finally able to move into an apartment of her own. She insisted it was probably the stress of settling in. While I had a bad feeling there was more to it, I'd never suspected leukemia."

The devastation combined with obvious guilt drained Jesse's features.

The waitress brought our burgers over, both of us muttering a thank-you as we stayed silent and still.

"I keep saying it, but I'm so sorry," I said, swallowing after I caught my voice crack.

"I know," he said so softly, his words were almost inaudible. "When Maddie was born, Tessa asked me if I could be Maddie's guardian just in case of anything, and of course, I agreed. Toward...the end...I told her that I wouldn't be insulted if she wanted to give Maddie to my parents instead, but she swore she still wanted me."

"Of course she did." I tried to smile despite the tears pricking my eyes. "You were always her first choice for everything."

"Well, this time, I keep wondering what the hell she was thinking. Maddie's therapist said to get her involved in an extracurricular activity, and Maddie asked to join soccer before I even had a chance to research or suggest anything."

I glanced at the huge burger and the mountain of fries in front of me, too sick for Jesse and his family to want to take a bite.

"That's a lot."

"It has been," he mumbled around a mouthful of food. "But I grasp at signs that she's maybe settling in with me. Like today. She looked like she was having fun or was at least excited about the prospect of having fun later on."

"And then you found out I was her coach."

A smile broke out on his face as he chewed.

"Yes, that was a little bit of a surprise. It shouldn't have been, same as I shouldn't have been surprised to see Penny there since I think she carried a soccer ball under her arm all through high school," he joked as he set down his burger.

"I think it's a good thing that you're her coach. A great thing." A grin split his mouth. "I know you'll do everything you can to make this an awesome experience for her."

"Well, I'm going to try," I said, picking up a fry and working myself up to taking a bite.

"I know you'll do more than just try. Maddie is in great hands with you. It's another good sign."

"Well, I'll take that compliment. I'm sure you're adjusting to being back on Long Island too."

"That isn't much of an adjustment. I came back and forth as much as I could, when I wasn't putting in crazy hours. The job I have now is busy but manageable, which it has to be since it's not just me to consider anymore."

I guessed Jesse had been unattached for a while if he could just pick up and move back, but that question, I was keeping to myself. If he wasn't ready for a drink with a friend at a bar, he probably didn't have much of a personal life. And while knowing he was single relieved me in ways it shouldn't have, I hated thinking of him so isolated.

"So, that's the whole story." He tipped back the rest of his beer and drained the glass. "Stop worrying about me and eat your dinner," he teased, nodding his chin to my full plate.

"Do you know what this reminds me of?" I mused as I reached for the ketchup bottle. "The first weekend after your dad gave you his Corolla, and we were supposed to go out but your parents had to visit your Aunt Lu because she was sick, so they left Tessa with you?"

Jesse's eyes shut as he nodded.

"We had the whole night planned out, and Tessa begged us to take her to that arcade." Jesse rolled his eyes.

"Yes, and she played pinball until her thumbs cramped, and we dragged her to the diner next door. She said she needed an extra big cheeseburger from playing so hard, but we had to cut it into pieces before she could wrap her hands around it." I chuckled despite the burn at the back of my throat.

"And then she only ate the fries." He laughed to himself.

"It wasn't a bad night, though. She was so tired and full, she passed out on the way home and..." I set down my burger, heat bleeding into my cheeks and down the back of my neck.

"I kissed you to christen my new car, thinking Tessa was still sleeping," he finished for me, popping his brows.

"Then she asked your mom the next time I came over why people kissed with their mouths open, because when you and I did it that way in the car, it looked gross. I wanted to both laugh and die at the same time."

"For a tall kid, she was sneaky enough. And Maddie is just like that. She's like a ninja."

"Your parents laughed at it." I pointed a fry at him. "It wouldn't have been such a cute story to my mother."

The laugh we shared eased my stomach enough to attempt to eat. I caught Jesse staring at me as I took the first bite.

"What? I thought you wanted me to eat."

"You know, not many girlfriends would have tolerated that. My sister *never* left you alone. Sometimes I'd have to drag you out of her bedroom and remind her you were there to see me."

"I was there to see you, but—" I swallowed, the meat going down slowly around that stupid lump that had reappeared in my throat. "She was very easy to love and never a bother. Any girlfriend who wasn't a jerk would have enjoyed her, not simply tolerated her."

"Be that as it may," he said, his sexy smile killing me. "I'd remind Tessa all the time how lucky we both were to have you."

Talking about the old times we'd shared with his sister felt good because she wasn't connected to any old resentments. I wished I could see Tessa one more time and meet the awesome woman I was sure she'd grown into.

I'd have to settle for coaching her daughter and looking out for her brother, no matter if the thoughts I'd leave with tonight weren't simply friendly and helpful. I doubted they ever would be, but thoughts and feelings were one thing, and actions were another. I had to at least keep control of those if any of this was going to work.

"Where are you parked?" Jesse asked me after we paid the check.

"In the back of the lot," I said as we made our way out the main entrance. "This was nice. I'm glad I broke league policy and abused the use of your cell phone number."

"I'll walk you. And I'm glad you did too," Jesse said, examining me as we headed toward my car.

I didn't know how to part ways this time. Did I offer to be friends again? Promise to watch over his niece? Or did I ignore it all—starting with the intensity in Jesse's gaze under the streetlights?

Before I knew it, Jesse wrapped his arms around me and pulled me flush to his body.

I stiffened from the surprise for a minute before I hugged him back and dropped my head against his shoulder.

After all the emotion of the day, I shouldn't have noticed how good he smelled. I registered a new cologne mixed with the salty and sweet scent that was always Jesse. My nose burned when he exhaled against me, his chest deflating as if he'd been holding it in for a long time.

"Thank you," he whispered as he inched away, dropping his hands before draping one over his eyes. "I'm sorry. That was beyond inappropriate—"

"But necessary," I said, grabbing his biceps. "I wasn't offended, if that's what you're concerned about. I felt the same relief."

The embrace had been unexpected but soothed something in me too. I wasn't sure if it was Jesse possibly accepting my help or the old comfort and thrill from being close to him.

"I understand wanting space to figure things out, but don't isolate yourself so much. Promise me that."

I grabbed his hand, letting my palm graze his as I squeezed. Familiar tingles ran up my arm as he smiled and squeezed back.

"I can do that. And if you don't mind a guy whining into his beer glass sometimes, it would be nice to do this again."

I nodded, letting out a long and hopefully quiet exhale to calm the old butterflies still spry enough to flutter in my stomach.

"I would really like that. And thanks for the vote of confidence as a coach. It's been a minute since I stripped off my cleats for the last time."

"Nah," he said, shaking his head. "I'm sure you've more than still got it, Legs." He pulled me in for a half hug and pressed a kiss to the top of my head. "Thanks again for tonight. It helped more than you know."

Legs. I'd forgotten about that nickname and how Jesse would whisper it in my ear before he'd run his mouth up and down my body, focusing on the insides of my thighs.

I wondered if the same dirty images flashed in his mind as his teasing grin melted away and he pressed his forehead against mine. Most of our time together had been sweet, but as we'd grown and explored each other, sweet had given way to passion so explosive, neither of us had known what to do with it.

My heels dug into the gravel of the parking lot as I watched Jesse head to his car.

Old memories shouldn't be sharp enough to hurt.

8

JESSE

"IT WAS *SO* AWESOME. YOU WOULDN'T BELIEVE IT, CADEN. I kicked the ball so far, and it made it into the goal twice! There wasn't anybody in front of the goal—"

"That's a goalie," I said from the recliner next to our new purple couch. When the lights were dim, it could pass for a dark gray, but I honestly didn't care if it looked neon green. Maddie had loved it from the second it was delivered, and she was telling Caden all about how much she loved soccer while sitting cross-legged on her favorite cushion.

So far, it was the best purchase I'd made since moving in to this condo.

I'd figured running after the ball and kicking it as hard as she could would have tired her out, but it was as if she came to life after we left each practice. For the past couple of weeks since she'd joined soccer, she'd been the chatty niece I'd remembered, before losing her mother had made her retreat into herself.

Hearing her babble to Caden was the best music to my ears. He'd come over this Sunday morning with a bag of steaming bagels and a container of cream cheese, saying he'd wanted to check on us and see how soccer was going. He was as great with Maddie as he had been with my sister when she was that age.

I was grateful, but fully aware the nosy asshole in him was the motivation for his random visit today.

"That is awesome, kiddo," Caden said. "I'd love to go to a game if that's okay."

"Yes, they said everybody could come. Grams and Grandpa said they want to come too." Maddie's eyes were still excited and saucer-wide. "Coach Emily is the *best*. She had us playing this game at practice yesterday called World Cup, where you kicked the ball and had to say what country you were from, and I did three countries. Two made it into the goal!" She held up two fingers in front of Caden's face.

"Wow," Caden said, flicking his eyes to me. "Coach Emily sounds pretty awesome."

"She is. Did you know she used to be Uncle Jesse's friend?"

"Yes, I did know that. I knew Coach Emily too, back in the day. We were all *friends* in high school."

Maddie was too excited to catch Caden's sneaky emphasis on *friends*.

"Did you know Sabrina too? She's her assistant. She's pretty nice."

"Oh really?" Caden's brows popped up. "Yes, I knew her too. Sabrina is *very* nice."

I didn't know if Sabrina and Caden had officially started something up again or were just seeing each other as friends. He'd hidden how torn up he'd been about his divorce with jokes, but I knew it ate away at him more than he'd admit. Spending time with Sabrina had always been an escape for him, and if it helped now, and they were both on the same page, I'd stay out of it since I was sure I wouldn't have to get in between him and some angry boyfriend of Sabrina's after school.

"Uncle Jesse, did you send Coach Emily the video from yesterday?" Maddie asked me and whipped her head back to Caden. "Uncle Jesse took a video of me kicking the ball in our backyard. We made a pretend goal, and I got it in like three times."

"I texted her this morning, Mad. I didn't want to bother her if she was out."

And I didn't want to know if she was. We'd started texting back and forth after that dinner, mostly about Maddie, with a little reminiscing in between. Conversation was becoming easier between us—or at least easier to find an excuse to start one.

"Is that what coaches do now? Make you practice on your own time and send video proof?" Caden laughed as he leaned back.

"No. Since Uncle Jesse talks to her, he offered to send it for her to see."

I held in a groan when Caden's brows popped up.

"That was nice of your uncle. I'm sure Coach Emily appreciates that."

As if on cue, my phone vibrated in my pocket.

Emily: *I love it. Tell her she's doing great, and I'm excited to see her play this week.*

Emily: *And nice job passing back and forth.*

I'd set my phone down when Maddie had asked me to pass her the ball like they did in practice. We were both showing off a little for her coach, although my niece's reasons were cute and not pathetic.

"What did she say?" Maddie asked as she popped off the couch.

"How do you know it's Coach Emily?" I held my phone out of reach before she could look.

"Because you were smiling at the screen. You always do that when she answers you."

Caden burst out laughing before he covered it with a fake cough.

Yes, I enjoyed speaking to Emily. Yes, I liked seeing her at the couple of practices we'd had, and it had felt good to joke around on the sidelines like old times. I looked forward to seeing her at the game this week with more anticipation than was probably healthy.

So no, I wasn't abiding by my own rules to keep my distance, but because she was Maddie's coach, I'd allowed myself the convenient excuse until the end of the season.

The smug look on Caden's face told me he wouldn't buy that, and if I was truthful with myself, neither did I.

Me: *You taught me well, I guess. I hope I didn't text too early.*

Emily: *You can always text me. And I've been up for a while. I promised my mother breakfast today since I've had to hear it all week about being too busy to call her.*

Me: *You better get over there and stop wasting time talking to me.*

Emily: *Getting into trouble because of you would be like old times. I feel warm with nostalgia.*

Caden gave me a look but didn't call me out on the wide grin making my cheeks ache.

"Did you play sports when you were in school?" Maddie asked Caden.

"Nope," Caden replied, still smirking at me. "Well, not really, anyway. Uncle Jesse and I used to run track in our last year of high school because it was an easy way to get out of the last class every day."

"You can do that?" Maddie's eyes lit up.

"No, you can't," I replied for him. "At least not in your school."

"Really?" Her bottom lip jutted out into a pout as her shoulders drooped. "You guys were lucky then. Did you like it?" She looked between us.

"Track? I liked it well enough," Caden said with a shrug. "There was really nothing to do but run, so I didn't have to learn any kicks or cool things like you will in soccer."

I was hopeful that soccer and reconnecting with her friends was helping her ease into a new normal. I'd gone to all the new school year events and had asked her teacher to let me know if there was anything going on in class or with her behavior that I should be aware of. In the last email exchange, her teacher had assured me that Maddie was doing fine so far and promised she'd keep me posted.

I still felt like I was just careening through parenthood by the seat of my pants, but things were going well enough to give me hope that I wasn't totally screwing it up yet.

"Do you want to play outside, Caden? It's not really that complicated to kick the ball back and forth if you want me to show you."

"I appreciate that," he said, tapping her chin with his knuckle. "Maybe before I leave."

"I think you have some homework to do. How about getting a head start on that, so tonight, we can do whatever we want?"

I stood from the recliner and held out my hand.

"Go break in your new desk in your room. Let me know if you need any help."

"Okay. See you later, Caden." Her lips drooped into a disappointed frown as she looped her arms around his neck for a hug.

"I'm here for a little while longer unless your uncle throws me out. Do what you have to do, kiddo."

She nodded and headed upstairs to her bedroom. Along with the purple comforter and sheets, I'd bought her a new desk and chair. My mother assured me it was the perfect little girl's room, but I knew a perfect room for her was still in her old apartment with her mother.

Sometimes, it seemed like we were slapping Band-Aids over all the ways Maddie was hurting with new toys and activities. But what other choice did we have?

"So, Coach Emily is a big hit, huh?" Caden said with a smirk as he sat back on the couch and crossed his legs. "I knew she'd be great with kids. She has that kind of way about her."

"And what way is that?"

"Relax," Caden said, shaking his head with a groan. "I meant that she has a nice, easy way about her. And it's kind of funny how you keep getting pushed back together."

"Keep? She's my niece's soccer coach."

"Think about it. You see each other for the first time in twenty years right after you moved back—"

"At the high school reunion the whole class was invited to."

"Okay, that doesn't count, I guess," he conceded. "But then the therapist tells you that Maddie needs an activity to keep her occupied. She picks soccer. You find Coach Emily. I don't know. I'm seeing a lot of dots." He moved his finger back and forth in the air.

"You would." I blew out a breath.

"Anyway, I didn't know that Sabrina was her assistant."

"I didn't know either until she was at the first practice."

Even though I'd sworn I'd keep quiet, I couldn't help asking anyway.

"I'm going to be blunt. Are you starting something up with her again?"

His smile faded to a scowl. "Didn't you ask me that already?"

"No. I asked you if you were hooking up with Sabrina. Not if you were starting something up with her. Different things."

"Either way, what's wrong with it? We have fun together when we go out. And I like her. I always did. Why should two people be alone if they don't have to be?"

"There's being alone, and then there's using people as placeholders." I raised a brow.

"I never said I was using her as a placeholder. I genuinely enjoy her company. If our time together leads to naked company, then..."

My head whipped to the staircase, hoping Maddie was far enough out of earshot.

"Consenting adults and all that. No judgment, right?" He stretched his arm along the top of the couch cushion and lifted a brow.

"I'm not judging you. I just hope you both know what you're doing."

"Right now, we aren't doing anything." He rested his elbows on his knees and raked a hand through his dark hair. "When do you see Coach Emily again?"

"Practice."

"But you'll text her later, right? I caught you mooning over your phone twice now. Just like old times."

"We text back and forth about Maddie mostly," I told him through gritted teeth. "Don't read into it."

He arched a brow. "About Maddie *mostly*. Excuse me for calling bullshit. Hell, I'm happy for you. No need to snap at me."

"I don't have time for whatever you're thinking is between Emily and me. We've managed to break the ice enough between us to be friends and take away most of the complications for my niece's sake."

"Right." He dragged out the word. "No complications besides the fact that your high school feelings are still an adult reality, but you're too chickenshit to say it?"

"I'm not."

"But you are, man." He laughed to himself. "What is the big deal? She's single, you're single—"

"Soccer is the first thing Maddie's been excited about in a long time, and she really likes Emily. I don't want to make it weird for her if we start something up and then it goes wrong."

"So, it's not weird now?"

I glowered at the smug smile curving his lips.

"It's a...containable weird."

A groan rose from Caden's throat.

"If, for argument's sake, you tried and it didn't work out, Emily wouldn't take it out on Maddie. You're both adults. You go to practice, go to the games, and suck it up for the rest of the season."

"It's not that simple." I pushed off the chair and headed toward the coffeepot in the kitchen. Thoughts of how not simple it was between Emily and me had given me many nights of shitty, restless sleep.

"It is from where I'm sitting, dude."

I could blame it on what Dr. Asher had said about not bringing anyone into Maddie's life who I wasn't sure would be there permanently, but there was more to my hesitation than that.

I poured cream into my coffee, inching the spoon around the mug because I didn't want to hear what I knew Caden was about to say—or should say.

"You forget, I was there that summer. You were all torn up over her for months. If you guys have another chance, I don't get why you wouldn't take it?"

"Because if I do," I said, focusing on the inside of my coffee mug, "then I am right back to where I was twenty years ago when I realized we had to break up."

Caden's brow furrowed. "I'm not following. You said you broke up with her because it wouldn't work with her going to school so far away."

"I broke up with her because I knew I couldn't be what she wanted or needed, regardless of whether or not she realized it."

"And how does that apply now?" Caden pressed.

"Now, I have a kid. A troubled kid who is grieving her mother. *I'm* grieving her mother. I'm taking her to a therapist and should probably pick one for myself at some point. I couldn't be what Emily needed then, and I have nothing to give her now. I won't hurt and disappoint her again."

I let out a long gust of air and dropped my head back.

"So yes, I'm a chickenshit. I fully admit it. Happy?" I downed the rest of the coffee, lukewarm from being out for so long and all the milk I'd poured into it, and I placed the mug in the sink.

Even though I insisted on space between us, I gravitated

to her all the same, and if I didn't watch myself, it wouldn't end well.

"I'm too fucking old for this. At thirty-eight, I shouldn't lose half a night of sleep because my high school girlfriend is back in my life."

"That stuff doesn't have time limits. Trust me, I wish there were some kind of magic switch to make you stop caring about someone, but..." He lifted a shoulder. "Time-lines for that kind of thing are out of our control."

He flicked his wrist to glance at his watch.

"Let me say goodbye to Maddie. I have shit to do today. I wish I knew what to tell you, but I would rather be the guy who tried and it didn't work out than the one who was too scared to do anything and had nothing but regrets in the end."

I nodded, agreeing with Caden but still clueless as to what to do about it.

"Her therapist even told me it's okay to go out and have a good time. That it's self-care. But it feels wrong to go out with Emily or anyone else, knowing how little I have to give."

"Anyone else?" Caden's eyes narrowed. "Are you getting offers that you're not telling me about?"

"I've had nothing but offers for *help* from the single mothers I've met on the team. Playdates, lunches, dinners to get my mind off things..."

Caden cracked up. "Are you serious? You're getting hit on at your kid's soccer practice? That is fucking hysterical."

"It's exhausting. And I'm not taking Maddie to any play-dates unless she asks. Because if she doesn't really know the kid, I have to stay there with her and—"

"Be cornered with more offers?" He snickered. "And

what does Coach Emily think of all the new attention you're getting?"

"I'm sure she's been too busy with the kids to notice anything or care."

"Hmm, I wouldn't be so sure. Watch her next practice. I agree with your niece." He laughed as he headed toward the stairs. "Soccer seems fun."

9

EMILY

"WHAT ARE YOU DOING HERE SO EARLY?" I ASKED SABRINA when I found her perched on the bench outside of the indoor field, jiggling her empty cup of iced coffee in agitation before she saw me. Our first game was at ten and I'd told the team to be here by nine, but I'd wanted to get to the field early to set us up for the morning and deal with any first-game nerves before the kids and parents were around to notice.

"What? It's our first game. I thought maybe, you know, I could help you strategize or something."

"Help me strategize," I repeated. "It's a scrimmage game between my kids and Penny's team. It doesn't even count on record. Other than making sure they pay attention and kick in a mostly straight line, I don't have a high-level game plan," I joked.

"Well, maybe we should. I could be useful."

"Useful?" I squinted at Sabrina and sucked in my cheeks to hold back a laugh. Sabrina had never played a sport in her life. She was a great cheerleader, but from the stands and not the sidelines.

"Well, yes. I could do more as your assistant than just hand out papers and water. Maybe I wasn't a soccer star like you, but I know things that could help you. *Rock Bottom Girl* was my favorite Lucy Score book, and I read it like three times. I'm sure I learned something about being a soccer coach that could be helpful," she said as we made our way over to our part of the field for the afternoon and dropped our bags on the bench.

"Okay, then." I came up to her and crossed my arms. "Do you want to draw a chart of X's and O's to show the kids how to line up when they get here, or just tell me what's bothering you that brought you here so early?"

"Fine," she huffed, shaking her head as she took a seat on the bench. "I'm here so early because I did something stupid, and I want to forget about it."

I held in a cringe as my mind immediately went to Caden. I knew they were hanging out sometimes, but I hadn't asked for any details. It was none of my business if they were falling into old habits, but I worried about her.

"Do I even want to know?" I asked her and took a quick sweep of the field. I waved at Penny as she set up the cones around the goals, but I didn't find anyone else. Before Sabrina confessed anything that wasn't suitable for children's ears, I wanted to make sure we were alone.

"I went on Facebook and looked up Austin." She held up her hands. "I know, I know. Nothing good comes from that. I was feeling low and had hopes that maybe the universe righted itself and he was miserable and ugly now."

She dug through the cooler and pulled out a bottle of water.

"I thought you were going to block him so the impulse wouldn't be there."

"Blocking doesn't work." She unscrewed the cap and

took a sip. "You can just unblock. Anyway, his baby is two, and his wife is pregnant again. Well, she's pregnant for the first time *as* his wife, not the woman he was seeing while he was married to me."

"Honey, I'm sorry." I squeezed her shoulder.

"Don't be, because I did it to myself. It was enough of a gut punch to knock the wind out of me and keep me awake, so here I am." She stretched out her arms.

"However you stumbled upon it, it sucks, and I hate that you were hurt all over again."

"I'm over it. For the most part, anyway. I'd been telling you for the longest time that we were having problems before it all blew up. We went over it plenty of times, and I'm too undercaffeinated to regurgitate any of it. But, yes." Her gaze drifted over the fake grass. "It still hurt."

I looped an arm around her shoulder.

"Yes, it does hurt when you see it, which is why it's not a good idea to look for it. But I've had plenty of my own weak moments on social media, so I really can't fault you for it."

"Thank you for not making me feel worse," she breathed out as her head fell onto my shoulder. "I needed a distraction. It was either come here or take Caden's offer to meet him later. He's a nice guy, but I can't do that again—and not in the state of mind I'm in. I can't hook up with someone just to forget someone else."

She rubbed the back of her neck and shook her head.

"It's not like high school, when it was a fun game. Now, I'll just feel more like shit."

"*Yes*," I said finally, because I couldn't help myself. "I am very, very happy that you came to that conclusion on your own. I was keeping my mouth shut, but I admit I was a little worried."

"It's good to know that I'm not too far gone, then." She

chuckled when she turned her head toward me. "How are you holding up? Nervous?"

"No. Or I shouldn't be." I peeled off my hoodie. "This game doesn't even count. I just want the kids to have a good time."

"I think some of the moms want to have a good time with Jesse."

A chuckle escaped me when she waggled her eyebrows. "Yes, that's...hard not to notice. But he's not interested."

"How are you so sure about that?" Sabrina drew her brows together.

"He told me that he's not interested in dating at all because he's focused on Maddie. In so many words anyway. These women are wasting their time."

"I don't know. Jesse is human, and some of them are very...direct. God bless."

Trying not to focus on how *direct* some of the mothers were had been a challenge last practice. One wouldn't let go of his arm the entire time—or at least every time I'd glanced their way—and kept leaning in close to whisper into his ear.

Girls had flirted with Jesse all the time when we were in high school, many just as brazen as these women were, and some would even do it right in front of me. He'd been polite but firm in telling them to back off, but I'd never been jealous or worried about it because I trusted him. While I still believed that Jesse didn't and wouldn't date, it didn't stop the almost overpowering inclination to march over and tell them to leave him the hell alone.

But I couldn't, could I?

Jesse wasn't mine. We were friends, and if a woman wanted to make a play for him, it was her right, as it was his to take her up on it.

And I had no reason to see red when I'd caught him smile and laugh at something one of the women said to him.

I had left the field that afternoon with a splitting headache from blowing my whistle too hard in misplaced frustration.

"Maybe he's not interested in dating, but he's a guy. They all have an itch to scratch. Even a perpetual golden-retriever-type like Jesse has needs." She held up a hand. "Just saying."

"Just saying, what?"

"If, possibly, the woman he's pretending to only want to be friends with let him know that she's interested in more, the soccer groupies would scatter. Just a thought."

"I'm not interested. We have history, but we're friends."

"Sure," she said, her eyes narrowed at me. "That's why I can hear your jaw ticking. Caden and I were just talking about it. You both have to be tired since it's exhausting just watching you."

"What do you want me to say?"

"Nothing to me," she said, holding up her hands. "But maybe if you told Jesse how you feel—"

"He's already said he's not interested. If Maddie hadn't joined the team, I probably would have gone another twenty years without seeing him again. If he *scratches* with some-one, that is his business and choice."

"You poor thing," she said, pushing off the bench and patting my arm. "You're not going to have any back teeth left when this season is over."

"Sabrina," I groaned, rooting around in my bag for my whistle. "I'm fine. Jesse is fine. Drop it." She raised a brow at me as I positioned the black lanyard string around my neck.

The frown pulling on Sabrina's lips only made me feel worse.

"I'm sorry, Em. I only want you to be happy. One of us should be." She huffed out a laugh.

"I know you do." I stepped closer and took a sweep of the area behind me. A few of my kids were heading over, but the field was mostly empty. "Friends is all we can be. For lots of reasons. This isn't one of the romance books I edit where a happily ever after is a given." I shrugged. "The ending may not be so great if I push it."

"I'm sorry. I'll stop trying to be anything more than your servant for today." She bumped my shoulder. "Put me to work, Coach."

"Hey, ladies. Ready for today?"

My head swiveled around to Penny's voice.

"I think so. I'll be happy if the kids have fun with no injuries. This is my first sort-of official game as a coach, not a player."

"In some ways, it's a lot less taxing. Other than the parents." She laughed and motioned to the man behind her. "This is Alex. He's our referee today."

"Nice to meet you," Alex said, holding out his hand.

"Same," I replied as I lifted my head. I was tall at almost five foot nine, but Alex had to be way over six feet.

"Alex is my brother-in-law. I roped him into being our ref for the afternoon."

His blue eyes crinkled at the corners when he smiled, an attractive contrast to his tanned skin. His blond hair was cropped short enough to spike at the front.

"And I don't like Penny or my brother enough to play favorites, so I promise to be fair," he said, holding up his hands, grinning as his crystal gaze stayed on mine.

"I don't think you can cheat during a scrimmage game, but good to know."

He laughed, still searching my face in a way that made me feel on display.

"Alex just moved here from California. Hence the surfer hair and tan," Penny said, tipping her chin to where Alex stood next to her. "He knows enough about soccer to realize when he has to blow the whistle. I wasn't picky when the ref I had scheduled texted me last night that he was sick."

"My sister-in-law is free and easy with the compliments," Alex said, folding his muscular arms over his chest, still focused on me.

"This is Sabrina," I said, squirmy enough under Alex's stare to shift back and forth on my feet. "We all went to high school together."

"They were the soccer all-stars," Sabrina said, moving her finger back and forth between Penny and me. "Not me."

"I see," Alex said, backing away. "Nice to meet you both. Have a great game!" He threw me a glance over his shoulder as he jogged to the middle of the field.

"Shit, he's hot," Sabrina whispered in my ear.

"Yes, he is," I agreed, both of us still gazing in his direction.

"For real," she said, elbowing my side. "And he's into you."

"He seems like a flirt." I shook my head. "He's probably into everyone."

"A flirt who didn't take his eyes off *you* the entire time. Jesse isn't going to like that," she sang.

"There is nothing for anyone to like or not like."

"Coach Emily!"

Maddie giggled as she barreled into my legs and squeezed her arms around me.

"Hey, kiddo," I said, hugging her back. Her hair was

pulled back in a tight ponytail with a maroon ribbon tied around it.

"My ponytail ribbon matches our shirts," Maddie chirped, pulling down the front of her team T-shirt.

"And it makes you easier to track on the field," I said, tapping her nose. "I love it."

"That's good to hear. I only had to watch the YouTube video on how to tie a ponytail three or ten times."

Jesse's smile was warm as his dark eyes held mine.

"Nice job, Uncle Jesse," Sabrina said, grinning at Maddie and giving her ponytail a gentle tug. "What are you going to do when she asks for a braid?"

"Probably sweat or call my mother," Jesse said with a chuckle. "And speaking of..."

I noticed Mrs. Evans's watery smile over Jesse's shoulder.

"Emily," she gasped before almost knocking Jesse over to pull me into a hug. "Let me look at you," she said, grabbing my arms to push me back. "My God, you haven't changed at all. Still so beautiful."

"Oh, I don't know about that, Mrs. Evans." I squeezed her shoulders.

Other than a little sparkle of gray mixed in with her brown hair, she was exactly as I remembered. So much so, I tried to swallow away the scratch at the back of my throat at just hearing her voice again.

"But thank you. You look amazing."

She waved a hand.

"You were always a sweetheart. I've heard a lot about you from my granddaughter." Mrs. Evans smoothed a tiny stray lock of hair from Maddie's ponytail off her forehead. "I told Maddie that I already knew her coach very well and used to see her all the time."

I pushed a smile across my mouth to stop the prick of

tears behind my eyes. Watching Mrs. Evans speak to Maddie the way I'd watched her with Tessa so many times triggered the grief I felt for this whole family, but I couldn't give in to it here. I'd pull Mrs. Evans aside after the game to tell her how sorry I was and cry—again—for all of them alone in my car on the way home.

"You can see her more now," Maddie said. "We have games every week, and she's Uncle Jesse's friend again. They text all the time."

"Well," Mrs. Evans said, biting her bottom lip as she threw her son a look. "That would be very nice. I'll go have a seat in the folding chair we brought. Have a great game, sweetie." She looked between Jesse and me and headed to the edge of the field.

"Maddie!" Jeffrey ran over to us, a soccer ball tucked under his arm. "Want to practice with me?"

"Ask Coach Emily if you can do that," Jesse told her, taking Maddie's arm when she started to race toward Jeffrey. "You may be in the way of everyone coming in."

"No, it's fine." I pointed to the empty patch next to the goal and far enough away from the chairs arriving parents were setting up. "You can for a few minutes. Just please keep it contained with small kicks back and forth."

"Okay," they both murmured before they scurried off.

"Nervous?" Jesse asked, his lips curling into a smirk. He wore a black Henley with the sleeves rolled up and jeans. Stopping my eyes from trailing his forearms down to where he'd stuffed his hands into his pockets was much harder than it should have been.

"This is just a scrimmage game, but I remember my days playing for a small league like this. I'm not worried about the kids, but the parents can be a little pushy. My mother was the pushiest."

He let out a throaty chuckle.

"Oh, I can imagine. You can always bring her here next game for reinforcements if anyone gives you trouble."

"Right? Even with a cane now, she can be pretty terrifying."

We shared a laugh, our eyes locked for an awkward beat after we stopped.

"You'll be great," he said, his eyes still holding mine as he eased closer. "You've got this, Legs."

I shoved his shoulder as my cheeks heated, trying to focus on the kids filtering in and not the sexy rumble of Jesse's laugh.

"Coach Emma, can I speak to you for a moment?"

Janie Cooper jogged toward me with her daughter at her side, shooting Jesse a quick smile before she came up to me.

"Emily," I said, wanting to remind her it was on the handout she'd received, but I doubted she'd looked at it or cared about her mistake.

"Aubrey has been practicing really hard, and I think it would be good for the team if you put her in first."

From the first practice, Janie had questioned everything I did, down to the warm-up games I played with the kids. I'd had a feeling she'd be difficult today and dreaded what she'd be like at a real game.

"That's great, Aubrey," I said with extra enthusiasm. "I already have it figured out who goes in when for today. I've worked it out so everyone gets equal playing time and can enjoy the snacks in between."

Aubrey peered up at me with a tiny smile as her mother scowled at me over her head. Aubrey was a cute kid and had fun at practice, despite Janie yelling for her to get the ball and kick harder.

"But the good players go out first. I didn't play sports in school, but isn't that a rule?"

"Ms. Cooper," I said, holding back a groan and trying for a polite yet firm tone of voice. Unfortunately, rude was sometimes the only way to get through to people like her, but I'd save that for the games that counted.

"This isn't a competition league. We keep track of wins and losses, but there are no local or state championships to strive for. I'm here to teach them soccer and make sure they have fun and that kids of all levels have equal playing time. A team like this is where I started to love soccer, without pressure from my coaches or my family." I held out my hand for Aubrey. "Right now, we're going to huddle up."

Aubrey peered up at her mother before taking my hand.

"Feel free to set up a chair on the sidelines with the other parents. I hope you enjoy the game."

"Have a good game, honey," Janie said, fake smile back in place as she aimed it at Jesse. "I suppose there's nothing else for us to do than to sit on the sidelines and watch our girls, right?"

Jesse took a slight step back when she reached for his arm.

"I brought a chair for my mother, but I'm going to stay over here to help Em and Sabrina. I'm used to it from all Emily's games in high school."

He snuck me a grin.

"Oh," she said, glancing back at me, phony smile still in place. "I didn't realize you knew each other from high school."

"Yes, Emily and I have a *long* history," Jesse said with a big grin that I wasn't sure was for show or not, but it stole my breath all the same.

"I see." I had to hold back a laugh at the disappointment

bleeding into her features. "We have an extra chair in case you need one—"

"I don't, but thanks."

She exhaled what looked like a frustrated breath through her nostrils.

"Well, I'll be right over there in case you...get tired."

She lingered for another minute and disappeared into the rows of parents at the edge of the field.

"You can sit with the kids over there," I said to Aubrey, pointing to where Sabrina was checking off attendance on a clipboard. "Once everyone is here, we'll line up on the field. Sound good?"

Aubrey nodded and headed over, not looking back at me or for her mother.

A laugh burst out of my chest when I met Jesse's gaze.

"I needed that," I said, pressing my palm against my forehead. "Nothing like a little comic relief before a game. That poor kid," I whispered to Jesse. "She's so much more relaxed when her father brings her to the field."

Jesse laughed. "So am I. Nice work. It's okay if I stay over here? I meant to ask."

"If you want to, sure. I know Maddie will appreciate it."

"I did want to stay close for her sake too, but I figured I'd linger over here in case you needed anything. Even though you have it handled, pushy parents and all."

"Thanks. After she was all over you last practice, I'm surprised she went away so easily."

"You noticed that?" Jesse drew his brows together.

"Well, it was a little obvious."

"I see," he said, giving me a slow nod.

"You see what?" I squinted at Jesse.

"You weren't jealous or anything, were you?" He raised a brow as his lips twitched.

"No," I said, a little too quickly, with a chalklike screech in my reply. "I was too busy trying to line up my kids to notice any single parents canoodling on the sidelines."

"Canoodling? You editors know a lot of words," he teased.

"You want to be cute? Now you're on snack duty. You can explain how we only have healthy veggie sticks instead of chips between goals." I jutted my chin toward the bag of food next to the cooler.

"So, you think I'm cute," Jesse said, snickering as he held my gaze.

"You're still decent, I guess." I scowled back at him as I adjusted the whistle around my neck. "But that doesn't mean I'm jealous."

"I'm flattered. Thanks," he rasped with a low whisper that curled my toes inside my sneakers. His smile shrank as the air thickened between us, too charged for a kids' soccer game—a game where I had to be present enough to coach.

Swooning over my high school ex-boyfriend was stupid on too many levels today.

"Emily!"

Alex jogged over to me, his beaming smile almost blinding me.

"You can gather up the first string now. Time for kickoff. I hope you're not nervous." Alex cracked a wide grin.

"Nope, we're all ready," I said, shooting him a half smile in an attempt to get him to shrink the beam of the megawatt grin on his perfect face.

"I'm sure. Penny said you were a pro."

"I stopped right before pro." I shook my head. "I'm just here to make sure my kids have fun and don't get hurt or pass out trying."

"Really? You look pretty pro to me." He smiled, and I

couldn't tell if he'd flicked his eyes up and down my body or was shielding them from the lights. "Anyway, good luck, even though Penny keeps telling me it doesn't count."

Maybe it had been too long since a man had tried to flirt with me, or that I'd noticed or cared if one was, but I was painfully clueless as to how to react other than to inch away.

I nodded a thanks and went back to our side of the field.

"Who's that?" Jesse asked, the playful lilt in his voice from a few minutes ago now gone.

"Penny's brother-in-law. He's the ref for today."

"You know him?" Jesse asked, glowering across the field to where Alex was adjusting the cones around the other team's goal.

"No. I just met him a few minutes ago. Why?"

"He acted like he knew *you* pretty well," he gritted out before uttering a humorless chuckle.

"He's friendly, I guess." I crossed my arms and marched up to Jesse. "You're not *jealous*, are you?"

"What? No. He just seems full of himself."

"And you could tell that in five minutes?"

"I could. Full of himself and pushy. It's a kids' game, not a bar. Not the time or place for whatever he was trying to do with you."

"I see." I tapped my chin. "Says the guy who went home with four containers of home-cooked meals from his fan club last week."

"It wasn't four—wait, you were counting? I thought you were too busy coaching," Jesse said, stepping closer to me while the corner of his mouth curled up.

"I hate to interrupt whatever this is, but I think you need to line up your kids, Coach," Sabrina said, nodding to where Penny's team was already lined up.

"I'll be right there," I said, holding Jesse's gaze as I followed Sabrina.

"Tell me again how you're just friends and neither of you is interested in anything else?" Sabrina whispered as we jogged toward the kids.

"Later. Right now, we have a game. Come on, guys." I pointed to the field.

"Yes," Sabrina said with a snicker. "We sure do."

10

JESSE

MADDIE'S BREATHS CAME OUT IN PANTS, WISPS OF HAIR falling from her ponytail and tickling her reddened cheeks. The other kids had trickled off the field after the game with their parents, most of them bored toward the end and ready to go, but we had trouble keeping Maddie in her seat.

"If I went back in at the end, I could have made a goal. I know it," she said, still gasping between sips of water.

"Making a goal isn't everything," Emily said, shaking her head as she settled on the bench next to Maddie. "Learning how to move the ball where you need it to go is what is important. You did great for your first game, so don't focus on goals yet."

"Here," I said, twisting open another bottle of water as I squatted in front of her. "Drink more and catch your breath like Em—Coach Emily—just said."

The first game seemed to have gone by before I could even blink. I handed out bags of snacks to the kids running on and off the field, and every time Emily would take Maddie out, she'd beg to go back in. Most of the players clustered around the ball, fighting to get control until they'd end up kicking in a circle.

Maddie gulped the bottle as I peered up at Emily. I wasn't sure if it was the memories of watching her play in high school or how fucking gorgeous she looked today, but the fight to keep my eyes off her the entire game had been as exhausting as it was pointless.

The rage simmering in my veins at the referee for eye-fucking Emily every time he'd glanced her way didn't help.

But what could I do? March over there and tell him to stop leering at her because she was my...nothing.

Emily was my friend, and I'd made it all too clear to her how I barely had time for even that. I'd insisted to her and everyone else that Maddie was the only woman I had room for in my life, and if that left Emily open for douches like this guy to hit on her, the only one I could be furious with was myself.

"I didn't think being on the sidelines would be this labor-intensive," I joked when Emily's gaze slid to mine.

"Honestly," she sighed, "neither did I. Their excitement is good. I guess I just need to teach them all to focus a little." She exhaled a long breath. "I think I got a little cocky. I thought I'd be better at this."

"That's not true." I shook my head. "You were great."

She lifted a shoulder. "I didn't play, but yelling every ten minutes to stop crowding around the ball because they wouldn't listen to me felt like a full-body workout by the end."

"Kids this age have a hard time listening, period, never mind when they're excited. I have short but very current experience with that." I motioned to Maddie, still chugging her water. "I think you did great, Legs. So stop worrying about it."

"Yeah!" Maddie agreed. "You're awesome." She scrunched up her nose and turned to me. "Wait, why did you call her Legs?"

"Because when she was a soccer superstar in high school —" I bent my head to whisper, my eyes on Emily "—she ran really fast."

I'd called her Legs because hers were long, lean, and gorgeous, and when I hadn't been telling her that, my mouth and hands had been showing my appreciation until she shivered in my arms.

Emily shook her head at me and swiped her hand along the back of her neck. I swore I spotted a blush staining her cheeks, and the thought kicked up my pulse. Knowing she may have been a little jealous by the attention I was getting on the sidelines gave me a thrill I had no right to have if I didn't intend to do anything about it.

Too bad intending to was a hell of a lot different from wanting to.

"Thank you both for that vote of confidence. I'll try to take your word for it. I think it was a great first game, but I'll be happy to sit on my butt all day tomorrow and edit."

I nodded, now thinking of Emily's ass in those tight shorts and those fucking legs as she'd run back and forth along the field today.

I hadn't heard much of what she'd said during the game either.

"Good game. Wow, you were working pretty hard there," Alex, the referee or whatever the fuck he was, told my niece as he took a seat next to Emily. He was pandering to a kid for an excuse to talk to her coach. But I'd already shown too many cards to Emily today about how I was trying not to feel about her. I couldn't point out this guy's all too obvious intentions.

"She was," Emily said, not looking back at Alex as she smiled at Maddie. "She reminds me a lot of me when I was her age. Although I always took my snack breaks." She tapped her toe against Maddie's sneaker.

"I bet," Alex said with that same slimy gleam in his eye before standing. "I told Penny I'd do this again if she needed the help. Although a game that counts is probably more pressure."

He stood, his eyes still on Emily. It took the restraint of every cell in my body not to pop off the bench and tell him to back off, but this wasn't the time or place—and if we were only friends, it never would be.

"Hope to see you again if I do."

"We'll be here," I said. "Have a good day."

"Have a good day," he said, moving his gaze back and forth between Emily and me as he shifted to leave.

"What?" I asked when I caught Emily staring. "I was being polite."

"So, I was the only one who thought *we'll be here* sounded like a threat?" Emily pursed her lips at me.

"Are you okay, Uncle Jesse?" Maddie asked before I could answer Emily, her eyes wide as she examined my face.

"Yeah, Mad. Why do you ask?"

"Because you made that rumbly noise my stomach sometimes does when I get really hungry."

Emily laughed but tapped her chest, pretending to clear her throat.

"That means your uncle should have eaten a snack while he was handing them out today." She clicked her tongue against her teeth and shook her head.

"Yes, even from where I was sitting, he looked a little cranky."

I shut my eyes at my mother's voice behind me.

"I'm not cranky."

She patted my shoulder without glancing back at me and reached for Maddie.

"What a game!"

Maddie popped off the bench and hugged my mother's waist.

"Did you see me, Grams? I almost kicked a goal twice!"

"I did. The ribbon was a great idea since I could spot you the whole time."

Mom tugged on the frayed edge of the ribbon before coming up to Emily.

"I made a nice big lasagna for tonight, and we would love it if you stopped by to eat it with us, Emily."

Maddie sucked in a gasp and folded her hands under her chin.

"Please come! Grams makes the best lasagna."

"I remember," Emily said, flashing my mother a warm smile. "I don't want to impose—"

"When did you ever impose? I used to make a big tray of lasagna whenever Coach Emily had a big game," my mother told Maddie while keeping her gaze on Emily. "Maybe we can restart the tradition this season."

Restarting anything where Emily was concerned was probably a bad idea, but I couldn't stop my mother any more than I could stop myself.

"Please," Maddie pleaded as she tugged on Emily's hand.

"We'd love it if you'd have dinner with us. Please," I said, my voice dipping to a lower and needier octave than my niece's. I couldn't stop wanting her, but I needed her to be at a distance for a lot of reasons.

The adoration my niece had for Emily was a big one. My own longing for Emily seemed like it came from my bones, deepening each day and costing me more sleep every night.

It would be so easy to get lost in her again, and I was already halfway there, despite my weak attempts to hold myself back.

"Okay, then. I'll bring dessert."

"Yes," my niece said, pumping her fist in the air before roping her arms around Emily's neck.

"I'm excited too," Emily said, sputtering out a cough after my niece appeared to almost choke her. "I better get home and change out of coach clothes. See you all later." She lifted her head, her smile shrinking a bit when her gaze met mine.

I dropped my eyes to the ground, the only way to keep from tracking her as she left the field.

"Did you really make that lasagna for everyone tonight or just one person?" I asked my mother when I lifted my head.

"I put it together this morning for later. I knew Maddie would be hungry and maybe we'd have...guests." She shrugged, hoisting the long strap for the portable chair over her shoulder.

"You don't usually plan that far ahead for *guests*." I slipped the chair strap off my mother's arm and put it over my shoulder.

"Sometimes you have to in order to get things moving. If this family knows anything," she said, her eyes narrowed to slits at me, "it's that time is limited."

"I know that. But I can't afford to—"

"Waste it? Along with any other chances and opportunities the good Lord is kind enough to give you? Yes, now you see my point." She patted my cheek, her honey-colored eyes shining as she scanned my face.

"Come on, sweetheart." She held out a hand for Maddie. "You have clothes in your room at our house. You can get showered and changed before Emily—I mean before dinner."

I let my head fall back, my eyes drifting up to the blue sky and puffy clouds my sister used to insist were marshmallows when she was Maddie's age.

"Stop laughing," I whispered as I followed my mother to my truck.

11

EMILY

I made it to Jesse's parents' house almost on autopilot, but once I arrived, I couldn't get out of my car.

I darted my eyes back and forth from their front door to the bakery box of chocolate cream pie on my passenger seat. They would spot me any minute now, and I'd have to explain why I was lingering in front of their house like a stalker.

The day before I'd left for Maine what now felt like a million years ago, I'd gone on a drive to pick up a few last-minute things for my dorm and had ended up here. I hadn't seen any of their cars parked in the driveway or in front, so I'd sat and stared at their house until I'd become disgusted enough with myself to leave.

I didn't know what I would have said if Jesse had been home and found me there, or what my intentions were after driving forty minutes out of my way to simply stare.

This was different. My heartbreak over Jesse had been fresh and raw enough not to care what any of his neighbors would think if they spotted me or if they'd report back to him or his family that I had been there. But the weight of how it felt to be here again still seemed as heavy.

The house looked exactly the same, down to the beds of pastel-colored roses under the large storm window. When I'd come here for the first time, I'd been so nervous, Jesse had told me to stop shaking as we'd walked up that same stone walkway to his front door. I had been barely fifteen and Jesse and I had already been inseparable, but having dinner at his house seemed like a huge step to making us official—as much as two young teenagers could be an official anything together.

My mother hadn't approved of my having a boyfriend at such a young age and had made sure to let us both know it when I'd brought Jesse over to our house. My grandfather had loved him, and both my grandparents had told my mother to calm down. Poor Jesse had endured dirty looks from her for simply existing each time she'd seen him, right up until graduation.

I'd thought that Jesse's parents would react the same way, but this house had become a second home for me from that first day. Mrs. Evans would light up whenever I'd come over, and Tessa would climb all over me. They'd made me feel like family, and I'd hated losing them all when I'd lost Jesse.

Mrs. Evans was still the same warm and wonderful human being, and I'd be welcomed with open arms as always the minute I rang the doorbell.

So, what was stopping me?

While the outside hadn't changed much, the inside wouldn't be the same. Tessa's giggle wouldn't waft down the steps as she ran over to greet me, and Jesse wouldn't pull me down the hallway for a passionate kiss hello when his parents weren't watching.

This house held more than just memories for me. I'd grown up here along with Jesse. Enough time had passed for the images to fade, but the old days ran through my mind so vividly lately. The time I had with Jesse, no matter how long ago it was, had meant a lot to me. No matter how many years had passed, I'd had moments when I might not have actively thought about him for a while, but I could never forget.

I leaned my head against the steering wheel and sucked in a long breath, letting it out slowly to relax and maybe get a damn grip on myself. Before I could tell if it worked, a knock on my window made me jump. I whipped my head around to Jesse's smirk on the other side of the glass.

I dropped my head back, chuckling to myself as I rolled down the window.

"The neighbors may think you're casing the place if you stay in the car any longer," Jesse quipped, a smile teasing the corner of his perfect mouth.

"Good point," I said when I dragged my gaze to his. "I'm sorry," I said, draping my hand over my eyes and peeking at Jesse through a crack in my fingers. "It's just..." My cheeks singed with embarrassment over getting caught without a clue how to explain.

"Weird?" He quirked a brow, peering down at me as he rested his hand on the roof of my car, treating me to the flex of his bicep as he leaned closer. I'd always thought he was the most beautiful boy I'd ever seen, but the man he'd grown into was too much to handle lately, never mind to look at for too long.

"I suppose that's a good word. But I couldn't tell your mom no." I grinned, my stupid heart jumping a couple of beats when his own smile deepened.

"No, you couldn't have. You know Patti Evans when she

has an agenda. She wasn't going to let you get away with just saying hello today."

"Your mom was always the best." I drifted my gaze toward the house. "I've missed game-day lasagna." I flicked my eyes back to Jesse.

Along with you, and now I'm not sure if I ever really stopped.

"Especially since my mom only made it on Christmas," I said, glancing back at the house. "It took a while to get used to eating it on just a regular day."

His blinding grin shrank.

"She said she always liked treating you to something after you worked so hard. And as I was at all of your games, I know you *earned* that lasagna every fucking time."

"Thanks," I said, warmth flooding my chest at the pride in his eyes. Jesse had never missed a game, making his dad take him to all the out-of-town ones until he'd learned to drive. Watching him on the sidelines today, cheering for Maddie with every kick, made me think of a time almost too wonderful and simple to believe it had ever existed.

"All kidding aside," Jesse said, furrowing his brow. "I hope we didn't pressure you. I mean, I know we did." He rested his elbows on the inside of my open window and laughed.

"I couldn't say no to your mom—or Maddie."

"Or…" Jesse said, raising a brow.

"Oh, you were easy," I said, waving my hand.

"I could just go home and heat up one of the casseroles from my fan club." His lips, now inches away from mine as he came even closer, twitched at the corners.

"I'm sure they're piling up. Maybe you should." I lifted a shoulder.

He dropped his chin to his chest, his throaty chuckle running right through me.

"I wanted to be here tonight," I said, my heart thudding in my ears as I prepped myself for my wimpy confession. "For everyone. Including you, so save the casserole for another night."

"I wanted you here too," Jesse said, his eyes holding mine as he opened my car door and extended his hand. "So, come inside."

I stood, my palm tingling as usual when it grazed his. It brought me back to that first jolt when our skin touched on the day we met, when both of us had reached for the same pencil and fallen into a four-year trance.

Core memories were good that way, staying part of your makeup despite the merciful lack of awareness.

Until something made you remember, and then you couldn't stop.

I dropped his hand to close the window and grab the pie, grateful for the opportunity to turn away from him and catch my breath.

"After you," Jesse said, his gravelly whisper stealing back the little air I was able to pull into my lungs.

Since we'd reconnected—or had been forced into each other's path—it had been easier to talk myself out of these odd moments in a text message. When one of us would bring up something simple from the past, like the pizzeria we used to sneak to by school, or how my mother would tell him to stay out of my sight during big games so I wouldn't be distracted, we could laugh without whatever this was simmering between us like it did when we were face-to-face.

When we talked in person, the feelings always got in the way. Whether it was remnants of how we used to be or something more current, it messed with my head all the same.

I'd never admit it to him, but he was right to cut me off

completely when we broke up. I wouldn't have been able to handle any kind of connection with him and move on.

All these years later, that was still a problem.

Jesse pressed his hand to the small of my back as he reached in front of me to push open the screen door. My entire body lit up at his proximity.

"Thank you," I muttered and stepped through the door, taking two big strides away from Jesse to shake off whatever had come over us both in the past few minutes and today.

"Emily!"

Mrs. Evans rushed up to me as if she hadn't seen me a little over three hours ago and scooped me up into another hug.

"Thank you for the invite, Mrs. Evans. I was just telling Jesse how much I missed game-day lasagna."

I glanced back at Jesse and the tiny smile ghosting his lips.

"I've missed game-day lasagna too. And now, with a soccer player in the family again, we can have it all the time."

The familiar deep rumble of Mr. Evans's laugh echoed down the staircase. His eyes, dark and kind like his son's, met mine. Other than the full beard, Jesse's father was an older version of his son, and time had been extremely good to both of his parents. His father seemed the same stocky kind of strong.

"Nice to see you again, sweetheart," Mr. Evans said, bringing me in for a gentle hug.

"Thank you. Nice to see you too." I cleared my throat when I noticed my voice squeak.

"I'm sorry I had to work today. Maddie already told me how amazing her first game was."

"You're here!"

I turned to Maddie's little voice. Just like her mother's, her voice seemed too small and soft for her tall body. She slammed into me and squeezed her arms around my waist.

"Easy, Mad," Jesse said, putting his hands on her shoulders. "You just saw Emily. You don't need to clobber her every time."

"Mom says hugs are free, so you should give them out whenever you want." Her smile faded. "Or used to say, I guess."

Jesse clenched his eyes shut as if he'd just been punched.

"Well, I'm a big believer in free hugs too." I cupped her chin as she beamed up at me. I wasn't sure whether to be relieved or want to cry at how easily Maddie had corrected herself that her mother wasn't around anymore to say anything.

"Did you come over a lot when you were Uncle Jesse's friend?"

"I did," I said, trying to ignore Jesse's stare in my periphery. "And your grams makes the best lasagna, but never tell my mother that," I whispered, pressing a finger to my lips.

She giggled, pretending to pull a zipper across her mouth.

I did a quick scope of the living room, noting the updated couches and recliner, but most of it seemed and felt the same. The scent of garlic wafted in from the kitchen and smelled good enough to make my nervous stomach rumble.

"I stopped at that famous bakery everyone talks about on Sunrise Highway and picked up a chocolate cream pie."

"That's very sweet of you. You didn't have to bring anything, but I'd never refuse something from *Hey, Batter*. You know that chocolate cream pie is my weakness." She tapped my chin with her knuckle. "It's almost ready, so all of you can take a seat in the living room until I call you."

"I'll help you," I said, following Mrs. Evans into the kitchen.

A lump grew in the back of my throat when I glanced behind me and found Maddie lining up her dolls on the living room floor—like Tessa would before she'd pull me down to play with her—and I couldn't swallow it away.

"You don't have to help. I'm sure you're exhausted from all those parents and kids," Mrs. Evans told me over her shoulder as she rinsed out a dish in the sink.

"If I can't handle a scrimmage game, I probably have no business coaching," I said, chuckling as I leaned against the counter.

"Did the kids find out that you're a superstar?"

I laughed at the excitement lighting up her features. Jesse and Mrs. Evans had loved to call me a superstar back then, and it seemed just as ridiculous yet wonderful now.

"Was. Past tense. I didn't do anything with soccer after college."

"Jesse told me," she said as she bent to peek into the oven. "Doesn't matter. I knew you'd go on to do great things, and I was right."

She straightened, regarding me with a warm smile that finally made the dam break.

"I'm sorry. So, so sorry," I sobbed, covering my mouth with my hand as if to will back the tears streaming down my cheeks.

She pulled me into a hug, patting me on the back of my head as I cried on her shoulder.

"I know, honey," she whispered, pushing me back to meet my gaze. "It's...it's a bitch." We shared a chuckle.

"I don't know what's wrong with me," I squeaked out,

wiping my cheeks with the back of my hand. "It's just, being here in this house with all of you, and watching Maddie play on the floor like Tessa and I used to..." I dropped my head into my hands and pinched the bridge of my nose as if that would shut off the waterworks.

"It's been a long time since you've been here, so it's all fresh. For me, too. When I spotted you on the field, I couldn't get to you fast enough." She laughed as she plucked out a tissue from the box on her windowsill and handed it to me. "I know Jesse felt the same way when he saw you again."

"We aren't..." I stammered as I dabbed at my eyes. "We're friends now. It's good," I said, nodding with a little too much enthusiasm.

"I'm not sure about that, but I think I've met my quota of interfering for the day." She patted my cheek. "But you can believe me when I say that we are all happy you're here tonight. Including my daughter, who asked about you every single day that summer."

"Did she?" There was the lump again, now too big to swallow away. "I wished I could have come back to see her and all of you, but—"

"I understood, and Tessa did too, even if she wasn't happy about it. She was pretty mad at her big brother for a long while. If it's any consolation, for months, he never made it through a single day without hearing your name, and I could tell it ate away at him every time."

"A little," I said, a real laugh bubbling out of me when I lifted my head.

"It's almost like Tessa is pushing you both back together." She raised a brow as she sifted through a drawer of silverware.

"I don't know about that, Mrs. Evans." I shook my head. "Granted, it's a lot of coincidence, but—"

"Maybe it's my old and foolish heart wanting to believe my daughter is still around or that there's a higher power with some kind of plan after all."

She handed me a stack of plates, a watery smile curving her lips.

"Whatever it is, I'm happy to have you back here at my table, with my son, who is trying to hold back how happy *he* is to have you here, and my granddaughter, who needs someone like you right now," she said, sniffling as she nodded to the dining room. "I'll keep watching the signs and hold on to the hope."

Did I believe a greater power had put me back in Jesse's path because it was fate, or just to screw with me?

I favored the latter.

"Hey, are you okay?"

Jesse grabbed my arm as I set the plates on the table.

"Fine, why?"

"You look...upset," he said, concern pulling at his features.

I clenched my eyes shut and nodded. I'd forgotten my crying jag on his mother's shoulder, and while I'd wiped away the tears, my eyes were probably still red and swollen.

"I'm okay, Jesse. It was just too many memories there for a minute."

His shoulders softened as a relieved smile coasted across his face.

"I know what you mean. When you went into the kitchen with my mother, I kept trying to remember when the last time you were here was. I know it was a lot of years ago, but I don't remember the exact last dinner—"

"I do," I admitted as I set down the last plate.

Jesse squinted at me. "You do?"

"Well, not the last dinner with your parents. But I remember my last meal here. We decided to have a taco night when your parents and your sister went on vacation and left you here alone because you were working that warehouse job for the summer with Caden. It was about a week before..."

Jesse shut his eyes, nodding as he leaned back against the wall.

"You picked me up after work, and we bought way too much from the grocery store to make tacos for only two people." I huffed out a laugh as I made my way around the table. "My mother actually bought that I was staying at Sabrina's house for the night. That was my last sort of dinner and my first and last breakfast here."

I hated my stupid brain and its airtight clarity when it came to my history with Jesse lately. I couldn't tell you what I'd had for breakfast this morning or dinner last night, but I could recall with complete detail devouring blueberry pancakes in Jesse's bed that next morning, starving since we'd abandoned our crazy dinner the night before to feast on each other instead.

"That was a fun night," Jesse rasped as the corner of his mouth tipped up, taking a quick glance behind him. "The kitchen was a disaster, but we managed to clean it up enough before everyone came home. Other than my mother asking why my sheets smelled like syrup, none of our parents were tipped off."

We laughed at the bittersweet memory. I blamed the fact that I'd—mostly—forgiven him for breaking up with me on losing that shield of anger I'd needed to ground and protect myself.

Even though we'd been young, too young to ever truly plan for a forever or even understand it, it had been good between us. Too good to last, but both heartbreaking and wonderful to remember.

"What's your other job? You said you have to sit on your butt all day and edit."

Jesse and I both straightened at the same time, the usual spell between us broken by his niece's question.

"I'm a book editor. I analyze manuscripts and make sure they have no mistakes before they get published."

Her tiny brows pulled together. "What are manuscripts?"

"That's what they call books when they're still being written."

She pursed her lips. "So it's like when my English teacher grades our essays?"

"Something like that. I make sure all the words and punctuation marks are correct and that the story makes sense. Do you like to read?"

"Sometimes. I love the Baby-Sitters Club books. Mom tried to read Harry Potter to me, but one book took like a month for us to read. I like short books." Her lips pursed as she slid into one of the dining room chairs.

"I like short books too, and The Baby-Sitters Club was always a favorite of mine. But it's awesome when I love a book so much I never want it to end. Then it's cool when there are a lot of pages." I took a seat next to her.

"I guess I could try a longer book if it's good. Could you pick one for me?"

She loved soccer, and now she wanted me to pick a book for her. This girl knew how to get to me almost as much as her uncle did.

"I would love to. Let me think on it."

A smile lit up her face.

"And maybe you could come to our house, and we could read it together."

My stomach sank when I spotted the deep crease on Jesse's forehead. I wanted to say yes, especially since she was so excited, but the tension in his features as he stared across the table stopped me.

"I'm sure Emily has a full schedule with coaching and working," Jesse said before I could figure out how to answer. "You can read the book she picks for you on your own and talk to her about it when you see her."

I was about to protest that it was no trouble, but maybe he'd said no because he didn't want Maddie getting attached to me in case I wasn't around after the season was over. It was probably best for me if I didn't get too invested in them both for that same reason. I didn't want to stop speaking to Jesse, but I didn't know what he could handle in the long-term, and from what I could tell, neither did he.

"Dinner is served," Mrs. Evans sang as she set the lasagna on a hot plate in the middle of the table.

"I'm sorry." I pushed away from the table. "I forgot the silverware."

She put a hand on my shoulder and shook her head. "My son will get it. Stay." She cut a look at Maddie. "You're our guest."

My skin prickled when Jesse placed a fork and knife next to my plate, grazing my arm as he moved away. Even if some of my crazy feelings for Jesse were reciprocated, that didn't mean he wanted me around on a permanent basis.

I got it and didn't fault him for it, but it stung all the same.

"Did you know that Emily was a professional soccer player?" Mr. Evans asked Maddie as he set a brick of lasagna on Maddie's plate.

"Not really." I shook my head at Mr. Evans. "Just high school and college—"

"Yes, I saw a video of her playing," Maddie said, grabbing her fork and cutting into her dinner.

"You did?" I muttered a thank-you to Mrs. Evans when she slid a piece onto my plate, and I peered down at Maddie, too into her dinner to look up.

"Yep," she mumbled, slurping up the strings of mozzarella on her lips. "Mikayla showed me on her tablet before the game. It's on YouTube."

"It is? Wow," I breathed out and fell back against my seat. "I guess I think of YouTube as after my time." I laughed, grateful for the change in subject.

"And she was amazing, right?" Mrs. Evans said. "I'd love to see that video."

"Honestly, so would I," I scoffed. "Do you remember where on YouTube?"

She crinkled her nose. "I don't know where she found it. It was a champion game. Mikayla said you can tell because of the flags on the field."

"She means championship," Jesse clarified, one side of his mouth tipping up in a smirk. "Because of course it was."

I rolled my eyes.

"It didn't look like you at first. Your hair was blond."

"Ah," I said, realizing what game it was now from the flags and my one year of blond hair. "That was a division championship game against UNH during my junior year of college."

"You were so fast! Even at the end when your kick was in slow motion. So cool," Maddie gushed, the words garbled around her full mouth of lasagna.

"Chew," Jesse said. "It's easier to taste it that way. And I told you Coach Emily was fast." He flashed me a relaxed smile, and I exhaled a small breath of relief that maybe he wasn't upset with me for overstepping.

I'd joked with Jesse about his fan club at soccer, but how could you not swoon over a man so dedicated to his little girl and protecting her from anyone who could hurt her, intentional or not?

It was impossible.

For a man always so worried about making mistakes as a parent, he was one of the best fathers I'd ever seen. He'd never fail Maddie or Tessa. His sister had known what she was doing when she'd insisted he be the one to take care of her daughter when she was gone.

"I'll walk you to your car," Jesse said later, following me out the front door after I thanked his parents once we'd finished dessert and promised I'd be back. I thought it was an okay possible white lie if another game-day lasagna would make Jesse uncomfortable.

"It's not necessary. You can watch me from the window as I walk the five feet to my car if you're worried."

"I know, but it's not the same. And I wanted to talk to you. About the book," he said, cringing as he pinched the back of his neck when we reached the curb.

"It's okay. I'm sorry I got carried away."

"You didn't. *I'm* sorry if I sounded harsh. It's just that..." He rubbed his eyes. "She already likes you so much. I'm not saying I'd ever want to lose touch with you again, but if you get busy or meet someone—"

"I completely understand, so no need to explain." I held up my hand. "You're being a good dad. You're pretty great at this parenting thing, even if you don't know it yet."

He laughed, tilting his head. "I don't know about that. Fuck knows I'm trying."

"You're doing more than trying." I squeezed his shoulder. "Would it be okay if I still picked a book for her? She already seems to love soccer, so if I could make her a reader…" I said, drawing a laugh from Jesse when I pressed a dramatic hand to my chest.

"Sure. And speaking of soccer," he said, reaching into his pocket. "Look what I found."

He handed me his phone with YouTube open on the screen. I pressed the arrow for play, and sure enough, I spied my long then-blond ponytail whipping behind me as I tore across the field.

"My God. My legs hurt just looking at this," I said with a chuckle. "I thought high school training was a bitch." I chuckled. "My coach almost killed me in college. A big reason why I decided to stop there."

Jesse watched over my shoulder as the video slowed, the ball soaring through the air like a scene in a movie before it hit the back of the net. Whoever had shot the video had added music over the actual sounds of the game, but I could almost hear the beautiful swoosh when the ball landed right in the sweet spot.

"Damn, I was good." I laughed. I couldn't make out Jesse's expression on the dark street, but I still felt the heat as his eyes burned into mine.

"You were incredible. Still are," he whispered as he stuffed his phone back into his pocket.

"I may not be as lean as I was back then, but I like my curves. My workout routines don't make me almost vomit anymore, and I can enjoy lasagna and pie without regret."

"You're perfect," he said, his voice so low it was almost inaudible.

"Thank you. For that and—" I glanced back at the house, laughing to myself when I caught Jesse's mother staring at us, then closing the curtain when I made eye contact "—for tonight. Your family is amazing."

I fidgeted with my car keys as I looked everywhere but at Jesse.

"And I guess you're all right too," I added, finally lifting my eyes to his. "Don't expect any casseroles from me, though."

I laughed with him until he grazed his knuckles over my jaw.

"Thanks," he whispered in my ear and kissed my cheek, lingering long enough to feel every centimeter of his lips on my skin. I prayed the goose bumps trailing down my neck weren't obvious in the dark.

"Goodnight," I croaked out, both wanting to run away and fall into Jesse's arms. I was too close to get away with either.

"By the way," I said as I climbed into the seat. "How did you find that video so fast?"

"I googled your name."

"Ah. I googled yours too a few times and may have done a Facebook search a time or two."

"This was the first time I've looked you up."

"Seriously? So you didn't check up on me. Even once. Wow, what kind of ex-boyfriend are you?" I joked.

"No, I didn't." Jesse didn't laugh with me. "But not for the reasons you're probably thinking."

"Jesse, it's fine. I'm not trying to make you feel badly because you didn't think to do it."

"Oh, I thought about it," he said with a chuckle. "I wanted amazing things for you and for you to be happy. But actually looking you up and seeing it? I wasn't sure I could handle that. I wanted to be right by your side, experiencing it all with you, even though it wasn't possible." He tapped his pocket. "Seeing this makes me mad I wasn't there in the stands that day, screaming so loud I wouldn't have had a voice after. Not just watching someone's video of it. The jealousy burns even now."

The night air grew thick between us before he shifted away from me.

"Text me when you get home. Thank you again for being here tonight."

I nodded, leaning away when Jesse shut my car door. I felt his eyes on me as I started the engine, and I gave him a wave before I drove off.

It didn't matter how long ago it was. It *all* still burned.

12

EMILY

"Here's to another *New York Times* best seller."

I clinked my glass to Mary's. She'd been one of my first clients after I'd gone out on my own, and half of my current client roster could be linked back to her. She was in her early sixties and stunning, her shoulder-length gray hair a soft silver that shimmered along with her blue eyes.

We used to be almost neighbors when I'd lived on the Upper West Side of Manhattan, but we still met for dinner occasionally, usually to celebrate publishing her latest book or if we'd needed an intense discussion over edits to the one she was working on. Either instance involved more drinks than I could usually keep up with, but I'd kept it to only a couple tonight since I was driving home.

"Here's to selling enough books to afford to keep writing them," Mary said before downing the rest of her martini. "It helps manage the disappointment when you aim low."

I laughed. "I absolutely see that logic. So what else is going on besides mapping out your next four book releases."

"Nothing, really. The kids are all out of college, and the

last one moved out as of last month. So, more time to write, which means more words for you."

"That's totally fine with me."

"Glad to hear it," she said. "What's new with you? Embracing the single life?"

"I don't know what you'd call embracing. I haven't had time to try to meet anyone."

"This place has some good-looking single guys." She turned, sweeping her gaze over the crowd behind us. "When I leave to get my train, you should try to make a new friend."

I had made a new friend out of an old friend, and that was probably the reason for my lack of motivation in meeting anyone new. I always loved seeing Mary, but it was great to spend the evening with someone who didn't know Jesse, our history, or our convoluted present.

Speaking to Jesse every day didn't help the confusion, and the unanswered text I'd sent this afternoon gnawed at me. He never went this long without responding, and other than my pesky attachment to him, something felt off.

"I'll see." I surveyed the group of guys in suits by the bar. "I'd bet most of those men are attached and wanted a drink after they got off the train before they go home to their families."

"You never know. One might be available enough for a good time." Her brows jumped.

"I'll see. I'm glad you made the trip in, but next time, I'll come to you."

"Don't be silly. I like coming to Long Island. It's like a small town but is big enough so that everybody's not in your business."

"Ah, spoken like someone who only visits and doesn't live here."

She laughed. "I suppose. It's not so secluded that there's

only one of everything, but it's cozy. I can see why you wanted to come back."

"It is, compared to the Upper West Side, I suppose. It's a lot more cost-effective to be back. I was lucky to find an apartment at a decent price since the coziness can get pricey, depending on where you look."

"I could see you having a nice small-town romance here. Maybe that could be next up. I can use you as inspiration."

"That sounds like a boring book," I said with a chuckle. "Don't do that."

"I better get my train." She flicked her wrist up to glance at her watch. "You're sure I can't treat you?"

"Nope. Least I could do for you making the trip," I said, grabbing the check when she reached for it. "Plus, I write it off anyway." I winked as I dug out my credit card.

She stood and pulled me in for a hug. "Fine. I'll treat you if this one does make the *New York Times*."

"You mean *when*," I said. "Safe trip back."

"You too, even though you're close." She pulled on her jacket and motioned to the bar. "And go have some fun."

"Sure," I said, waving as she made her way out of the entrance. I handed the waitress my card and scanned the dining area. The restaurant was an old library, and the walls were decorated with replicas of classic titles. I'd chosen it more for proximity, but the food and drinks were good, and it was fun to pretend to eat in a library.

I'd set up my life in such a way that I was the one to make all my own choices. While I had no regrets, I wished I had a juicy story that Mary could pillage for her next best seller.

I signed my receipt and pulled on my jacket, taking another glance at the bar, and I stilled when I spotted someone familiar. I could only see him from the back and couldn't make out his face. His shoulders worked under his dress shirt as he hunched over whatever he was drinking.

But I would know Jesse anywhere.

No matter how long or short his hair was, it always curled at the back of his neck, right below his ears. It had been adorable when we were younger, and it was downright sexy now, no matter how much I didn't want to notice.

I darted across the room when Jesse wobbled on the stool as if he was about to fall off. As I approached, I spotted two empty stools on either side of him. Why was Jesse drinking alone? I searched for Caden in the crowd, hoping he was here with Jesse and maybe had just gone to the restroom, but I saw no drinks on the bar other than the one clutched in Jesse's hand.

We'd snuck a beer or two in high school, but I'd never seen him drunk. I didn't know what his drinking habits had been once he was of legal age, but getting this drunk alone didn't seem like him. My blood ran cold at why he'd be here like this.

I grabbed his arm as he veered to one side, muttering a curse as I lifted him upright. His confused gaze slid to mine as he searched my face.

"Jesse? What's going on?"

His hooded eyes widened in recognition, a sleepy smile drifting across his mouth.

"Hey, Legs," he said, slurring his words with a husky rasp. "To what do I owe the pleasure? Fuck, you look good." He curled his arm around my waist and yanked me closer.

I winced at the potent stench of whiskey on his breath before he buried his face into the crook of my neck.

"Are you here alone?" I spied a suit jacket crumpled on the floor in front of him and leaned over to grab it. "Is this yours?"

His only response was a groan as he nuzzled my neck.

"Jesse!" I pushed his shoulders back to search his face. His loosened tie dangled over his shirt, open to the second button with one flap of the collar up, I supposed from the way he was leaning against the counter.

"I parked across the street this morning to take the train into the city for a work thing." He swung his arm behind him and pointed toward the parking lot with his thumb. "I stopped here for a drink, which led to another and to another." His head bobbled, his eyes almost shut other than the tiny slit I noticed in one eyelid. "After the second drink, I figured I'd call Caden later to get me, so I just kept drinking."

"Did you call him yet?"

"I texted him," he said, bending to glance at his phone screen and almost knocking his forehead against it before I caught him in time to pull him back. "At least, I think I did. I'll text a cab or Uber or something later."

"No, you won't. I'll take you home."

"What for? I have no one to go home to. I'm a free bachelor tonight," he said, this time the words coming out more garbled than slurred.

"Where's Maddie?"

"I pulled her out of school for a couple of days so my parents could take her to that indoor water park out east to distract her from tomorrow. But I couldn't forget tomorrow. I tried, though." He picked up his glass and slammed it down with a hysterical chuckle.

It was a holiday weekend, so there was no game tomorrow.

"Distraction from tomorrow?"

He nodded, crumpling his face. He blinked away whatever had just come over him and tilted his head back, sucking up the last drops of liquor.

"They'll be back in the morning, so we can all go to the cemetery later."

My stomach sank even more.

"To see Tessa?"

"Yep. I have to go home and look for a shovel to bury the cupcake Maddie and my mother baked. At least I don't have to set my alarm to call so early in the morning this year to make sure I'm the first one to tell my baby sister happy birthday. I was the first every fucking year, you know. I guess I still could, we never shut her phone off, but she won't answer. Be spooky as shit if she did, right?"

His head fell back, a hysterical and eerie laugh falling from his lips.

Shit.

Tomorrow was Tessa's birthday, the first one her family would celebrate without her. He'd probably come here to be numb or grieve for his sister without her daughter or anyone else watching. Either way, my heart cracked right down the middle for this broken and devastated big brother who seemed to have finally had enough of pretending through his pain.

"Jesse, I'm so sorry."

"I know you're sorry," he clipped. "Everybody's sorry. Instead of singing 'Happy Birthday' to her like I've done every year since she was born, I have to visit her headstone instead. It's fucking unfair, Emily." I caught a quiver in his chin when his voice cracked.

"I agree," I said, rubbing my hand up and down his back. "It's very fucking unfair."

He dropped his head into his hands, and I couldn't tell if his shaky breaths were from rage or tears.

"Excuse me," I called to the bartender, waving the arm that I wasn't using to keep Jesse from falling over. "Can we settle his bill? Quickly?" I jerked my head to Jesse and raged at the bartender's nonchalant nod. I had no idea how much he'd had to drink, and I guessed since it was becoming crowded, they couldn't police everyone. Still, a man almost sliding off his seat should've been cut off a while ago.

I propped my purse onto the bar and dug out my credit card, flinging it at the bartender when he set the bill in front of us.

"Sorry, I didn't mean to throw it. I just need to get him home."

Sympathy flitted over his features as he furrowed his gray brow at us.

"No problem," he said. "I'll run this now, and you can be on your way." He darted his eyes from Jesse to me. "Do you need help?"

"Hopefully not if you run the card in the next five minutes." I barked out a nervous chuckle, adjusting Jesse's arm around my neck.

Jesse wasn't a bulky guy—his body was nothing but lean muscle as he pressed it against me—but he was well over six feet tall. I needed to pile him into my car and get him through his front door as soon as possible because I couldn't carry him alone if he lost consciousness.

"All right, Jess. Let's go. You're coming home with me."

"Now you're talking," he said, a lazy smirk on his lips as he slipped an arm around my waist again. I was worried enough about him not to be so light-headed at his body flush against mine. And if hanging on me like this would help get him home quicker, he could rub up against me wherever and however he wanted.

I'd register all the inappropriate sensations ping-ponging through me later.

"We'll figure out a way to get your car tomorrow morning. It's early enough that you can sleep this all off before tomorrow," I told him as we trudged to my car. "You'll most likely feel like shit, but you'll be awake."

"Oh, Legs. You always worried about me too much."

"I'm freaked out about what would have happened if I hadn't been here tonight and seen you, but that's a conversation I need to have with sober Jesse," I said, propping him up against the side of my car to get the passenger door open. "Right now, I need to get this one into bed."

"I've been dreaming about being in bed with you for most of my life. That sounds great to me," he whispered, his lips soft and wet as his words fanned hot against my neck. He was drunk and clueless about what was falling out of his mouth, but the heat in his eyes had a raw honesty to it.

One I couldn't entertain tonight and, after getting a glimpse of how he was really suffering, maybe never.

I thanked God when he managed to climb in without my help.

"Tell me your address," I told him as I cued up the GPS on my screen.

"I could just tell you how to get there, Em. I'm not that drunk that I don't know where I live."

"But in case you pass out on the way there, I need your address. Pretty please with sugar." I forced a tight smile and narrowed my eyes.

He leaned forward and entered his address with slow stabs of his finger.

"There," he said, peeling my hand off the steering wheel and bringing it to his lips. "Since you asked so damn nicely."

My eyes sank shut, the wet warmth of his mouth and the scratch of his stubble getting to me in ways they shouldn't have tonight. The urge to kiss away all his troubles and make it better shouldn't have been so overwhelming, another reason why I needed to get him home as soon as possible.

I slipped my hand away and pulled out of the parking lot, hoping the GPS was right and Jesse's condo was only twenty minutes away, and praying he would make it that long.

I kept my eye on him in my periphery as his head swung back and forth over the headrest.

"Seriously, though," I said, tapping his leg to make sure he didn't nod off when he became quiet. "What would you have done if I hadn't been there?"

"I wouldn't have driven anywhere, if that's what you're worried about."

"I know that. But you were alone. That's dangerous."

"I guess if I was still awake, I could've kept trying Caden." He laughed to himself. "Ah, see, I told you I wasn't parent material. I fuck up all the time."

"Jesse," I started, more relief flooding through me as the GPS told me the destination was only a mile away. "This has nothing to do with that."

"Yes, yes, it does. I shouldn't be a parent. I should be an uncle. But I'm not an uncle. I'm a father because my sister is dead."

His words were laced with so much anguish and anger, I wondered if he'd ever had the chance to feel his sister's loss, or if he'd even allowed himself to.

I pulled into a spot in front of his condo and shut off the engine. He seemed slightly more alert as he blinked his eyes open. When he reached for the door handle, he managed to unlock it, but I feared he'd face-plant right into the grass when he tried to step out.

"Stay there," I told him, curling my hand around his bicep to pull him back. "I'll help you."

I raced over to his side and pulled his door the rest of the way open. He managed to push off the seat and stand on his own, but I had the bad feeling he was either going to be unconscious or sick very soon.

"Give me your keys," I said, crooking my finger at him.

"I can open my door, Emily," he growled, stumbling when he glanced back at me.

"I'm sure you usually could. Don't make me go into your pocket and get them, Evans."

"Is that supposed to be a threat?" He arched a tipsy brow at me. "A beautiful woman putting her hand down my pants?" He snickered as he stepped in front of me, holding up his arms. "Go get them, gorgeous."

His eyes narrowed to slits, simmering with lust and want and so many things I couldn't give in to. Not like this.

Judging by his behavior and words tonight, the booze had loosened up all the feelings Jesse held back. Even if he meant what he was saying, he wouldn't be so open and brazen about it once his brain cleared.

I slipped a hand inside his pants pocket, feeling for his keys while trying not to feel for anything else. I blew out a relieved breath when my finger slid along a hard metal groove. I managed to slip them out of his pocket quickly while I kept my eyes on his door, not his face.

I didn't want to waste precious time arguing, but so much of this felt wrong, both the way he wanted me to touch him and listening to what he wouldn't have wanted me to hear.

I'd take care of him and make sure he was safe. He'd be

mortified he'd put me in this position tomorrow—if he remembered it. The key opened both locks, and I eased the door open, pushing Jesse in front of me to get him inside first, and locked the door behind me.

"Okay, while you're more or less awake," I said, throwing the keys on his side table, "let's get you changed and into bed."

"I like this take-charge Emily." He came toward me, exaggerating each small step, and wove his hand into my hair. "I'll be your good boy tonight." A crooked smile curved his lips.

"Jesse, stop," I sighed, cringing when I spotted steps behind him. "I'm guessing your bedroom is upstairs. Can you make it, or do you want to lie on the couch while I get your clothes?"

"I can make it. I don't want to mess up the new couch," he said, pulling me toward the living room. "I bought that couch for my niece because she likes purple," he said, both of us wobbling as he took me over to the couch and plopped down on one of the cushions. "This is her favorite cushion. I bought her a desk, but she likes to do her homework here if I sit there." His whole body swayed as he pointed his finger toward the other end of the couch. "She loves me."

"Of course she loves you. You take good care of her." I cupped his chin and gently shifted his face until his gaze slid to mine. "It's a great couch. Are you sure you don't want to stay here?"

"No. I need to sleep it off." He pressed his hands to the cushion and stood, swaying again but not enough to lose his footing. Maybe he was sobering up a little? His eyes were still glossy and vacant but seemed a touch more alert when they met mine. "You can go now if you want."

"It's fine. I said I wouldn't go until you were settled in

bed." I slid my arm through the crook of his elbow and led him to the staircase. "I'll move toward the wall so you can hold on to the banister, but go slow, okay?"

He nodded as we took each step one at a time at a cautious pace until we made it to the second floor. I stepped in front of Jesse when we were far enough away from the steps not to fear him falling back, and I pulled him by the hand toward his bedroom. I peeked into Maddie's room, purple-themed down to the curtains, bedspread, and desk chair.

He'd really done all he could to make this a home for her, even if it may've broken his heart to do it.

I gave him a gentle push toward the bed, his hazy gaze now focused on the carpet after he dropped onto the edge. I rummaged through his drawers and found a T-shirt and boxers, looking over my shoulder as I tossed them onto the bed.

"Change. I'll get you a glass of water and some ibuprofen before you doze off..."

Something caught my eye as I pushed his drawer closed. It was the edge of a newspaper clipping along the back panel, faded enough at the edges not to be anything current.

When I looked closer, I recognized the St. Kate's masthead at the top of the article. The school sent newsletters by mail to solicit donations, and Sabrina and I would get a kick out of the updates we'd find on classmates and students who'd attended St. Kate's with us but in other grades.

My heart seized when I saw a grayed-out photo of me. They'd made us take pictures for the college website and social media page when I'd started college. We were told to hold a soccer ball and glare at the camera like "We are about to kick some ass." I guessed St. Kate's had lifted it from there to publish, and my mother and I had missed this issue.

How long had he had this? He'd only just moved in to this condo a few months ago. Did he always keep it in his dresser drawer? I hadn't asked, but there had to have been women in his life over the years.

He'd been flirty to the edge of inappropriate since I'd found him, but he wasn't the first man I knew to get handsy when he was drunk. The liquor and unresolved grief had made him act like this, but keeping this photo meant something different. Something a lot more.

I was about to press it back where I'd found it before Jesse noticed I was lingering by his dresser, but he was free and easy with the truth tonight. Instead of staying up all night deciphering what this could mean, why not just ask?

"Didn't look me up, huh? What's this—"

Jesse stood, his boxers pulled up to his waist with the band twisted, and no shirt on. My eyes roamed his body, the smattering of chest hair now darker across his chest and the smooth grooves of muscle. I pinched the photo in between my fingers, almost tearing it as I couldn't stop staring.

"My mother had that. They used to send that stupid newsletter to their house, and she cut out the picture and saved it. She gave it to me to show Maddie."

"But you kept it?" I asked as I examined his face.

"I did. I wanted to show Maddie. Maybe I will. But you still looked like my girl in that picture. I didn't want to share it yet." He yawned, falling back onto the bed with a squeaky bounce.

My eyes stung as I slipped into his bathroom, filling up a cup with water and grabbing the ibuprofen from the medicine cabinet.

Everything I'd learned about Jesse tonight wasn't for me to know, but I couldn't forget it. He might not have kept it for twenty years, but it was precious enough to him not to share.

I had a lot to figure out, but I needed to make sure Jesse was in bed and out cold before I headed home for what was probably going to be a long, sleepless night.

"Take this, and I'll go—"

I froze at his doorway, the plastic cup crinkling in my hand as Jesse's gaze met mine, his eyes still half closed as he sprawled out on his bed, drifting his hand back and forth over the bulge in his shorts with a sleepy smile.

"Come help me, Em. Touch me."

Jesus Christ.

"Take this," I clipped, crooking my finger for him to sit up. I handed him the cup and held out my hand for him to take the ibuprofen from my palm. "Take this and lie down."

"Yes, ma'am," he said, low and husky, as he shoved the pills into his mouth and tipped back the cup.

"Was I a good boy?" He jutted his lip in a pout.

"Yes. Now go to sleep."

I turned to throw the cup into the trash can next to his nightstand when he grabbed my wrist and yanked me onto the bed.

"Touch me. I need you."

I shook my head. "No, Jesse. You're drunk. I won't touch you when you're drunk."

"But you'll touch me when I'm not?" he asked, raising a brow as he propped his elbow onto his pillow. "What if I said please? Pretty please with sugar." He brushed his lips against my cheek, painting a trail of tiny kisses to my ear.

"Jesse, stop it." I sat up, shoving him back. "You're not thinking clearly. I know you're hurting, but—"

"I've only let myself do this once. I mean, once while thinking about you." He shut his eyes and laughed to himself. "I wouldn't do it that summer, even though I missed you so fucking much I couldn't see straight. If I came thinking of you, I'd never get you out of my head. Not that I ever really did," he said, brushing the hair off my forehead. "You were always in there somewhere."

"When did you?" I asked, wondering what the hell was wrong with me. I'd gotten him home, and now, that was where I needed to go. Away from him and this ache in my heart and between my legs that had no cure.

I had no time for questions I couldn't handle the answers to.

"That night after the reunion. I was so happy you didn't hate me anymore. And you looked so damn beautiful." He cupped my cheek, setting my skin on fire from the skid of his thumb along my jaw. "I was a sloppy kid back then. Lost in how good it was to be inside you and how sweet you tasted. Now, if I had the chance, I could give you what you need. I'd make it *so* good, Em."

"Jesse, please stop," I said, forcing air out of my lungs to form words. The ache at my core was a full-on throb, all my blood flow now in my clit with nowhere to go. "You don't mean what you're saying."

"The fuck I don't." His jaw clenched as he hovered over me. "I mean *everything*."

I shimmied out of his hold to push him back on the mattress. "I'll go home and forget about all of this, just like you will when you wake up. But I mean it about never drinking alone like that again. Do you have an extra key so I can lock up?"

"If you can't touch me, kiss me. I swear I want you to. Please, baby."

My chest squeezed at the crack in his voice. He was hurting, and all I'd wanted to do tonight was make him feel better. But kissing him wouldn't only be for his benefit. I needed him too. More than I'd wanted to acknowledge and now couldn't deny.

I let my fingers curl into his hair, and I scraped my nails along his scalp. He moaned, guttural enough for the vibration to run right through me. I inched toward him, easing my lips onto his until they barely touched. I backed away, hoping it would appease him enough to lie back down and pass out.

He shook his head and looped his arm around my waist, drawing me closer until we were almost chest to chest. He brought his lips back to mine, slanting his head before dragging his tongue along the seam of my lips. My mouth opened on a gasp before I let him in, my hands back in his hair as the kiss caught fire, our teeth scraping as our tongues tangled, both of us licking into each other's mouths in long sweeps, chasing a twenty-year thirst we'd managed to push aside until it consumed us.

He rolled me on top of him, gliding his hands up and down my back as his erection pressed against my core. I repeated *one more minute* over and over in my head, but I couldn't make myself stop. I skimmed my hands down his arms and over his strong shoulders, bringing them to the back of his neck as I pulled him closer, deepening the kiss I should never have let happen at all, never mind let go this far.

"Okay," I murmured against Jesse's lips as I finally tore my lips away. "I need to go, and you need to sleep."

His head sank into the pillow as his breathing slowed. It was as if our crazy kiss had pacified him enough to grasp on to some peace, if only for the moment. I kissed his forehead as his eyes fluttered.

"No," he breathed out, clutching my wrist with his eyes

still half shut. "Stay with me. Please," he said, settling on his side and pulling my back to his front.

I let my head fall back into the pillow and groaned. I gently squirmed out of his hold enough to slip away, when I noticed the purple cushion on the chair next to his bed. The entire house had notes of purple, all, I was sure, courtesy of Maddie.

I plopped my head back down as Jesse brought me closer, his breathing soft and even against my neck.

Whether he knew what he was saying or not, I couldn't leave any more than I could stop kissing him, even if it would further complicate things between us. It didn't matter if he probably wouldn't remember asking me to stay or the mind-blowing kiss we'd shared that felt as soul-searing as it was wrong. I let myself drift off, feeling some of the solace that had finally put Jesse out, and savored the stolen moment before I'd have to give it back.

13

JESSE

I SQUEAKED MY EYES OPEN AND CLENCHED THEM RIGHT BACK shut as pain ricocheted across my temples. I cupped my forehead, shielding my eyes before I squinted at my window, the sun peeking through just enough to make my splitting headache even worse.

I didn't remember much of last night or how I'd even gotten into bed. How much had I had to drink to almost black out?

I eased up to sitting and glanced at the clock on my nightstand. Panic laced through me for a minute as I shot up to get Maddie, then remembered she was with my parents.

On a trip to distract them all from my sister's birthday today.

Despite the painful haze I'd woken up in, I couldn't forget that. I'd inhaled most of a bottle of whiskey trying. I'd felt off from the time my parents had picked Maddie up, like a fungus or residue lingered on me that I couldn't wipe away or shake. I felt my sister's loss every day, but I was too busy holding things together for Maddie's sake and so afraid of being a screwup as a parent that it hadn't sunk all the way in that my sister was truly gone. I'd managed to hold it back from seeping into that last layer, the one that made it permanent.

When I'd spoken to Maddie on the train back from my meeting, she'd sounded like a typical kid after indulging in all the water rides and, I was sure, all the junk food my parents could throw at her. I didn't want her to hurt or dwell on the loss of her mother, but I wanted her to remember her enough to miss her today.

Maybe that was my fault.

I hardly brought up my sister, not by name anyway. I'd constantly ask Maddie if she was okay and told her if she was sad, she could talk to me, but neither of us ever mentioned Tessa. I wondered if Maddie didn't mention her for the same reason I didn't—we were afraid of both missing her too much and making the other upset if we brought her up.

When Maddie had told me she'd helped my mother make the *best cupcake* for her mom's birthday before they'd left for the park, because it "doesn't matter if it's fresh or not since we're just going to bury it," something broke inside me. The deep crack in my chest I'd tried so hard to ignore had finally burst open.

My sister couldn't celebrate her birthday, eat the cupcake her daughter had helped bake for her, or call me a dork after I'd woken her up at the crack of dawn to sing "Happy Birthday."

I'd had months for it to settle in and to start to accept it. I'd thought enclosing Maddie and myself into a bubble and putting all my focus on being what she needed, all while ignoring how much it hurt to lose my baby sister, was the best way to move on and heal.

Yesterday, the pain had become too deep and all-consuming to ignore, and now I couldn't escape it.

Once I'd decided to drink myself into oblivion, I'd texted Caden to get me, but I couldn't recall anything else after. The entire night was like a fuzzy dream that began to fade before I could register any of the details. The image of punching my address into a GPS screen fluttered in my mind, but I couldn't see who the driver was.

Who had brought me home?

I groaned as I pushed off the bed to stand, pressing my finger into my temple to stop the pain. I had never been a big drinker, but either my age made a night of alcohol that much harder to recover from or I'd just drunk *that* much. Maybe a combo of the two. I shrugged it off until I noticed the dents on both sides of the bed, as if I hadn't been alone here last night.

Had someone been here? Had I brought someone home and not realized it? I pushed my finger deeper into the side of my head, trying to get my brain to unclog enough to remember something.

My blood ran ice-cold through my veins, the chill waking me up enough to panic again. Did I bring a stranger home into the house that I shared with my niece? That was not okay, regardless of whether she was here or not.

I grabbed my phone, hoping Caden would give me some kind of explanation of last night. Maybe he'd stayed because I was that pathetic and sick to make sure I didn't choke on my own vomit during the night.

I'd take whatever shit he wanted to give me about the state of mind I was in if he was the one who'd brought me home.

I couldn't let this happen again. I'd go to therapy and straighten myself out, and if I'd just embarrassed myself in front of my best friend and hadn't brought any strange women into this house, I'd never drink another drop.

I had a flood of missed calls from Caden and one text from Emily lingering on my phone screen.

Emily: *Caden gave me a ride to the train station parking lot to get your car. I should be back in a little bit.*

I fell back on the edge of the bed, groaning out a sigh of deep relief. Emily was the one who'd gotten me home.

But, wait. Emily had stayed here?

Fragments started to piece together along the edges of my memory.

Emily holding me up on the barstool, throwing her credit card at the bartender and begging him to run my bill quickly as I buried my head into the crook of her neck. The memory of her perfume, roses mixed with vanilla, as I'd clung to her.

I dropped my head into my hands as more details crystallized in my foggy brain.

I'd let myself rub up against her as she'd dragged me to her car and had told her to pick my keys out of my pocket. Then I'd jerked off in front of her and begged her to help me.

This wasn't as bad as bringing a stranger home, but fucking awful all the same.

Jesus Christ, what the hell have I done?

My unresolved grief wasn't the only thing I'd let out of my system, thanks to the booze.

I wanted Emily, so much I could barely think about anything else. But I was too much of a mess to be in any position to ask for more than friendship. I'd proven that last night in spades. What she had to think of me now... How could I even begin to apologize for this? I could only reason away so much of what I'd done and said last night as pain over missing my sister.

Even through all my disgusting behavior, she'd managed to get me home. And she'd stayed.

I didn't deserve her. Not back then, and especially now.

Grabbing a T-shirt from my drawer and a pair of shorts, I headed to my bathroom to splash some cold water on my face and figure out my damn life—or at least what to say to Emily once she came back.

I ran the water until it was cold enough to shock me and brushed my teeth to get rid of the rancid taste of stale whiskey. I met my bloodshot gaze in the mirror. My eyes were rimmed with dark circles and deep crinkles in the corners. My outsides looked as screwed up as my insides felt, exhausted and barely holding my shit together.

I smoothed out my sheets to start making the bed when another memory hit me. Emily's mouth on mine as she writhed on top of me, my hands coasting up and down her back and pressing her beautiful body into mine.

Fuck. The missing, broken parts of last night slowly came back to me, and while I couldn't tell what did or didn't happen as it all pieced together, that kiss was real. I could still taste her as I swirled my tongue inside her mouth, swallowing her soft moans as I wove my hand into her hair and held her mouth on mine with all the strength I'd had left.

And she'd kissed me back.

The rest of the night might have been a drunken blur, but there was no way my whiskey-soaked brain had conjured that up. I could still feel her, her full breasts pressing into my bare chest, grinding her hips against me as her core rubbed against my aching cock.

Every part of my body had ached for Emily for what

seemed like my entire life. When I'd begged her to kiss me, it had been my soul talking, not my alcohol-fogged brain. My drinking binge had cost me the barrier of common sense. Now that I had it back, I had no clue where to go from here.

I needed to apologize for not being in my right mind and making her uncomfortable with the inappropriate things I'd said and the sloppy way I'd hung on to her as she'd dragged me home.

But I had no regrets about that kiss or a single second of her in my arms.

And now, along with everything else that had poured out of me last night, I had to face what that meant.

I pulled on my shirt and shorts when I heard my front door open and close. My chest tightened as I made my way down the stairs. I'd figure out what to say to Emily as soon as I found the guts to look her in the eye.

"Morning, sleepyhead," Emily said as she tossed my keys into the glass bowl I kept by the door. "Your car is parked safely in your driveway. Caden said he's picking up the greasiest breakfast he can find and coming back soon."

She came up to me, a small smile lifting her lips, the lips that still tempted me just as much in the cold light of day. I had a shit-ton to unpack, but I wasn't confused about how I felt. It scared me enough to run from it, just like when I was a teenager, but it was time to face that, along with everything else.

"How are you feeling?" she asked, trailing her gaze over me and lingering on my mouth. Something flashed across her face before she blinked and took a half step back.

Her quick retreat was all the confirmation I needed that the kiss had really happened, and I hoped the blush running down her neck meant she thought it was as good as I did.

Because when I let my mind go there, it was *really* fucking good.

"Better than I deserve. Thank you for getting me home last night."

"You're welcome. I'm glad I was there, but I'm still scared of what could have happened if I hadn't been." She shook her head, her mouth pulled down. "You can't do that again. Please don't make me worry about you. Caden is worried too, but I'm sure you'll hear about it over breakfast," she said, lifting an eyebrow.

"I won't, and I can promise you that. Can you sit for a minute to talk?" I motioned to the living room behind me. "Take a seat on the couch. Please."

She nodded and followed me to the couch.

"Maddie picked this couch, or you just picked something purple?" Emily asked as she slid her hand along the soft material.

"She picked the picture off the computer, and I ordered it. Along with the rest of the purple you see scattered around the house. I guess I told you that last night?" I took a seat on the other side of the couch and rested my elbows on my knees.

"Among other things." I caught a grimace before she nodded.

I wanted to take her hand, but I'd crossed too many boundaries in the past day already. Instead, I inched toward her.

"I am so sorry. A lot of last night is fuzzy, but I remember enough to know that I was completely out of line. You were trying to help me, and I didn't make it easy. I never would have acted that way had I been in my right mind, please know that."

"Jesse," she sighed. "Of course I know that. I'm just really worried about you. I know Tessa's birthday hit you hard, and probably the next milestones without her will too. But drinking alone like that? I know you wouldn't have gotten into your car, but someone could have robbed you or worse. I hated seeing you that vulnerable."

Her brows drew together as she moved a hesitant inch toward me and grabbed my hand.

"I know you think keeping yourself isolated is the way to focus on Maddie, but you're hurting too. It's like when they say on airplanes to put your own oxygen mask on first before you help anyone else. You need to be able to breathe, Jesse. And I don't think you are."

"I know." I nodded. "It's why I'm going to find a therapist this week." I squeezed her hand back.

"I am very glad to hear that." She smiled, wide and breathtaking enough for me to have to look away. "I'm sure Caden has other things to say, but as long as you promise me it won't happen again, I'll let it go."

"Wait," I said, pulling her hand toward me when she stood. "I want to talk about something else. And I think you may know what."

"Jesse," she said, darting her eyes from mine. "You were drunk and upset. Whatever happened last night, just forget about it, okay?"

"What if I don't want to forget it? What if I told you there's one part of last night that, while I hate the state I was in when it happened, I don't have a single regret that it did. Sit down, Em. Please. Pretty please with sugar."

She groaned, rolling her eyes as she sat back down.

"Okay, I'd wanted to give you a day to recover, but now *I'd* like to apologize."

I flinched back. "*You* want to apologize? For what?"

She averted my gaze, darting her eyes around the room.

"You weren't thinking clearly. I feel like I took advantage."

"Took advantage?" I barked out a laugh. "You're serious?"

"It was an emotional night," she said, dragging her hand down her face. "I was so upset when I found you like that. At least, that's what I'm blaming it on for now." She grimaced when her eyes came back to mine.

"Emily," I said, squeezing her hand when she dropped her gaze to the carpet. "Of all the stupid things I did and said last night that turn my stomach with regret, kissing you was absolutely not one of them."

"Like I said, it was an emotional night. The both of us weren't really at our best."

"You found me blitzed out of my mind, drunk and handsy and stupid, got me home, and stayed with me to make sure I was okay. You were amazing last night, Em. You always are."

"You asked me to," she whispered. "You needed me. So, I stayed."

If she only knew how much I needed her. Instead of a sloppy drunk confession, I should have just admitted it a long time ago.

I cupped her cheek. "Whatever your reasons, I appreciate it." I grazed my thumb back and forth along her cheekbone, skimming her lips as I let my hand slide away. Her mouth parted as our eyes stayed locked, a groan rising from my throat as I traced my finger along her jaw.

"Breakfast is served. Unless you're hanging over the toilet, then it's breakfast for me."

Our heads whipped around to Caden's voice drifting in from my front door.

"Shit. I didn't mean to interrupt."

"You didn't," Emily chirped, jerking away from me and popping off the couch. "I have a ton of editing to do today. I'll check on you later, Jesse." She smoothed a piece of hair falling out of her hair tie behind her ear, her shoulders softening for a moment. "I'm thinking about all of you today. Let me know if you need anything."

"I'll do that."

She nodded, squaring her shoulders before she came up to Caden.

"Thanks for the ride. Watch him today," she told him in a loud whisper, giving me one last glance over her shoulder before heading out my door.

"Jesus, what the hell happened last night?" Caden looked between me and the path of Emily's hasty exit.

"A lot," I said, wincing as I squeezed the back of my neck.

"Good thing for you, I have nothing but time this morning," He held up a white plastic bag. "We can talk as you eat."

I fell back against the couch, letting out a long exhale before I stood and followed him into my kitchen.

"Extra-large coffee," he said, motioning to the paper cup on the table. "I'll dig out the food, and you can start."

"Fine," I said, lifting the cup to my lips for a long sip. "You know today is Tessa's birthday."

"I do," Caden nodded. "I planned on being here this morning but didn't expect you to go on a bender last night."

"Neither did I," I huffed. "I couldn't handle it and got

drunk on my way home from my meeting in the city. Emily found me and brought me home."

I took another long gulp. He'd used extra cream and sugar, but the coffee was hot enough to burn my throat on the way down.

He glared at me and set a bagel with bacon, egg, and cheese on the table. It was wrapped in paper, already transparent from the grease.

"Do you remember this?" He reached into his pocket and dug out his phone, unlocking the screen before shoving it into my face.

Me: *I'm at McCays by the station. Come get*

"Come get?" I read out loud. "Well, at least it was you I texted."

"By the time I saw it and I made it there, figuring *come get* meant pick you up, you were gone. You didn't see the ten missed calls on your phone?"

I shook my head and took a bite of the sandwich.

"I didn't look at my phone until this morning."

"You're very fucking lucky that Emily saw you. This is how people end up on Netflix documentaries. They do stupid shit when they're out and alone. Maddie and your parents haven't had enough loss?"

"I know." He said the same thing Emily had, but thinking of Maddie and my parents enduring more pain because of my stupidity made my stomach roll.

"Trust me. This will never happen again. I'll talk to Dr. Asher and get the name of a therapist that I can see. Last night was a scary wake-up call."

"Good." He took a seat at the table and crossed his arms. "So, what did I interrupt with Emily?"

"I was pretty fucking awful last night. I said some very inappropriate things as she was trying to get me home. Got a little too close to her. From what I can remember of it, it was bad."

"I guess the alcohol loosened everything else up too." He eyed me over the rim of his own coffee cup.

"More or less, but we weren't talking about that when you walked in. I asked her to kiss me. Begged her. And she did. It's the only part of the night I can recall with vivid certainty."

Caden sputtered his coffee before setting it down.

"Well, shit. What else happened? Did she stay here?"

"Yes, that part is a little fuzzy, but she told me I asked her to stay right before I knocked out. I apologized for everything else but kissing her because I'm honestly not sorry. I mean, sorry it happened like that, but—"

"It would have happened eventually. You were blitzed enough to finally get out of your own way. What did she say after that?" Caden eyed me as he took a chomp out of his breakfast.

"She said something like, 'I guess I'll be going now that Caden is here.'"

"Ah, damn it." He winced as he dropped his head back. "My father always said I have a special wrong-place-at-the-wrong-time talent."

"Well, maybe a little." I had to laugh. "But after last night, I think she needed some space. At least, I do. I think it's going to be a long day once my parents and Maddie get back."

"And then tomorrow, you're going to go get her, right? Stop this stupid game."

"I want to, but how? I'm obviously not holding things together that well. I swear to God, it feels like twenty years ago again. Emily is everything I want and nothing I can keep."

"But it's not twenty years ago. Stop fixating on that, for fuck's sake. She's here, not six hours away, and you're both adults. Do you have baggage? Yes, but show me someone our age who doesn't. You're missing the big difference between then and now."

"I'm missing a lot right now, so enlighten me."

"You want her? Fight for her. She stayed, didn't she? And she kissed you on her own? You're sure it wasn't a figment of your tipsy imagination or your sloppy drunk ass trying to kiss *her*?"

"Nope, it happened, all right. Even in my fucked-up state of mind, I asked her to kiss me and didn't just go for it. She even apologized to me just now because she was afraid she took advantage."

Caden's chest shook with a laugh as he cupped his forehead.

"Do you remember how the guys used to give you shit in school for having the same girlfriend for four years straight?"

"That, and how Emily was too hot for me." I shrugged. "So?"

"We all had drama left and right, as you can recall. How Sabrina and I became— Anyway, I'm losing my point. Even my immature teenage ass understood why you never broke up. You fit. It was that simple."

"Until it wasn't," I muttered and drained the rest of my coffee.

"That's the thing. It *is*. Get out of your head and fight for her. Before someone else does."

14

EMILY

"Have you been online today?" Sabrina asked, her eyes dancing as she ran over to me on the field. We only had a few games left and we were about even in wins and losses, but the kids were having fun and so was I. Soccer had once again become my joy, albeit for different reasons.

"I haven't," I said as I threw my bag behind our bench. "What did I miss?"

I'd avoided Jesse other than short texts and quick small talk at practice this week, but the thought of how I'd found him still upset me, and I was still worried sick over him. I'd believed him when he'd promised never to drink alone like that again, and I hoped what had happened last weekend had shocked him enough to deal with his grief rather than bury it for both his and his niece's sake.

When I wasn't worrying about Jesse, thoughts of finishing what we'd started played on an endless loop in my brain, along with what I would have done if he'd asked me to touch him and kiss him when he was sober—when I wouldn't have to wonder if he really meant it.

Not that I didn't believe he'd meant it. Drinking had

loosened his inhibitions, but the pure lust in his eyes was real. So real, when I closed my eyes at night, it haunted me. I could still feel his arms around me, thicker and stronger than when we were young, clutching me like a lifeline. My fingertips tingled with the memory of tracing his broad shoulders when he'd pulled me on top of him, groaning into my mouth as it was glued to his.

Jesse and I could never just be friends. The pull between us was too strong, but friendship was the only thing on the table because he'd said he couldn't offer anything else, and I didn't know if that would ever change.

I'd spent a lot of time, more than I cared to remember, waiting for Jesse. For the first few weeks after our breakup, I'd still expected him to come to my house and take it back. I'd even searched for him in the stands during my first few college games, wishing for a romance-novel-worthy reunion where I'd run into his arms and he'd tell me he couldn't live without me.

Then I'd stopped waiting—for him or anyone else. He'd always have a big piece of my heart, but I'd needed to guard the rest of it.

"First of all, you didn't tell me you met with Sharon."

"I didn't. Not really. We spoke over video one night for maybe fifteen minutes. She said she wanted to pick my brain for something she was working on about female entrepreneurs."

"Well, she highlighted you in a post across all her platforms. It ended up in my Facebook feed because she tagged you. And the funniest part, she took one of our high school yearbook pictures and photoshopped it to look like you're posing like besties." She handed me her phone.

"Ten thousand likes already?" I said, bringing the phone closer. "Oh wow. Raina Nello liked the post."

"Who's that?"

"She was on the US World Cup team back in the nineties. My grandfather always cut out articles that mentioned her and would show them to me. She was an Italian American woman and a soccer star, and because I played and was half Italian American, he felt she was relevant to my interests." I laughed, a little breathless from being starstruck. He'd brought her to my attention, but I'd followed her career throughout college, even when I'd decided not to try to go professional.

"And I recognize that picture. That was the photo we all took on the lawn for graduation." I tapped the screen with the tip of my nail. "Remember when they made us assemble into the numbers of our year to take an overhead shot? She ended up behind me, and I remember her complaining about not being more in front."

"She edited out an entire crowd? I am super impressed. She's got skills." She took back the phone and angled the screen to her face. "It's a nice piece, though. I could see you getting a lot of new clients from this."

"I'm busy enough, and I like to get new clients by word of mouth. But I guess it's nice of her to do, regardless of her angle."

"It was the best laugh as I got ready for today." She slid her phone back into the pocket of her leggings. "I was hoping it would cheer you up."

"I don't need cheering up. I'm fine."

She pursed her lips and nodded. I'd ended up at her apartment the morning after I'd taken Jesse home and spent the night. She'd listened to the whole sordid story and, to her credit, had stayed mostly stoic without forcing any advice because, really, what was there to say? Either we addressed what was between us, or we stayed away from each other for another twenty years or for good this time.

But she'd been hovering a little over the past week, as if she was waiting for me to finally break.

I was close but keeping it to myself.

"I mean it," I told her, trying to infuse my voice with the confidence I didn't have. "Really."

"Okay, fine," she said, nodding to the corner by the bench. "The kids are already lined up. I love how they're trained."

"They are," I said, a smile sneaking across my mouth. They still had trouble channeling their energy on the field, but I loved their excitement, even if it exhausted me by the end of a game.

"Hey, Emily. Can I talk to you?"

Alex had been the ref for the last couple of games, and while I wouldn't admit to Jesse that he was right, Alex always lingered by me more than other coaches. I was cordial but distant, as I didn't need opposing teams thinking his attention on me meant that my team would have an unfair advantage. He was good-looking enough, but I wasn't interested. Not only because of my current Jesse problems.

I appreciated a confident man, but Alex toed the line between confident and full of himself. At least full of himself to the point of not taking a hint or ignoring it.

"Sure, what's up?"

I glared at Sabrina over his shoulder as she fluttered her eyelashes behind him.

"I saw on Facebook you're a big-time editor. Penny told me a little about it, but I didn't realize you had so many famous clients."

"I don't know if I'd say big-time, but—"

"I've had a manuscript I've wanted to publish for years

but never had the guts to try. Maybe we could have dinner, and we could talk about it?"

"I'm not taking new clients right now. My schedule is pretty booked."

"Well, it's been sitting there for years. It can sit some more until you're ready." He smiled, his voice dropping to a new raspy octave. "I just thought I could get some ideas from you."

I peered over at my kids, all staring at us. At least Jesse wasn't here to get all alpha over Alex today and seethe every time he'd try to speak to me. The last time we texted, he'd mentioned that his mother was bringing Maddie today and he'd try to catch the end of the game after his work meeting was over.

Alex was one of those people who wouldn't let it go until you agreed to meet. Without an audience, I hoped I could fully let him down as a potential client or anything else he had in mind.

"I have some time this evening. There's a coffee shop by Sunrise—"

"I'll buy you dinner instead. It's the least I can do for you making the time." His smile deepened, and my sneakers felt like they were in quicksand. "How's Julianna's at six?"

"Hey, Coach. Time to start soon," Sabrina called out, tapping her watch.

"Fine. Julianna's at six. I'll meet you there."

"So, it's a date. Awesome. Have a good game," he said, beaming at me as he jogged off without giving me a chance to correct him.

"Okay, kids," I said, ambling over to where they sat on the grass. "Like I told you last game, pass the ball rather than crowd—"

"Coach Emily has a date," Mikayla, a beautiful little girl

with black hair and wide dark eyes, announced to the entire team.

"Is he taking you to dinner or drinks?" Jeffrey asked. "My uncle told my dad yesterday he only does drink dates at first so he can leave fast if the girl is boring."

"Well, my cousin says that a guy who doesn't ask you to dinner isn't worth going out with." Mikayla flipped her silky pigtail over one shoulder.

"You can't have a date at a fast-food restaurant," Candie, my tallest girl, piped in, her blond curls swaying as she shook her head. "My mom didn't speak to my dad for like a whole week after he took her to McDonald's on a date night. I don't know why she was so mad. I love McDonald's."

My eyes fell on Maddie, peering up at me with an expression I couldn't decipher. Her gaze was curious but not upset. I wondered what, if anything, she'd picked up on between her uncle and me, but maybe she just thought of us as friends.

I'd hoped the kids hadn't heard Alex say date or would know what that meant, but I guessed they knew more about dating than I did.

"She's going to Julianna's," Mikayla told Candie. "They have the good warm bread with the oil and pepper plate. *That's* a date." She smiled and gave me an enthusiastic thumbs-up.

"Okay, guys, this is all great advice, but you have a game to play," Sabrina said, clapping her hands. "Listen to Coach Emily." Her eyes were wide when she found my gaze. I grimaced back and nodded, grabbing my whistle as I surveyed all the young eyes on me.

"Okay, everyone. Let's have a great game and have fun," I said, trying for an easy and relaxed smile before I blew the whistle for them to line up. They scurried to the field, but

Maddie lingered behind and padded over to where Sabrina and I stood behind the line.

"Everything okay, Maddie?" I asked, my heart dropping to my stomach at the concerned crease in her brow.

"My mom went on a date a couple of times. She got really dressed up and wore these," Maddie said, flicking her earlobes. They were the gold butterflies she always wore that seemed too big for her ears, but I let her wear them when she played since they were posts and didn't dangle.

"She must have looked very beautiful, just like you."

She beamed up at me, getting me choked up as usual, but now I could add guilt to the mix of emotions—even though I wasn't sure where it was coming from.

"So, you have a date with the ref," Sabrina quipped as the kids lined up.

"He said he saw I was a big-time editor on Facebook and wants to talk about his book with me. I figured I'd meet him for coffee so I could just say no and be clear about it without the kids around, but he cornered me into dinner."

"Fucking Sharon," she said and burst out laughing.

"Fucking Sharon," I agreed and headed to the field to watch my kids play and forget what I'd gotten myself into.

JESSE

"Hey, you made it!"

My mother waved me over when I arrived at the field. I'd hated missing most of the game today, but we were working on a company-wide system upgrade, making a Saturday morning meeting necessary for our international branches. I'd already seen Maddie kick a few goals, so while it sucked to miss today's game, my mother was able to come while my father worked.

I was "embracing the village," like my new therapist had suggested at our first appointment yesterday. I'd thought I'd have to wait weeks to see someone, but Dr. Asher had managed to get me an intake appointment this week. I'd called her office on Monday, expecting only to be able to leave a message, but she'd gotten on the phone with me right away to ask what happened. I spewed out most of the story, how I'd gotten drunk while I was out and alone because of all the repressed grief, and before it all got even more out of hand, I needed help.

I'd left out the part about all I'd confessed to Emily and how the kiss I hadn't had the balls to go for sober had shifted the entire dynamic between us—or pulled us enough out of daily denial to make it painfully awkward in every interaction we'd had since.

I'd left that for the therapist I'd pay for to deal with, not the one extending sympathies because my niece was her patient.

Dr. Asher had thought it was important to see someone as soon as possible, while it was all still raw, and as I sat there for over an hour at my first appointment pouring everything out like a big breath I'd been holding in, I had to agree that timing was everything. I had a long way to go, but the first step in the right direction was already a massive relief.

Maddie had lost her mother, but she still had family who loved her and had an active role in raising her. I was her guardian, but I wasn't alone. *We* weren't alone. And like Emily had pointed out, if I didn't take care of myself, I wouldn't be much good to my kid or anyone else.

"Barely, but yes. How's it going?" I bent to kiss my mother's cheek as I surveyed the field. I smiled as Maddie raced across it with a cluster of kids, her eyes narrowed while she focused on the ball as she passed it to Jeffrey next to her. After a few games, even though I was no expert, it was easier to point out who might continue with soccer. The kids had stopped crowding the ball as much and mostly just ran back and forth behind the kids who appeared to know what they were doing and were more than happy to take over.

"It's almost over. One goal for today, but she's a force. Doesn't like to give up the ball," Mom said with a chuckle. "She's stopping to eat the snacks, at least, since running up and down is giving her an appetite, I think."

Emily had said she saw a future in soccer for Maddie if she continued to love it and would want one. *I* wanted a future with Maddie's coach but was working on the best way to ask.

Burying that cupcake in the dirt in front of Tessa's grave had felt a lot more final than her funeral had, but the closure I'd run away from for so long had come with an unexpected relief. I'd dug out old pictures of Tessa and showed them to Maddie, and we'd talked about her more this week than we had in the past eight months.

It still hurt and always would, but once I'd accepted that Tessa was gone for good, it was easier to keep her memory alive—or had been so far. I'd decorated the house with some photos of Tessa and me as kids, including the last one we'd taken together the day I'd helped her move in to her first apartment, her bright and hopeful smile so much like her daughter's.

If she'd had this much faith in me, I had to learn to have faith in myself.

"I'm sorry I missed it," I said as I scanned the field, waving to Maddie once she spotted me. I clenched my jaw when I noticed Alex was the ref for today, as he'd been the last couple of games. I bet he was requesting Emily's games, and I wasn't the only one who watched when he always veered toward her team's side of the field to talk to her.

But if Emily wasn't mine, there was nothing I could say. If I was lucky enough to change that, I'd have no problem setting him straight and I very much looked forward to it.

"You came!" Maddie yelled as she slammed into me. I swore she'd grown two inches since she'd moved in with me, as I didn't have to bend as much to meet her eyes.

"Of course I did. And that is the only Saturday meeting I'll need to have for a very long time, so I won't miss any more games." I smoothed the hair off her sweaty forehead.

"Sorry I didn't get to say hello."

I craned my neck to Emily's voice as she came up to my mother.

"Don't be sorry. You were busy," Mom said, rising from the folding chair to give her a hug.

"Hey, Jesse," Emily said, her smile for my mother fading once she spotted me, thanks to new tension between us. I found it better than the denial creating space between us that—I believed—neither of us wanted.

"See you later," Alex said, a wry grin aimed at Emily as he touched her shoulder. "Thanks again. And good game, kiddo," he said, throwing my niece a surprised smile as if he'd forgotten there were any kids on the field.

"See you later?" I narrowed my eyes at Emily. "What is there a league thing today?"

"She's going on a date," Maddie offered. "He asked her before the game."

"He asked...*what*?" I raised my head and found Emily's sheepish gaze.

"It wasn't exactly like that—"

"So, he didn't ask you out on a date in front of a bunch of eight-year-olds?"

I caught my mother's scowl and took in a deep breath to calm down and lower my volume.

"Here," Maddie said, unfastening her earrings and dropping them into Emily's hand. "You can wear them on your date and be even prettier. I heard my mom really liked you, so she would be okay if you wore her earrings for a night."

"Oh my gosh," Emily whispered, staring at the earrings in her hand before closing her fingers around them. "I remember these earrings, and I'd be honored." She cleared her throat and smiled down at Maddie. "I really liked your mom too."

Maddie's mom would want her to wear those earrings

on a date with *me*, and it was all I could do not to scream that. But this was the price I had to pay for hesitating.

This was wrong. She shouldn't be going on dates with slimy referees or anyone else but me. When Caden had said to fight for her, I'd never thought I would actually have to. Did I think she'd just wait around for me? How fucking stupid and arrogant was I?

I kept drawing these bullshit boundaries between us since Emily had come back into my life. Waiting until I had my shit together wasn't an option if I didn't want to lose her for good.

So, I would fight for her.

Because enough was enough.

"You guys have a good day," Emily said, sweeping her gaze quickly over all of us. "I'll take very good care of these, I promise." Her eyes darted to mine for a moment before she shifted to leave.

"Did you hear when and where Coach Emily's date is?" I asked Maddie, my eyes still lingering on Emily as she left the field.

"Six, I think, at Julianna's."

I expected my mother to glower at me or pull me aside to whisper to get a grip, but a small smile ghosted her lips as she came closer.

"How about a sleepover?" she asked Maddie. "You can tell Grandpa all about the goal you kicked today, and we'll order dinner. We can follow Uncle Jesse home in my car, and we can pack a bag for tomorrow."

Maddie pursed her lips and grabbed my hand.

"But I haven't seen Uncle Jesse all day."

"He's got some work to do," my mother whispered, arching a brow when she met my eyes over Maddie's head. "An *overdue* project."

Maddie crinkled her nose. "But you said you were done with work."

"I am, Mad," I whispered, kissing her forehead. "But this is important too. I promise we'll have a popcorn movie night tomorrow, so make sure to remember all the game details for me."

She gave in with a reluctant nod and peered up at me. "The popcorn-maker popcorn, not microwave?"

"Yes, only the best popcorn for my favorite niece." I tugged on her braid, courtesy of her grandmother.

"Thank you," I mouthed to my mother.

She nodded and leaned in to kiss my cheek.

"Go get our girl."

I'd spent a lifetime letting the world have the girl, now woman, I'd loved because I'd thought she was better off without me. I was done, but I hoped not too late.

But for now, I'd head home and help my niece pack a bag for a night at her grandparents' house.

I had a date to crash.

16

EMILY

What did I get myself into?

I wasn't thrilled with the way he'd pushed for a date and had my suspicions of whether he really needed an editor or just an excuse to talk to me. But I'd already agreed, and he was the brother-in-law of a good friend, so I'd make the best of it.

And if nothing else, the good bread with the oil plate Mikayla had mentioned sounded great.

A real date with Alex or anyone else didn't appeal to me, and that was a problem. I still had so many feelings for Jesse —feelings I was fairly sure were mostly, if not all, reciprocated. Whatever had been between us in the past remained in the present, but that didn't mean we had a real chance now.

I'd edited enough romance books with the "right person, wrong time" storyline, and it was always so glorious when it came full circle in the end. Our full circle was much different and not as romantic.

The love was still there and neither of us was going anywhere, yet life still kept us apart. I was happy to have him in my life as a friend, but asking or hoping for more seemed a pointless exercise in futility.

Alex was nice enough and very attractive, at least in a conventional sense. He didn't have the soulful brown eyes, a smile that liquefied my knees, or know enough about me from all that time ago to be one of the few to really know me now.

I parked my car, practicing an easy smile in the mirror behind my visor, and climbed out of the driver's seat. When I turned around to click the key fob, goose bumps pebbled on my neck, as if eyes were on me from somewhere. Six o'clock had become a darker twilight in late October, and although the parking lot was full, no one appeared to be near or in their cars. The eerie dark silence sent a weird shiver up my spine.

I let out a long exhale. I was being ridiculous and needed to get a grip. Maybe working from home had given me a little paranoia, but I slid my key in between my fingers just in case my odd instincts were right and I needed to jab someone in the eye.

"Ready for your date?"

I froze, my head swiveling around to Jesse's voice. He cocked an eyebrow from where he leaned against the front of my car, arms crossed as if he'd just caught me doing something wrong.

Granted, that was another odd feeling I had in meeting Alex tonight, but Jesse had no right to regard me that way.

"What are you doing here?"

Jesse came toward me, his slow footsteps echoing in the empty lot.

"My niece told me the time and place since Alex decided to announce in front of a team of kids where he wanted to take you, and here I am."

"Yeah, I got that. But why?"

"You know why. We both do."

"No, I actually don't," I huffed, crossing my arms over my torso to create some distance between us. "You have made it very clear that we are only friends. And I get it and understand why. But what I still don't get is why you're here. You don't want me, but I can't date anyone either. Does that seem fair to you?"

He flinched. "Is that what you think? After everything last weekend, you still think friends is all I want?"

"I really don't know what you want. We have—" I pointed my finger back and forth between us "—chemistry. Old feelings, history. But you can't get all possessive when you've made it clear for a *very* long time that we can't be together."

I hadn't realized until I growled out the *very* that my frustration with Jesse went beyond this pseudo-friendship we had. It was still him deciding what we could or should be together—and being without a say still infuriated me.

"Look, I have plans tonight. We can talk about this later."

He stepped in front of me.

"Chemistry and old feelings." He uttered a humorless laugh. "You want to know why I'm here? Because for what feels like my whole goddamn life, I've given up the only woman I've ever really loved for stupid fucking reasons, and I'm done."

"Because someone asked me on a date, now you're done? Everything is different." I took in air with shaky breaths, like what he'd just said hadn't knocked the wind out of me. "I can't deal with this now. We'll talk about it later."

I tried to go inside but couldn't move past the angry wall of Jesse.

"Please just go," I whispered, darting my eyes from his piercing stare.

He shook his head, skimming his thumb back and forth along my bottom lip. "I'm not asking this time."

Jesse grabbed the back of my head and crushed his lips to mine. I pressed my hands against his shoulders to push him back, but once he flicked the seam of my lips with his tongue, I stopped fighting and melted against him.

"So good," he murmured against my lips, pressing me to him with one hand on the small of my back, while he wove his other into my hair, wrapping his fingers around a fistful. "Nothing ever compared to this."

Nope. Nothing did, and it messed with my head for what seemed like *my* whole goddamn life.

I poured all the love I didn't want to feel, along with the anger of tonight, twenty years ago, and all the time in between, into that kiss. The kiss on his bed had been full of desperation from two people who'd always wanted to love each other but hadn't known how.

It used to be so easy to love Jesse. The hard part came when I had to figure out how to stop.

But as it turned out, I never had.

Teeth scraped, tongues tangled, Jesse's guttural moan egging me on as I ran my hands all over his body.

Time stopped, and the rest of the world faded away as it always had where Jesse was concerned. The parking lot had seemed empty, but that didn't mean there weren't eyes on us from somewhere. I didn't and couldn't care, and that was what scared me most of all being back in Jesse's arms.

When we finally broke apart, I ran my hand over my swollen lips and the raw scrapes on my chin from his stubble.

"I'll go," he panted, framing my face. "I'm alone for the

night. You can come to me, or I'll meet you wherever you want." He pressed his lips to my forehead and rained kisses over my eyelids and cheeks.

I dropped my head into my hands, taking easy breaths through my nostrils to slow the rapid thump of my heart.

I already felt bad for Alex. I was the world's shittiest date, and I hadn't even walked into the restaurant yet.

Heading back to my car on shaky legs, I stepped inside and pulled down the visor. I grabbed some fast-food napkins out of my glove compartment and wiped away my smeared lipstick. My lips were swollen and the skin around my chin was angry and irritated from beard burn, but I tried my best to cover it with powder and some gloss.

"Hey, sorry I'm late," I said, breathless, when I spotted Alex at the table.

"No worries. You're only five minutes late." His easy smile as he pulled out my chair made the guilt twist that much harder in my gut.

"Oh, that's not necessary," I said, waving a hand as I sat down. "Thank you."

"Beautiful women should be treated nicely." He cocked a brow as he sat down.

"Thank you again." My lips burned as I pushed a smile across my mouth. Burning from my ex-boyfriend shoving his tongue down my throat in the parking lot. This was a date that I had been put on the spot to accept from a guy I wasn't that into, but shame washed over me anyway.

"I should be thanking you. I know it was spur-of-the-moment."

"Well, maybe next time don't have those moments in front of kids. Kids who love to talk like my players do. It's not a big deal, but I don't want the parents to get a bad impression, and your sister-in-law wouldn't want that either. She's little but scary."

"We all know that." He chuckled as the waitress brought the bread to the table.

The steam from the flaky crust wafted toward me as she poured the flavored olive oil into a shallow bowl next to the basket. *Thank God.*

"I had no idea you were in publishing."

"Editing," I corrected around a mouthful of bread. "The article highlighted the more well-known authors I work with, so it made it sound like I was in publishing. I did work for a large publishing company out of college, but I like being on my own. What do you do for a living?"

"Finance. Stocks, that kind of thing. My book is about baseball, but I only have about twenty chapters. I'd love to have someone look at it, but I don't know who I'd give it to."

"Well," I said, clearing my throat after I swallowed. "I'm slammed, and my schedule is booked for the next few months. I don't even get the chance to read for pleasure lately. I can ask some friends if they could fit it in."

"Sure, that sounds fine. The book was just my conversation starter. Asking you out to dinner on the field felt a little odd. Especially since Penny told me not to."

I stopped swirling my second piece of bread in the puddle of olive oil.

"She told you not to?"

He smirked and bobbed his head. "She said you and one of the parents on the team had a history that she wasn't sure was current or not. I think I know which one since he always looks like he wants to take a swing at me when I ref a game."

A chuckle fell from my lips. "Jesse is my high school boyfriend. We recently reconnected when he signed his niece up for the league."

"His niece? I thought he was one of the dads."

"He is. It's complicated."

As was every other damn thing when it came to Jesse.

Small talk wasn't bad. Alex was confident but maybe not as full of himself as I'd assumed. He was funny and even a little charming. I caught myself staring at him between bites of my shrimp scampi. How much easier would my life be if I were into this guy instead of the one who'd been waiting for me in the parking lot earlier tonight?

Jesse seemed sincere, but being sincere and putting the action to the words were two very different things. The best thing for me would be just to move on, with Alex or someone else.

But I knew I wouldn't. Maybe I could've pushed myself to go through the motions with someone else like I'd done for the past couple of hours, but my heart? That wouldn't budge.

I had been stuck on the same person for more years than I'd wanted to acknowledge, and that kind of helplessness pissed me off.

"I'll let you know if I can find someone to take a look at your book." My pulse raced as Alex walked me to my car. Not because I wanted him to kiss me, but I wasn't sure how to react if he did.

Plus, it'd been a lot of years since I'd kissed two guys in one night, at least without copious amounts of alcohol in my system.

"No rush. It's probably a dumb premise anyway."

"The Yankees are *never* a dumb premise." I smiled as I leaned against my driver's side door. "Thanks for dinner."

Alex leaned in, and I froze, fighting the urge to draw back from what I knew was coming. I expected his lips to land on mine, but they shifted at the last minute as he brushed them against my cheek.

"This was nice." He stuffed his hands into his pockets. "I'd be open to doing this again, but..." He trailed off and shrugged.

"But what?"

He chuckled and shook his head. "I hope Jesse knows what a lucky guy he is. Drive safe."

I smiled, not having it in me to voice a denial that would sound hollow even to my own ears. After I opened the car door and locked it, I dropped my head to the steering wheel.

Hadn't I wanted this at one time? Jesse had come back into my life and told me he wanted me again, as I'd always dreamed he would. I'd wished for it even though I'd known it would never happen. So I'd grown up and moved on, making myself the priority in my life so I'd never be in that awful position again.

Yet, somehow, I was here anyway. The only difference was that this time, I had a choice.

But when it came to Jesse, it wasn't so easy to choose me.

17

JESSE

I'D DRIVEN STRAIGHT HOME, FIGHTING THE URGE TO DO NINETY in case—or in hopes—Emily would meet me there. The silence as I sat on my couch almost had me climbing the walls. One of Maddie's shows was always on the TV along with the dinging from whatever game she was playing, so a quiet house was rare and, right now, maddening.

I'd made so many mistakes when it came to Emily. I could almost forgive myself for how I'd let her go in high school, but when I'd found her again, I should have had the balls to admit to the feelings that were too deep to ever go away.

Life had a funny way of coming full circle. I'd thrown her out of my life when I was eighteen, not allowing her to have a say or even a word. Now, I'd laid it all on the line and left it up to her, and the thought of losing her again and for good this time made me want to jump out of my skin.

I deserved the suffering but was selfish enough to keep fighting for her all the same.

I checked my phone for the millionth time and found a blank screen. It'd been almost three hours since I'd kissed

Emily in the restaurant parking lot and had asked her to come to me later. Did she go in and have dinner with that guy? Did she go straight home after, or did he take her somewhere?

If I was going to get her back, I needed to work on her time, even if it killed me—or ate away at my insides as it was, and it had only been a few hours.

I flung my phone on the table and headed to the kitchen. I couldn't lose her again, but with every minute that ticked by without a word or even a fuck-off, I was terrified I'd been too late.

I'd bounced from relationship to relationship for so many years, to the point I didn't even try for one anymore. I'd figured I was meant for a bachelor's life and tried my best to write off how happy I'd been with Emily as first love between teenagers.

Then I saw her at our reunion, and it was like that first day I'd knocked all the pencils off her desk. I'd come alive in a way I hadn't in too many years to remember, and all the *old feelings* I'd forced myself to dismiss had come back in a rush, along with another set of complications brought on once again by my insecure, frazzled mind.

I debated ordering something or going for a drive to quell my nerves when the chime of my doorbell, along with an angry knock, filtered down my hallway. A smile broke out on my face as I headed to the door. She sounded pissed, but she cared enough to come here and say so, and I took that as a great sign.

Fighting for her would take time, but making her mad enough to seek me out felt like a tiny victory.

Sure enough, I opened the door to a furious Emily. Her eyes were narrowed to slits as she tapped on the brick next to the doorframe. Her chest heaved up and down with quick breaths, and she glared at me as if she wanted to rip me apart.

"Come in," I said, moving aside for her to cross the threshold. I wouldn't ask her if she was okay because that answer would be no, she wasn't, and it was because of me and my antics tonight.

But again, I'd gotten her here.

She stalked past me, raking a hand through her tousled hair as she stormed into my living room and threw her purse on my couch.

"I'm guessing you're still mad." I shoved my hands into the pockets of my jeans and inched closer, biting back a laugh when her brown eyes, almost black with fury, grew wide.

"Still mad? Are you serious? When did you decide all this?"

"When did I decide what?" I asked, still making a slow approach toward her and keeping myself at a far enough distance in case she wanted to hit me.

"When did you decide that you loved me and that you wanted me back?"

"About four blocks away from your house the night we broke up." I lifted my shoulder in a sad shrug.

She took deep breaths through her nostrils as if she was ready to charge at me.

"I'm so close to punching you right now."

"I can see that."

"That was twenty fucking years ago." Her words quivered as if she was about to explode. "And you've been back in my life for months. You wouldn't even agree to a hypothetical cup of coffee at first because you weren't ready for anything. Which I understood under the circumstances, but then you wait until another man asks me out on a date to decide that you've changed your mind."

"I never changed my mind." I ate up the distance between us in two steps. "I couldn't keep you then, and I thought I couldn't be what you needed now. But there was never a day, never a second, since that first day we met when I didn't want you."

I stood over her, holding her angry gaze.

"Yeah, it's been twenty fucking years. It could be a hundred, and you'd still be the one. The *only* one."

She shoved my shoulder, her jaw tight as her eyes went glossy.

"Stop saying things like that."

"Why did you kiss me last week?"

She rolled her eyes. "You were drunk. I thought if I kissed you, it would appease you enough that you'd pass out."

"That's all?" I whispered, pressing my hand to the small of her back to pull her close. "What about before? The restaurant parking lot. You seemed to be pretty into it for only *appeasing* me."

I cupped her chin, gliding my thumb over her mouth and letting out a hiss when, despite how anger still radiated off every inch of her, she parted her lips to bite it.

"I meant what I said that night, even if I slurred the words out. I'd make it so good, baby. *We'd* be so good." I dipped my head, brushing the hair off her shoulder to paint kisses down her neck, and slid her jacket off. She didn't move but didn't push me away. I dove in harder, trailing openmouthed kisses behind her ear and pressing her closer to me when she slumped in my arms.

"Jesse, please," she breathed out, breaking out of my hold and heading for the door. "I can't... It's all too much."

"No, it's just fucking right," I said, coming behind her as she grasped the bottom railing of my staircase. "It was always you, Em. I know you need some time to believe me, but I won't stop saying it." I buried my head into the crook of her shoulder and ran my lips up her neck. She leaned into me, right against the aching bulge about to burst through my zipper.

"I mean it. I'll wait. I've been waiting for you for a long time, even if I only found the balls to admit it now." I caught her cheek lift. "I'll do whatever you want."

I cupped her cheek, turning her head to face me. I brushed her lips, lingering longer once she relaxed in my arms. When her mouth parted on a groan, I slid my tongue against hers, the kiss slow but full of hunger and laced with relief. Maybe I hadn't gotten through all the way yet, but she wasn't fighting me. I swallowed her sweet moans as she reached back to hook her arm around my neck and draw me closer. I slanted my mouth over hers as I took the kiss deeper, skimming my hands up and down her thighs and slipped one under her blouse, teasing the soft skin on her stomach.

"I mean it, Em," I murmured against her lips as I brushed my fingertips along the lace of her bra. "I'll do whatever you want."

She grabbed my wrist, her nails piercing my skin.

"Touch me, Jesse."

My cock pulsed at her gravelly plea, and she didn't have to ask me twice.

I slipped my hand into her panties, my own knees almost giving out when I found her soaked and dripping on my fingers.

"You're drenched. Shit, Em," I grunted out, tracing circles around her clit, already as hard as I was. "You remember how good it was? How hard I could make you come? I had to hold my hand over your mouth so you wouldn't scream," I whispered, sucking her earlobe into my mouth as I teased her, resisting the urge to fuck her with my fingers. "But I'd feel you every time. Remember?"

She dropped her head back against my chest, her eyes shut as she nodded.

"Lately, all the time," she said as a whimper escaped her.

My hand shook as I forced myself to go slow.

"Remember that first night I tasted you? You were so sweet I couldn't stop, even when your legs shook against my face."

She nodded, rocking her hips against my hand.

"I could come just thinking about that." I cupped her chin and turned her head to face me. "And I have."

I took her mouth in a sloppy, desperate kiss. This wasn't slow. It was greedy and wet and loud as she gasped into my mouth with every circle I traced around her clit.

"Do it," she said, her voice dropping to a raspy plea.

"Do what, beautiful?" I asked as I slid two fingers inside, any semblance of control I had gone as I pumped them inside her, her pussy already squeezing around them as I twisted them deeper. "I'll give you anything you want."

"Taste me. Fuck me with your mouth. Please."

I spun her around and dropped to my knees, unbuttoning her jeans and yanking the zipper down so fast I swore I heard a tear.

"What a dirty mouth on such a sweet girl."

I held her hooded eyes as I shoved her jeans and panties down her legs. I peeled off her boots and tapped her heels for her to step out. I'd only gotten one side off when I couldn't take it anymore and hooked her leg over my shoulder, giving her pussy one long lick before I kissed her hard and deep, tasting every sweet inch of her. I let out a garbled moan, my eyes rolling back as she coated my tongue like the sweetest sugar when I snaked it deep inside her.

She speared her hand into my hair and pushed my head between her legs. We'd gone from zero to sixty tonight—hell, in the past twenty minutes—but I couldn't stop. I'd been starved for this, for her, for too long.

We still had a lot to talk about, but the buildup had us both too blind with want to think straight.

I dragged kisses along the inside of her thigh as my fingers still worked inside her. I peered up at Emily, smiling as her head flailed back and forth.

"You're so close, aren't you?"

She jerked against me when I brushed my lips over her clit.

"I've waited so long for you to scream my name."

She dipped her chin, a hazy smirk at the corner of her lips, still swollen from my kisses.

I adjusted her leg over my shoulder. "Hold on, sweetheart."

I sucked her clit into my mouth as my fingers pumped inside her. I wanted to drown in her but took slow breaths to stop myself from coming in my pants from just the taste of her and the sounds she made.

Her body went rigid from the waist down as she screamed, bucking her hips against my face as her thighs quivered against my cheeks.

"Jesus," she muttered, breathless as she folded over, one hand over her eyes and one on my shoulder to steady herself.

"Jesse," I corrected. "But you can say that the next time I make you come." I pressed a kiss to the back of her knee and stood.

I smiled when I spotted the scowl on her face, her eyes still hooded as they found mine.

"Talk to me," I said, taking her face in my hands. "What do you need?"

"I need to help you," she said, her voice a scratchy whisper as she unbuckled my belt and unzipped my pants. I moaned as she wrapped her hand around my cock, gliding it up and down as it jerked against her palm. "Like you asked me to."

"I'm not going to last," I gritted out, trying with every cell of my body to hold back, but I was already too close. She bit her bottom lip as she pumped faster, her eyes on mine as she gave me a slow nod.

I came in long spurts, too fast to put enough distance between us to not make a mess.

She dropped her head to my chest as I held on to her, my heart thumping against hers as we stood chest to chest.

"I need to clean up," she said, glancing down her body with a wince.

"Same." I kissed her forehead. "But don't go. Please."

"I don't think I'm in any condition to go anywhere, Jess." She flicked her eyes down to her soaked blouse and lifted her leg, dangling her panties on her ankle.

"After we clean up, I want you to stay. Not the night if you don't want to, but long enough to talk. Okay?"

"Okay," she said as she stepped into her jeans. "Not that I have a lot of brain cells left after that." She laughed, but it didn't make it all the way up to her eyes. I spied the fear and the doubt, but she wasn't running. Not yet.

I could work with that.

Emily followed me upstairs, stopping at the doorway of my bedroom.

"Could I borrow a hoodie for tonight?"

"Sure," I said, stepping into my bedroom and rummaging through my drawer until I found a sweatshirt. "Here you go. You can wait for me in the living room if you want. Just give me a minute."

"Thank you," she said, taking the hoodie from my hands and holding it up by the shoulders. "Glad you're still a Yankees fan."

"Why wouldn't I be?"

"My grandfather liked when you used to watch the games with him. He used to yell at my mother to give you a break."

"I remember," I said, returning Emily's easy smile when she lifted her head. "It was all in Italian, but they kept looking back as they argued, so I assumed it was something about me."

"You would have been right. I'll go change. This takes me back," she said, snickering as she headed for my bathroom.

I shut my eyes and laughed.

"I was hoping to show off some skills now that I'm not a teenager anymore, but"—I bunched my shoulders—"turns out I still have no control when it applies to you."

She shook her head. "Skill was never important."

"Well, thanks. Not sure how to take that."

Emily cupped her hand over her eyes.

"I mean, not that you didn't have skill or you don't. But we...us... It was never about that. As long as it was you, that was all I needed."

I watched her head down the hall and disappear into the bathroom, knowing exactly what she meant. Every time was mind-blowing and explosive in its own way, and I'd attributed that, or I'd tried to, to being young and lost in the wonder of it all.

Then Emily came back into my life, and every spark of electricity still burned bright between us in a way it never had with anyone else. She consumed me now just as easily as she always had, and it scared the shit out of me as much as it did then.

What we had together wasn't due to age, innocence, or puppy love.

It was just us.

18

EMILY

I PULLED JESSE'S SHIRT ON, PRESSING MY NOSE TO THE COLLAR and taking a greedy inhale before I smoothed it down. Just like when I used to keep a collection of Jesse's hoodies, I had to roll up the sleeves. I had never been a tiny girl, but Jesse's clothes always dwarfed me. It had been my favorite thing whenever I'd wear anything of his, like I had Jesse draped all over me and, as usual when it came to anything from him, I couldn't get enough.

Guys had come and gone since Jesse, but I'd never worn another man's clothes, even the one I'd lived with and almost married. If I looked back with an honest gaze, I'd probably catch a lot of little ways that I'd been intimate with Jesse but wouldn't consider with anyone else.

As I grew older and wiser, I'd kept anyone trying to love me at a long arm's length but had never realized I was doing it. On the few rare moments I'd let my guard down, I'd been blindsided and hurt enough to keep a permanent distance.

Now, I was jumping back into the risk I'd avoided for most of my life. It wasn't that I didn't believe Jesse or that I thought he'd ever hurt me on purpose. Even though it was hard for me to accept, I now understood that back then the only reason he'd been so cruel was because he'd thought he had no choice.

As sincere as I knew he was, or as he thought he was, he still had issues to sort out. And while one therapy appointment was a step in the right direction, it wasn't an instant cure.

What if I agreed to another chance, only for Jesse to decide later that was too much?

I'd already fallen hard for both Jesse and his niece. Even while trying to stay away, I worried about him and constantly had to fight the urge to ask what he needed and how I could help.

I hadn't decided whether that was because we were meant to be or I just couldn't let go.

I headed downstairs and spotted new pictures on the wall behind the couch. I leaned in, kneeling on one of the cushions to get a closer look. I was familiar with the one in the middle of the wall. Jesse wore a cap and gown as he draped his arm around an eight-year-old Tessa. Had I not been there and taken the photo, it would have been impossible to tell if it was Tessa or Maddie by Jesse's side. I'd never seen a mother and daughter so identical.

One was more recent, with an adult Tessa beaming at the camera next to her brother. She was gorgeous and so tall, not much shorter than her well-over-six-feet brother. I tried to picture the little girl who'd loved to climb on my lap possibly a head taller than me. My heart broke for Jesse all over again as I fixated on the photo. Their love for each other was so evident, it was palpable.

No wonder his grief ran so deep.

"Are they crooked?" Jesse joked.

"I don't remember these photos when I was here last time," I told him, still scanning the wall. "Not that I had time to really take anything in while trying to get you in bed before you puked or passed out."

He laughed and came up behind me, resting his chin on my shoulder.

"Those are new. I only hung them up this week."

"Tessa was always so beautiful." I pointed to the photo of Tessa, Jesse, and Maddie at what looked like her college graduation. "She grew up stunning."

"She did. These photos were my first therapy assignment." He wrapped his arm around my waist. "Part of why... I was the way I was last week is that I haven't allowed myself to talk about her much, so Maddie didn't feel like she could either. I have more to put up. These are just the first batch."

"I'm glad it went well," I said, turning to sit on the cushion.

"It's only the first appointment." He plopped down next to me. "I should have started going on my own when I first took Maddie. Maybe a lot could have been avoided."

"Maybe, maybe not. I'm still proud of you for going at all."

"Thanks," he said, picking up my hand and lacing our fingers together. "I'm glad you still feel a little pride for me after finding me such a hot fucking mess last week."

"Well," I said, my dopey heart fluttering as Jesse skimmed his finger up and down my palm. "You did tell me you wanted to be my *good boy*."

His head snapped up. "I said that? Jesus Christ." He pressed our joined hands to his forehead. "Please don't tell me any more."

"It's fine. I let you say whatever you wanted to keep you upright." I slipped my hand from Jesse's and stood from the couch.

He gave me a tiny smile, his eyes searching my face.

"What?" I flitted my eyes down my body. "Do I have it on backward or something?"

"No, I just like looking at you." He cracked a grin. "In my house, in my clothes. It's a sweet kind of surreal, like when I saw you at the field the first day, only without the stomach-turning panic."

"I can agree with all of that. I like looking at you too. Now that I don't want to punch you—as much."

"You don't look like you want to punch me at all now." He stood, cupping my cheek. "Or before."

"I keep it hidden," I said, a nervous laugh bubbling out of me as Jesse inched closer.

"I don't know about that." He grazed his thumb over my lips. "You came in pretty fired up."

"When I finally decided to come here, I got pretty worked up on the drive. I still can't believe you did that tonight."

"Which part?" He framed my face, running his thumb back and forth over the seam of my lips. "Coming to stop your date, kissing you in the parking lot, or making you come next to my staircase?"

"You've had a busy night," I croaked out, lolling my head to the side as he nuzzled my neck.

"I guess I have," he muttered, running his tongue over the sensitive skin behind my ear. I felt his smile against my skin when I jerked in his arms.

"We need to talk," I said, letting my head fall back as he ran his lips down my throat.

"I know," he said, his voice dropping low as he fisted the bottom of his sweatshirt and dragged it up my torso. "And we will. I just can't stop touching you." He cupped my breasts, dipping his fingers inside the cups of my bra before yanking them down.

I should have been saying something like "No, we need to talk now" or "We need to slow down". The only words falling from my lips were "Fuck yes" as he sucked a nipple into his mouth, dragging it between his teeth before licking a path across my chest.

"You still love this, huh?" he murmured with my other nipple in his mouth.

"Mmm-hmm," I mumbled, grasping the back of his head as I tried to pull the rest of the hoodie off with my other hand.

"Need some help, baby?" Jesse straightened. His hooded eyes were full of a carnal heat I didn't remember from our younger days. A smirk tilted his mouth as he pulled the shirt over my head and let it fall on the carpet with a soft thump.

"My God," he said, his eyes wide as they roamed my body. "You're so gorgeous. I can't even look at you," he growled, diving a hand into my hair and crushing his mouth against mine.

"That's something every girl wants to hear." I laughed as he kissed down my chest and across my stomach.

"I can barely look at you because you're too damn beautiful. It's too much." Jesse skated his palms down my chest and hooked his thumbs into the waistband of my jeans. "It's always been too much, but I'm not giving it back this time."

My hands quivered as I delved them into Jesse's hair. I wasn't sure if it was from being so turned on that my vision was hazy or the promise of him not giving us up. He was right, it had always been too much, and I had no doubt that once he was inside me again, I'd be completely ruined.

But wasn't I already?

This was too soon, and despite knowing that, I couldn't stop it. Even though I had the urge to pay attention to every second in case I had nothing but the memories for the next twenty years.

He grabbed my wrist as I fisted the material at the bottom of his T-shirt.

"Upstairs. I want you in my bed—as nice as against the staircase was," he said before lifting me by the waist and hoisting me over his shoulder.

"Jesse, stop. I can walk," I said, trying to push out of his hold as I bounced against his back.

"I'm returning the favor," he told me over his shoulder. "You helped me up the stairs to get me into bed. I'm just paying you back."

"But I didn't carry you. Stop." I laughed as he set me down on the bed.

"Now, where were we?" He peeled off his shirt and hovered over me. "Right," he said, holding my gaze as he popped the button open on my jeans. I lifted my hips for him to slide them down my legs, but he stopped, furrowing his brow as he peered down at me.

"What's wrong?" I panted out. If we hesitated, I'd come to my senses, and the ache at my core was too in need of relief to entertain any of that.

"You're sure?"

I dropped my head back in frustration.

"You've got to be kidding me. You're backing out *now*?"

"Hell no, I'm not backing out. I want you so much I can't see straight. But I want you to be sure."

I needed a ton of time to work up to sure, if I'd ever get

there at all. What I did know, and what I could never deny, was that my love and need for this man ran soul-deep. Deeper than logic or self-preservation and everything else I'd grasped on to since I'd lost him.

"I need you," I cupped his neck, avoiding his question with a confession. "Please," I begged, pressing my lips to his as I arched my back off the mattress.

His eyes glossed over as he smoothed the hair off my forehead.

"You have me." His lips curved as he reached around me to unhook my bra. "All of me." He slipped the straps off my shoulders before tossing it next to the bed. "You never need to ask."

He held my gaze as he sucked my nipple back into his mouth, pressing his hand to my stomach when I bucked my hips off the mattress.

Instead of almost ripping my jeans in half, he inched them down slowly this time, slipping his hands up my legs and over the insides of my thighs, with a mix of lust and reverence in his gaze.

He rose from the bed, tearing off his jeans and boxers in one swoop.

I let my gaze rake over his body, fixating on his long, hard cock as it bounced against his stomach.

"Like what you see, Legs?" He climbed back on the bed after he rummaged through his nightstand drawer. He held up a foil packet and tore it open, rolling it on his hard length as he smirked at me.

"You're all right," I tried to tease as I wrapped my legs around his waist, smiling at the groan rising from his throat as I clenched them tighter.

"Are you sure you call me Legs because I was fast...or because of this?" I joked, lifting my hips off the bed.

He slid his hand across the nape of my neck before he took my mouth in another hungry, desperate kiss. I rocked against him, the tickle of his chest hair against my breasts setting me off already as I scraped my nails down his back.

"I called you Legs because this, right here," Jesse rasped, slipping a hand between us. I mewled as he teased my clit with more torturous little circles before he slipped a finger inside. "Between your beautiful legs is my favorite place to be." He kissed me again, licking inside my mouth with long, needy strokes. "Feels so good to be home."

He slid inside me with one thrust, my core still sensitive from earlier but very ready for more. I tightened my legs even more as Jesse moaned into my mouth, slamming into me so hard, I was afraid he'd put a dent in the wall.

Sex between us as teens had always been rushed. We were either on curfew or waiting to hear that key in the door from someone arriving home before they were supposed to, but this desperation wasn't because of a time limit or fear of getting caught.

This was something different. Something more than just racing toward a finish line or getting lost in the feelings and each other.

This was deeper in every sense of the word. Deeper and dangerous and more telling than I had the guts to acknowledge.

"It's so good. Too good," he grunted out, his gaze locked with mine as a bead of sweat snaked down his temple.

"Are you okay?" I asked him, grabbing his face. A smile danced across his mouth as he clutched the back of my head.

"I'm in heaven, baby. Come join me?"

He slid his hand between us again, pinching my clit as

he moved deeper and faster. I sat up as the throb at my core ricocheted down my legs.

I laughed to myself, thinking of Jesse worried about skill. If he were any better, he'd kill me.

"That's it. I feel you. Hold on, baby," he panted out and clutched on to me as his release tore through him, still moving inside me as his breath slowed.

He collapsed on the mattress next to me, grabbing me by the waist to draw me into his side.

"I love you," he whispered into the crook of my neck. "So much."

Tears pricked my eyes as he kissed across my cheek, lingering on my mouth.

"It's okay," he said, pressing his lips to my forehead. "You'll believe me soon." I didn't realize I was crying until he swiped away a tear with his thumb. "Until then, convincing you should be fun."

I gave him a soggy smile. I wanted to be convinced, but I didn't know how to silence the steady voice of doubt in my head.

"How about…" he said, rolling back on top of me. "I'll take care of this—" he flicked his eyes down to his waist "—and we'll talk. Maybe you could even stay the night, and this time when I wake up, I'll remember that you were here." The hopeful glint in his eyes made my nose burn. "And tell me, was I a *good boy*?"

"Two orgasms in a little over an hour. I'd say that makes you a *very* good boy."

He peered down at me with a wicked grin.

"I'll be right back." He kissed the tip of my nose and headed into the bathroom. "Don't go anywhere."

I let my head sink into the pillow as I stared at the ceiling. Life had a funny way of playing out. I'd never wanted to go anywhere. Once upon a time, I would have happily given up everything to stay by Jesse's side, but I wasn't sure how I felt about being back.

I sat up, gathering the sheets around my torso as I swept my gaze over the trail of clothes on the floor. I'd come here to yell at him for his audacity tonight and the whiplash he'd given me since his drunken confessions last week, but I was no better. I'd let him kiss me in the parking lot and then allowed him to do everything else to me once I strode through his door.

I had no willpower when it came to Jesse, and as right as it felt to be in his arms again, it was terrifying.

I brought my knees into my chest and took slow breaths in and out.

"Hey, what's wrong?"

I didn't turn around when the bed dipped behind me or when Jesse pulled my back to his front.

"Nothing. I'm fine."

"You don't seem fine. I think you're shaking a little. Talk to me."

I turned my head to his worried gaze and squared my shoulders.

"I'm a little overwhelmed right now. Between tonight and the past weekend—"

"I know." He sifted his fingers through my tangled hair. "I can swear to you that I didn't plan on any of it either. Well, other than trying to stop your date tonight. I fully intended to do that."

A laugh slipped out of me as he kissed the top of my head.

"I think I need a break."

Jesse flinched as his entire body went rigid.

"A break? What do you mean?" He scooted around me until we were eye to eye.

"I'm so sorry for all the mixed signals I'm giving you right now." I draped a hand over my eyes, avoiding the hurt and panic in Jesse's dark gaze so I could say what I had to. "I don't regret the parking lot, or—" I jerked my chin to where my jeans were splayed on the carpet "—or even kissing you the night I took you home. I loved all of it, but we need to pump the brakes a little."

"Pump the brakes?" he repeated slowly, scrubbing a hand down his face. "I really fucked things up when we were kids, didn't I?"

"It's not even that. Believe it or not, I understand how it feels to be so scared to lose something so important to you that all you want to do is run. Because that inclination is pretty damn strong for me right now."

"I don't want you to run." Jesse's eyes were wide as his nostrils flared. "Emily, I lov—"

I pressed my finger to his lips. "I know you do. It's not about convincing me. You have a full plate, and I have a lot of baggage—and not only from that night. I'm not saying stop. I'm saying"—I tilted my head to the side—"ease up a little."

I tried for an easy smile.

"I am going to go home. I'll take a rain check on another sleepover." He nuzzled his cheek against my palm as I skated my thumb back and forth along the scruff on his jaw.

I swung my legs over the side of the bed, so damn tempted to take back all I'd said and spend the rest of the night naked in his arms.

I slid on my panties and jeans, careful not to turn around as Jesse rustled behind me. If I got one more look at his handsome and crestfallen face, I wouldn't leave.

And I had to.

I grabbed my blouse from where I'd left it in Jesse's bathroom and slipped it on before heading downstairs.

"This is dry enough to go home in." I smirked at Jesse as I pulled the hem down. "Thank you for lending me your hoodie." I scooped it off the living room floor and handed it to him.

He stared at the shirt in his hands before he shook his head and stood over me.

"Keep it." He fisted the material to widen the collar and lifted it over my head, holding my eyes as he pulled it down. "I'd say add it to your collection, but I assume you've burned what you had."

"Not burned," I said, clearing my throat when I noticed the squeak in my voice. "Donated."

He chuckled and pulled me into his arms, leaning his forehead against mine.

"Can you text me when you get home?"

"Of course." I framed his face and brushed his lips, light enough not to start anything else, but I couldn't resist one more tiny kiss. "And you don't have to walk me. I'm only parked in your driveway."

"Doesn't matter," he muttered, stepping ahead of me to open his front door.

I'd hoped for a quick getaway tonight, my urge to get away from Jesse just as strong as never wanting to let him go.

But I needed a minute. And as much as he wanted to be all in, I believed he did too.

"Thanks for getting me here safely," I teased as I stepped into my car. "I promise I'll text you when I'm home."

Jesse didn't laugh or smile or even look at me.

"Goodnight, Em. Drive safe."

He shut my door, squeezing my chest with all that sadness pulling at his features. I forced a smile and threw him a small wave before I started my engine and backed out of his driveway.

As I turned away from his street, I had a new sympathy for Jesse. Driving away from the person you loved was the worst feeling in the world, even when it was the right thing to do.

19

JESSE

I DROVE AROUND FOR WHAT SEEMED LIKE FOREVER TO FIND A damn spot in the hospital parking lot. I finally found one so far away from the entrance, I had to jog what felt like a mile to get to the emergency room doors.

"Sir, can I help you?"

The clerk lifted her glasses from the chain dangling around her neck and slid them on.

"Yes, I'm here to see Carmela Patterson. She was brought in by ambulance."

She nodded, sifting through the papers on the desk before turning back to me.

"She's still undergoing tests. No one can be back there right now, but you could have a seat." She pointed a bright-pink fingernail toward the waiting room behind me.

I was about to argue when I spotted Emily, hunched over her tablet in the corner of the empty waiting room.

"Thank you," I muttered as I rushed over.

As I approached, I found a sleeping Emily, her eyes shut as her head rested against her hand. She'd texted me this morning that her mother had been rushed to the hospital in the middle of the night and that she couldn't make the game today, but I didn't know how long she'd been here.

I wished she would have called me right when it happened, but she probably didn't because she knew I had Maddie and couldn't leave without someone to watch her— or at least, I wanted to believe that.

As excruciating as it was, I'd given Emily space after she'd left my house last weekend. When I'd thought I finally had her back, she'd left. She'd said she didn't blame me for how I'd broken up with her, but when I trudged back inside after she'd driven away, alone with remnants of Emily still all over me, I couldn't help thinking I'd finally gotten what I'd deserved.

I still spoke to her every day, but we hadn't known how to act around each other at soccer practice this week. She hadn't avoided me, but neither of us could make eye contact. Every time I'd looked her way, I'd thought of her in my arms, in my bed, the taste of her as she came on my tongue. My mind and body would react to the memories if I stared too long, so I'd tried to focus on the rest of the field instead of the woman I'd always loved.

But if I wanted her, I had no option other than to wait, and I couldn't push, even if the paralyzing helplessness made me want to jump out of my skin.

It would take her a while to trust me enough to rely on me, but knowing she didn't—at least not all the way yet— stung.

I put a gentle hand on her shoulder and kissed the top of her head.

"Jesse?" she whispered, squinting at me as she jerked her head up. "What are you doing here? Maddie has a game."

"I didn't want you to be here alone." I slid into the seat next to her. "How long have you been here?"

"Since three, maybe? Mom was able to call for help after the fall but lost consciousness right after. I haven't even seen her yet. All they've told me is that they're running tests." She dropped her head against my shoulder. "I feel like I've been here forever."

I was more familiar than I wanted to be with how time could basically stop in a hospital and how hours and days could go by without realizing it.

"But I'm fine. We only have a few games left. I don't want Maddie to miss it."

"She's not missing it. Caden is taking her today, and he'll bring her home later."

"Oh, that's good. Maybe he can help Sabrina today too." The corner of her mouth lifted in a tired smile. "I think she's used to the kids, but it's a lot easier when there're two of us."

"They'll be fine." I kneaded the back of her neck. "I wish you would have called me."

"You wanted me to call you at two in the morning?" She rolled her eyes at me.

"If something is wrong, yes, I do."

She shook her head. "You have a kid to worry about."

"I have *you* to worry about."

She rubbed her eyelids, her silence making me feel even worse, but I'd wait to argue that point until after she found out her mother was—hopefully—okay.

"Is there anyone you need me to call?"

She shut her eyes and shook her head.

"Nope. My cousins all live in Vegas now, and we hardly speak other than a Christmas card."

"What about your mom's friend? Ann, I think her name was—"

"Anna. She passed away a couple of years ago. That was part of why I moved back and found a place so close. Mom wouldn't admit it, but I could tell she was lonely." She fell back against the vinyl cushion of the chair and crossed her arms. "So, we are pretty much alone. It's not news, but it hit much different after sitting here for the past few hours."

Her gaze floated to the back of the room.

"I used to think it was easier that way. Too many people in your life means too many expectations and too many ways they can disappoint you."

Her eyes clenched shut for a second when they met mine.

"I didn't mean you. Well..." She laughed to herself. "I didn't mean *only* you. It's weird how life gets smaller as you get older, you know? When my grandparents were alive, our house was bursting at the seams with family and friends. Not just on holidays, but Sundays too. You remember."

"I do." I nodded and stretched my arm along the back of her chair. "I've never eaten more at one meal like I used to at your house."

"Right?" Her eyes were bloodshot and tired, but I wondered how much of the exhaustion I spied in her gaze was from lack of sleep. "Then grandparents pass away, friends move, and everything you thought would last forever dwindles."

She uttered a humorless laugh when her eyes found mine.

"I had my friends at work and in the city and always had Sabrina. But being *with* someone, that I was never good at." She flashed me a wry grin. "I can only blame you so much."

I chuckled but didn't reply so she'd continue.

"I always felt like things were decided for me before I had a say in any of it. I liked soccer and I was good at it, so my mother pushed me into making that a way to pay for school. Then the only college that would give me a full scholarship was six hours away from everyone I cared about, but I had no choice but to go. Then...We don't need to rehash that when I'm on two hours of sleep." She pressed her palm to her forehead and let out a yawn.

"The first real choice I ever made about my own life was the day I told my coach to take me out of the running for the draft into a professional league. I said I'd play out the rest of my time in school and work hard, but that wasn't what I wanted to do once I graduated." She shrugged. "Felt good."

"I'm sure it did," I squeezed her knee and drifted my thumb back and forth on her thigh. I never thought I could feel worse about hurting Emily when we were young, but the lost look in her eyes cut me so deep I couldn't look at her for a moment.

"I dated. For fun, since I didn't have time for anything else in college. I was even engaged once. I made it all the way to the last deposit on the wedding venue before I broke it off."

"What happened?" I asked more out of curiosity than jealousy, although the thought of another man's ring on her finger turned my stomach.

"He told me he'd changed his mind about having kids. But it shouldn't matter to me if I really wanted to marry him. That it shouldn't be a deal-breaker because if I loved him, he should be enough."

She lifted her gaze from the floor and shook her head.

"He wasn't. If we tried and it didn't happen, that was one thing. But if I went ahead and married him, knowing that something I'd always wanted was automatically off the table, it would feel like another concession. And I'd had enough of those." She sniffled before exhaling a long gust of air. "Alone felt better than settling. And that's what it had seemed like I'd be doing if I married him."

"Do you still speak to him?"

"Oh no," she scoffed, her chest rumbling with a laugh. "He called me a cold bitch and told me good luck being anyone's mother."

"I'll kick his ass if you tell me where he lives."

She patted my hand where it still rested on her thigh.

"It's not worth it, and he was right. We were together for a couple of years, and while that's something he should have been up front about earlier, it shouldn't have been the reason for me to walk away and not even be that sad over it. Maybe there is something wrong with me."

"There is not one fucking thing wrong with you."

"I told you I had baggage." She smiled, lifting a shoulder. "You remember high school Emily. She was a lot less complicated than this one is, Jess."

"No, she wasn't." I cupped her neck. "She's still beautiful from the inside out. I see you with Maddie and with all the kids on the team, and you loved my sister. Your heart is too big for you not to be an amazing mother if that's what you want."

I peeled her hand off her leg and brought it to my lips.

"It's big enough for you to take care of your pathetic ex-boyfriend when he was so drunk he still doesn't remember everything that happened that night. You're the complete opposite of a cold bitch, and I never want to hear you say that again."

"Either way," she said, her hand limp against mine, "I'm alone. It's what I wanted, right? I work alone, I live alone. And if anything happens to that ornery lady back there," she said, her voice cracking, "I'll really be alone. I guess I'm just now realizing how *lonely* alone is."

"You're not alone." I crouched in front of her so she'd have nowhere to look but at me. "You have me. Since that first day and, whatever you decide, for the rest of my life. As long as I'm alive, you aren't alone."

Big tears snaked down her cheeks, but her expression didn't change. Our eyes stayed locked until we turned to the buzz of her cell phone on the seat next to her.

"Sabrina is FaceTiming me," she said, squinting at her phone. She swiped her cheeks with the back of her hand before she tapped the screen. "Hey, everything okay?"

"We are all okay." Sabrina's voice was garbled as she moved the phone around. "The kids just wanted to say hi."

I took a seat next to Emily to see the screen. Maddie and all the other kids on the team waved their hands and screamed their hellos at once.

"Don't worry, Coach Emily," Maddie said after she pulled the phone toward herself. "We're going to win for you."

Emily snuck me a smile.

"Thank you, Maddie. That means a lot to me, but I just want you to do your best and have a good time today."

The camera dropped to the grass before Caden's face filled the screen.

"Don't worry about a thing, Em. Sabrina and I have this covered. And listen," he whispered as he brought the phone closer. "I've been watching the other team practice, and if we just trip the big kid, I think we can clear the way—"

"No!" Emily yelled. "Jesus, Caden, they're kids."

"This one looks like he's got a five-o'clock shadow. Does anyone check their birth certificates?"

"Caden," I growled, taking the phone from Emily. "Just have them kick the ball back and forth and give them snacks in between. No need for sabotage."

"Fine," he sighed. "But we got this. Just take care of your mom."

"Thank you," Emily said before jabbing the screen to end the call.

"I really hope he doesn't tell the kids to trip anyone." She pressed her hands to her cheeks.

"I think he was kidding. Mostly. But Sabrina will keep him in check."

She nodded, her eyes roaming my face as another heavy silence fell over us.

"Ms. Patterson?"

Emily jumped up from the seat as a doctor came up to us.

"Yes. How's my mother?"

Emily's chest deflated when he smiled.

"Lucky. Her hip has a minor fracture, so I don't think she needs a replacement. But she will need surgery. Orthopedics will be by this afternoon to look and come up with a plan moving forward. She has a nice bump on her head but just a minor concussion."

Emily leaned against me as the tension melted from her shoulders.

"Can I see her?"

"She's up and awake and asking whatever nurse stops in when she can eat."

She pressed a hand to her chest.

"That means she's going to be okay," she said, turning to me with a watery smile.

"I'd say so," I said, chuckling as I wrapped my arms around her waist.

"You can go see her now," the doctor said, motioning to the double doors behind her. "She's in curtain three."

"Thank you," Emily croaked out.

She cried into my chest, her shoulders shaking as she let out a soft sob.

"Don't cry," I crooned as I rubbed her back. "It's going to be fine. She's okay. And if we don't find her a muffin or something, she's probably going to raise some hell back there."

She backed away with a soggy chuckle, her face still in her hands.

"Come with me," she said, grabbing my hand.

"It's okay, Em. I'll wait out here for you."

She shook her head. "She needs to get used to you again."

The beautiful and easy smile spreading across her lips, along with her assumption I'd be sticking around, ignited a glimmer of hope in my chest.

"Hey, Mom," Emily whispered after she pulled the curtain open.

"Why are you whispering?" Mrs. Patterson crinkled her nose. "It's morning, isn't it? Everyone's awake."

Mrs. Patterson had always been a petite woman, but she seemed even tinier in the hospital bed. Her cropped blond hair was now white and shorter, sticking up as she ran an IV-covered hand through it in frustration.

"They told me you had a concussion, so I didn't want to make your headache worse. Thanks for the scare, Mom." Emily kissed her cheek and took a seat next to the bed.

"I didn't plan on the new blood pressure pills making me dizzy enough to fall. Thank God I keep my phone in my pocket." She turned her head and tapped Emily's chin. "You've been up all night, haven't you? Sorry I scared you, cookie."

"It's fine, as long as you're okay."

I was about to step out, feeling all kinds of intrusive watching them when Mrs. Patterson scowled at me over Emily's shoulder.

"Are you going to come say hello or what?"

I laughed at the hint of a smirk on her face.

"Good to see you, Mrs. Patterson." I came up to the bed and squeezed her hand. "Not here, of course, but happy to see you again."

"You're almost forty, for Christ's sake. Call me Carmela."

"I'm sorry to interrupt." A nurse peeked inside the curtain. "Your insurance card says there is a secondary plan, but we can't find the number."

"I can help with that." Emily rose from the seat to follow the nurse, stilling for a moment before turning to her mother. "Be nice."

A chuckle escaped me as I took a seat on the opposite side of the bed.

"I was wondering when I'd see you." She raised a brow at me as she shifted on the mattress.

"You were?" I leaned closer, not sure if it was her concussion talking.

"As soon as Emily said she ran into you at the reunion and that she was coaching your niece, I figured it was a matter of time." She hissed as she leaned toward the bed rail. "Can you fix this pillow for me, please?"

"Of course." I held her hand as she bent forward, and I adjusted the two pillows at her back. "Better?"

"Yes, much. The pain medicine they gave me has me nice and loopy, but it's hard to get comfortable." She settled back on the bed, frowning as sadness flashed across her face. "I'm so sorry about your sister. What a doll she was. I called your mother when Emily told me."

"Thank you. Mom never said she spoke to you."

"We used to talk all the time back then. You two never knew that either. You used to worry us, being so intense." She clicked her tongue against her teeth and shook her head. "Believe it or not, I always liked you. You were a good kid then and now, taking care of your sister's baby and making a good life for her."

Pride swelled in my chest at her warm and easy smile. After years of trying so hard to be on her good side, I never would have guessed I was already there.

"When you're a single parent, you have to be a little scary. Comes with the job. If you haven't learned that yet—" she pointed a finger at me "—you will very soon."

"I haven't had to be scary yet, but I'm ready. Having learned from the best." I smiled and patted her knee.

In all the years I'd known Emily's mother, this was the first time I ever witnessed her truly laugh. When her face lit up, she reminded me a lot of her daughter.

"What choice did I have? Who was going to keep you in line? My father?" She waved a hand, her nose turned up in disgust. "He was more in love with you than my daughter was. And my mother fed you until I was sure you'd throw up one day, and you never told her no. I was on my own."

"I never faulted you for that." I shook my head. "In fact, I told Emily that I admired you for it. She was special and deserved the best." I eased forward and raised a brow. "You were right to never let me forget it."

She nodded, studying my face. I'd bet if she sat up and punched me for hurting her daughter, IVs attached to her arms or not, it would still really hurt.

"I promise that I will never hurt her again. I love your daughter very much."

"I know that. I knew that. Why do you think I hovered so much? Kids in love don't exactly think too clearly. Adults too." She looked away. "I'm glad you were here for her today. Although I'm sure she didn't call you to come, and you just showed up."

"You'd be right."

She shut her eyes and nodded.

"She grew up to be a tough nut to crack, but I have no doubt you will. You just have to prove that you're not going anywhere."

"I'm not, Mrs.—Carmela." *God, that felt weird.* "I'm hers for the rest of my life, and if it takes that long to prove it to her, I will."

"Oh, don't be dramatic. It won't take that long. I should still be alive by the time it happens."

I burst out laughing before I could help it.

"Hey there." Another nurse drew back the curtain. "The food cart is outside if you'd like to get anything. I know you've been saying you're hungry."

"I'll grab you some breakfast." I stood and motioned to the cart. "What would you like?"

"I doubt the selection is big, but coffee and some kind of pastry would be great, thank you." She grabbed my arm before I headed out. "Two things before I forget. Don't let her be alone tonight." Her mouth flattened. "She's shaken up, even if she won't admit it. So, don't leave her, okay?"

"I had no intention of it. What else?"

"I'm old and traditional and will expect you to ask my permission before you propose to my daughter."

I blinked a few times as I tried to figure out how to reply.

"It's only been a few months since we've—"

"It's been eons, trust me. I knew if you ever came back into her life, that would be it. And here you are. Now go to the cart before they leave and I have to wait until lunch."

I had no reply as my jaw went slack.

"Go." She pointed to the cart. "And if you get me a cheese Danish" —a smile curved her lips— "I may even tell you yes."

20

EMILY

"I NEVER THOUGHT THAT SITTING DOWN FOR SO MANY HOURS would be so exhausting," I told Jesse from the passenger seat of his car.

When the call from the hospital had woken me out of a dead sleep, I had been too shaken up to drive and had called an Uber.

Jesse had offered to take me home after Mom was settled into a room and mostly comfortable with pain meds. Her doctor had told me that I could go back home and come back in the morning. My mother had thrown me out when I resisted, yelling at me to leave and get some sleep.

After we'd lost my grandparents while I was in high school, it had been just us, but we'd still had our extended family. Little by little, our family had shrunk to only each other.

I didn't know if marriage was in the cards for me, especially after the way my engagement had ended. I'd figured I'd be permanently single but had no problem with being on my own.

But today, as I waited to find out if she was okay, I realized that I was never truly *on my own* if I still had my mother. If something had happened to her today, I wouldn't know my place in this world without her.

And that realization had terrified me to my core.

"Hospitals are exhausting." Jesse's voice pulled me out of my musings. "I know how it is to be there all day, sometimes all night, and those chairs aren't exactly comfortable. I always left tired, with a big knot in my back."

He chuckled, but his smile never made it to his eyes.

I knew he was thinking about his sister, and I couldn't imagine what it was like to see someone young and vital become so ill that your family had to spend endless amounts of time with her at a hospital.

"Yes, I still have a crick in my neck from falling asleep in the waiting room. I can't wait to change and get into bed."

Jesse pulled up in front of my apartment and shut off the engine, regarding me with a tentative gaze. I'd spewed out a lot in that hospital waiting room, surprising even myself at some of the words falling from my mouth. Fears I'd kept hidden far in the back of my mind rose right to the surface and had a crippling hold on me.

A weird weight had been lifted after my surprise confessions, even if I had no idea what to do about them.

"Thanks for the ride home and for...everything." I leaned over to kiss his cheek. "I'm glad you came."

"Me too, Em," he said, stretching his arm across the back of my seat. "I have a suggestion. How about you stay with me tonight?"

He held up a hand before I could reply.

"I will sleep somewhere else, and you could take my bed. Maddie would love it, and I don't think you should be alone. You had a long, scary day. We'll order some dinner, and we can hear all about the game that hopefully didn't involve any suspicious injuries."

I dropped my chin to my chest and laughed.

"Hopefully."

"We're here now, so you could go inside and pack a bag for tonight and the morning." He jutted his sharp, stubbled chin toward my door. "I'll make us all a nice breakfast and drive you back home. So, come home with me. I mean—" he winced, and I had to laugh "—come be with us tonight. Please."

I should've told Jesse goodnight. Staying at his house tonight would complicate things even more between us, no matter where I slept.

Dread filled my stomach as my gaze drifted to my front door. I didn't want to go home to an empty apartment tonight.

I wanted to be with Jesse.

And after everything today, I was too tired to question what I should or shouldn't do or what I really wanted.

Especially when what I wanted was pretty damn clear, even if I was afraid of it.

"Okay."

Jesse's head jerked up.

"Seriously?"

"Are you taking it back?"

"No, of course not. I'm just surprised that's all it took. I had a whole second part of the speech planned for when you said no."

His sheepish grin made me want to grab his face and kiss the hell out of him.

"Well, I guess I'm just that tired and hungry. And your bed is pretty comfortable."

I cringed when he arched a brow. His chest was comfortable too, and his pillows were soft and fluffy to rest my head on as Jesse plowed me into his mattress. But that wouldn't happen tonight or anytime soon.

Or it shouldn't.

"It is comfortable, and it's all yours. I can either sleep on the couch or on the futon in the guest room. I just don't want to leave you tonight."

"I appreciate it. Want to come in?" I motioned to my door. "I don't know how long I'll be, and I'll feel bad if you're just sitting out here in the car. Plus, you don't want to look like me, loitering in a car and casing the place, right?"

Jesse's head fell back with a chuckle.

"Very good point. Sure, I'll come in."

I padded up my walkway, Jesse's steps echoing behind me as I unlocked my door.

I'd picked this apartment because of its proximity to my mother and an easy setup for working. I had the far end of the living room blocked off for an office and a kitchen big enough to cook in without feeling cramped. Two large bookcases lined one wall, filled with old favorites and some finished products from clients, with pictures spaced out along my hallway.

I had one bedroom with an almost floor-to-ceiling window and a bathroom big enough to soak in the tub without my feet dangling over the side.

I'd always found it small but spacious, perfect for what I needed it for. But now, it seemed tiny to me—and stifling.

The usual familiarity of home felt like an old, itchy sweater, making me squirm until I could wiggle out of it.

I needed to think about what all that meant. But for tonight, I'd go to Jesse's house, somehow shake the urge to crawl into bed with him, and get some sleep.

I'd seek some clarity for this internal mess I'd uncovered later.

"This is a nice place." Jesse swept his gaze over my living room.

"Thanks," I told him. "It's small, good for what I need it for, right?"

A chuckle escaped me, my words so defeated and pathetic they left a sour taste on my tongue.

I headed to my bedroom, rummaging around the bottom of my closet for my overnight bag and stuffing it with a change of clothes for tonight and tomorrow. I tried not to overthink as I packed the bare minimum and slipped into my bathroom for a few toiletries. I stopped packing my bag when I felt Jesse's eyes on me.

"You keep looking at me like I'm about to combust or something." I narrowed my eyes as I shut my drawer.

Jesse smiled, propping his elbow against the doorjamb of my bedroom like every fictional and high school fantasy brought to life. The ones I fought against but that snuck into my brain anyway.

Even in a T-shirt and sweatpants, he was so handsome it was painful.

"Like I've said, I just like looking at you." The corners of his mouth lifted. "And maybe I'm watching you a little more closely to make sure you're okay. I promise I won't hover or push tonight."

"I didn't want to be alone tonight. I'm looking forward to Maddie talking my ear off and distracting me."

A slow smile broke out on Jesse's face, making him even more beautiful and calming me for a moment after my shaky breath left me in a whoosh. He'd been around enough for me to get used to the pull toward him, but the events of the past couple of weeks heightened my awareness of him to the point of distraction.

Staying at his house tonight was going to be an Olympic effort in willpower, my growing weakness already evident as I packed my toothbrush.

"I had a feeling. I'm happy that I could be there for you. I'm just warning you that you might be in for kind of a long night because I don't see Maddie going to sleep anytime soon once she finds out you're staying with us."

"That's okay. At least I can give her the sleepover that her mom always used to beg me for. I never had the heart to tell Tessa that my mom wouldn't let me stay at her house or go into why." I smirked at Jesse. "I did have a couple of sleepovers at her house, but nobody knew about them."

Jesse laughed, deep and throaty and sexy as hell.

"That is true. Only we knew about those." He lifted the strap of my bag off my shoulder and slipped it onto his. "Although I think my mother may have had her suspicions after taco night, but by the time she started to question things, I was already too torn up over losing you for her to punish me. I'm guessing, anyway."

His crooked grin slayed me like always. That was when he looked the most like the Jesse I remembered. The one I'd loved, and although we'd taken a big hiatus from each other's lives, the one I still did.

That was more of a given than a revelation.

———

"I DIDN'T KNOW YOU WERE COMING OVER." MADDIE GASPED and almost knocked her uncle over when she noticed me behind him. She squeezed my waist a little too hard, but I bent to hug her back.

"Is your mom okay?" Maddie searched my gaze with worried eyes and too much understanding for a little girl.

"She's okay, but she'll be in the hospital for a few days."

"Emily is staying with us tonight. You can drop the 'Coach' while she's here." Jesse smiled at me over his shoulder.

"Interesting."

I turned to find Caden sitting next to Sabrina on the couch, both looking between Jesse and me with the same wry grins.

"Can you stay in my room? I have a new beanbag bed that I use to play video games, but I bet you can sleep in it too." Maddie bounced with her hands clasped under her chin.

"Emily is staying in my room, and I'm taking the futon. I'm afraid I'll never get out of the beanbag bed if I try." He tugged at her ponytail. "We're ordering dinner if you guys would like to stay. How did it go?"

"Great!" Maddie scurried over to me. "We won! By, like, a lot."

"Really..." Jesse said, squinting at Caden. "By a lot."

"There was no sabotage. Relax. Your team was just fired up today. It was fun. Open to help out anytime, Em."

"And we have a surprise for you. It wasn't a big game or anything, but the team thought you'd like to have the ball since they won for you today." Sabrina handed me a soccer ball. "They all signed it for you."

"Oh my God," I breathed out, careful when I took the ball out of Sabrina's hands not to smear any of the signatures. "They suggested this?"

"Maddie and a couple of the girls did, but we had to stop them all from fighting over who would sign next," Caden said as I turned the ball around to count the names.

"They love Coach Emily." Sabrina wrapped her arm around my shoulders and squeezed. "And thanks for the offer of dinner, but we're going to head out."

"Yeah, they're great kids, but after an afternoon of yelling on the field, I want to soothe my scratchy throat with a nice IPA."

"For real," Sabrina sighed. "I want a greasy meal and a drink before I collapse tonight." She grabbed her coat from the rack next to the front door and leaned in. "But in case anyone calls me in the morning, I'll be up bright and early."

I elbowed her side and pursed my lips.

"I'm sure you will."

After Jesse shut the door behind Caden and Sabrina, nerves fluttered through my stomach. He turned to me, popping his brow as he glanced up the stairs.

"I'll take your bag up to my bedroom. You and the boss can talk about what to order for dinner." He flashed Maddie a smile and headed up the staircase. As my gaze fell on his hand as he held on to the banister, my cheeks and neck flushed hot remembering both his hands and mouth all over me the last time I was here.

"Did you know the diner delivers?" Maddie said, shaming me out of my graphic fantasy about her uncle.

"I did. I could go for a burger and some chocolate cake."

"Wow, I was about to say the same thing." She patted the cushion next to her. "Uncle Jesse can order on his phone. Did you ever hear of the Ramona books?"

"I love the Ramona books. They were the first series of books I read. Which one are you reading?"

"The first one. *Beezus and Ramona*. It's really good. I know it's not a long book, but maybe we could read it after dinner?"

My heart leaped at the hopeful look in her eyes.

"If Emily isn't too tired, I'd say that is a great idea," Jesse said. "And if she is, she'll be back so you can read another time."

He smiled when he met my gaze, warmth flooding my chest and muting that annoying voice of reason I needed tonight.

"Okay." Maddie nodded. "We decided on the diner."

"Whatever you ladies want is fine with me. Not that I was asked."

Jesse caught my gaze and winked.

"Oh, my grams found some of my mom's books this week." She popped off the couch and rushed over to a box in the corner.

"She highlighted a lot. We aren't allowed to do that in school, or we get into trouble."

"I notate. I mean, I have little stickers I put in my favorite parts of a book to read again. I never like marking up the actual pages unless it's on my computer screen."

She put a familiar book in my lap.

"This one has a lot of highlights, from the first page too."

It was a contemporary romance, one of the first I'd edited for Mary and the most common one I'd see on bookstore shelves. I picked up the book, a little nervous as to what highlighted parts Maddie might have noticed, as it was one of Mary's spicier stories.

"See? Look." She leaned over me and flipped open the cover. "This page is just names, though."

A gasp escaped me before I could help it.

"What is it?" Jesse asked, his forehead crinkled as he stepped over to us.

"It's...my name. This book is one of mine." I picked it up and turned it around to show Jesse. "Tessa highlighted my name. She knew."

"This book is one of yours?" Maddie's brows drew together.

"Yes. Well, kind of. Remember when I said that I edited books? I worked on this one." I tapped the page. "Your mom must've recognized my name."

I peered up at Jesse, watching us with tears in his eyes as his throat worked.

"She read *all* the time. With me every day, and she kept a pile of books on her nightstand."

"I must have just missed her reading days when I...when I last saw her." It was hard to form words as a lump in the back of my throat stunted the air coming out of my lungs. "I'm glad she grew up to be a reader."

"That is so cool. Your name is printed in a book."

Jesse grinned at me. "It's very cool. Emily was always a big deal."

I smiled back, so many emotions running through me, I had no idea which one to go with.

"I'm going to look if your name is mentioned again."

I swiped the book from her hands as she started to skim.

"I'm in the acknowledgments, but that's it. This is an adult book, so let's keep to Ramona and The Baby-Sitter's Club for now."

I cringed at Jesse and set the book back into the box.

"I'm a really good reader. My teacher says that I read almost two grade levels ahead, so it's okay for me to read an adult book."

"No, it's not." Jesse kissed the top of her head. "Go upstairs and get changed while I order us dinner."

Her shoulders slumped as she stood from the couch.

"Emily is here until tomorrow, and you can read anything else you want."

She nodded and trudged toward the staircase.

"Wow," I breathed out, reaching back into the box for the book.

"Wow is right," Jesse breathed out. "I can't believe she never said anything and figured out that was you." He jutted his chin toward the book in my lap.

"Not that hard to figure out." I chuckled, lifting a brow at Jesse. "She could have seen my name and did a search or maybe stumbled upon me on social media. All my pages say that I'm a freelance editor. At least someone in your family may've cared to snoop a little bit."

I drew a smile out of him.

"I'd like to have this, if that's okay." I flipped the pages and spotted a ton of blue and yellow highlights. "I've been thinking about your sister a lot. I wish I could have known her as an adult." I held up the book. "This makes me feel like I kind of did. At least, I hope she was mostly an adult when she made all these highlights."

Jesse didn't laugh or react as I peered up at him.

"If you want to keep it, it's fine—"

"No, of course you can have it. It's just—" he raked a hand through his hair and shook his head "—I can't believe my sister is still busting my chops when it comes to you." A sad laugh tumbled from his lips. "I'm honestly not surprised."

I didn't know what to say when he flashed me a weak smile. It was a sucker punch to the gut for me too, yet a comfort at the same time.

"I'll order us dinner. I should just get a whole cake for the two of you."

"Okay. Here's two books."

Maddie plopped two books on my lap as my gaze lingered on Jesse, heading to the dining room as he scrolled his phone.

"I know Uncle Jesse said we could read after dinner, but if we silent-read like my teacher lets us do, I won't get into trouble."

She pressed her finger to her lips.

"That works for me. Pick any book you want."

She cuddled into my side and opened one of The Baby-Sitter's Club.

"I'm so glad you're here," Maddie whispered as she hugged my neck. "I hope you can come back again."

"Me too."

I kind of loved the thought of Tessa never letting her brother forget about me, and despite how I'd always thought he'd thrown us away, he hadn't. Even as a scared kid, he'd loved me enough to put me first, even if he hadn't realized it at the time. As a man, he was loving and protective and so wonderful.

"Should I turn the page now?" Maddie asked, squinting up at me.

"Oh, sorry," I stammered, leaning my head against hers. "Go ahead."

Jesse caught my gaze, a wistful smile curving his lips as he headed upstairs.

Fate was hard to ignore when it was this damn loud.

21

JESSE

"So, no one tripped anyone, right?"

My niece shook her head at me. "No. They were all bigger than us, and we still won!" She banged her fist on the table.

I sucked my cheek in to hold back a laugh.

"Bigger doesn't mean better." Emily tapped Maddie's shoulder. "Yes, they can push harder on the field and move you out of the way faster, but some of the best soccer players I knew in school were a lot shorter than me. It's all about the skill."

"And *we* had the skill."

I cracked up when Maddie did a little dance in her chair.

"Don't get cocky, Mad. What else happened at the game?"

"Nothing really, except I have a question. Are Caden and Sabrina boyfriend and girlfriend?" Maddie asked around a mouthful of chocolate mousse cake.

Emily's narrowed eyes met mine.

"Why do you ask?" Emily asked Maddie but held my gaze.

"Just because they like to touch each other a lot."

"Touch each other?" I snuck Emily a look. "They were touching at the game today?"

"Well, like, they were always giving each other high fives, or sometimes Caden would put his arm around her. Mikayla said that's a *very* boyfriend-like thing to do." She straightened in her seat.

"And Mikayla knows about boyfriends?" I asked.

"Yeah, she's had a couple."

My head whipped to my niece.

"A *coup*—"

"I'm sure she *thinks* she's had a couple," Emily tried to clarify, draping her hand over mine when she most likely noticed the protruding vein pulsing on my temple. I was not ready for this shit when my niece was only eight years old— or ever.

"She said that if a boy likes you, he likes to touch your shoulder or hold your hand so he can stay really close to you. She said Caden and Sabrina *definitely* had that vibe."

"Caden and Sabrina have been friends for a long time. They're familiar with each other. That's probably what Mikayla noticed."

I hoped Emily's explanation would satisfy Maddie enough to change the subject.

I had no idea what was going on between Caden and Sabrina and never really did. If they were going to get together or had already and hadn't said anything, I was happy for them. I had my own relationship issues to deal with and really wasn't in a place to think about or judge anyone else's.

"Like you and Uncle Jesse." Maddie nodded and looked between us.

"Like what about me and Emily?"

"You've known each other a long time, so you're familiar. Why you always stay so close to her during games."

The corner of Emily's mouth twitched as she stood and gathered the empty paper containers from dinner.

"I guess you could say that." I peered up at Emily, smiling when she found my gaze. Staying close to Emily was an instinct as natural as breathing. Even at the reunion, when I wasn't sure if she hated me or not, I'd taken the seat right next to her and hadn't veered too far for most of the night.

While she was sleeping at my house tonight, I had to figure out a way to fight that. At least my niece provided enough of a buffer between us, but when she went to sleep, no matter where I stayed in this house, it would be hard to drift off, knowing that Emily was here.

I'd asked her here because I didn't want her to be alone. I wanted her here because I wanted to be with her, however she'd let me. I feared maybe this was all I'd get, that even with all the love I believed we still had between us, it was too complicated to be together.

Even if, from where I was sitting, it was pretty damn simple.

"Can I play some video games before we read?" Maddie asked.

"Sure, just keep the volume down."

She scurried onto the living room floor to turn on one of her game systems. She played the portable ones in her room, but I let her hook the console up to the big screen.

"Thank you for dinner tonight. And for tonight, in general. Maddie is a nice distraction."

"That she is," I agreed, following Emily into the kitchen. "And you don't have to clean up. You're a guest." I took the bag of trash out of her hands.

"You've made a really nice home for her here, now that I've had time to see all of it after Maddie gave me a tour." She leaned against the sink, crossing her arms over her torso and plumping her breasts against the round neckline of the snug T-shirt she wore over even tighter yoga pants.

Emily could have come here in a potato sack, and I'd still find it hard to keep my eyes, and my hands, off her.

"It was a little hard to pretend I haven't been here before."

"It shouldn't have been that difficult. Some rooms are new to you." I stuffed the containers into my recycling bin. "Maybe not my bedroom or anything down here." I motioned behind me toward the living room.

Her cheeks flushed as she shot me a wry grin.

"True." She cleared her throat and tightened her ponytail. "About that, I feel bad for taking your bed. I'm totally fine with staying on the couch or the futon. But even though I'd like to think I'm fairly in shape, I can't do Maddie's beanbag bed." She chuckled. "I'll get my stuff from your bedroom—"

"No, you'll stay in my bed. I'm not going to have you sleep on the couch or anywhere else. I want you to get some rest."

"And you think being in your bed is going to be relaxing enough for me to sleep?"

I couldn't decipher the expression on her face. I spied dread, maybe a little longing, and from the way she moved back and forth on her feet, nerves.

Maybe I wasn't the only one jumpy over a night together under the same roof.

While that thrilled me a little, I still couldn't push. Emily had to come to me.

I inched closer, tapping her chin with my knuckle.

"I won't be in it to tire you out, so you should sleep fine."

I cupped her neck, goose bumps pebbling under my thumb as I skimmed it back and forth.

Her lips parted as her eyes, dark and full of as much fear as pure want, fixed on mine.

"Too much?"

She laughed and dropped her head against my chest when I lifted a brow.

"Sorry," I murmured into her hair and kissed the top of her head. "I'm here for you, however you want me to be."

She lifted her head, her sweet smile killing me as she grabbed on to my T-shirt.

"And that means a lot to me. Thank you."

"You don't have to thank me, Em. I was hoping a little company and cake would help." I skimmed my hand down her back, noting the twitch of her muscles along the path of my touch.

"It does." Her voice dipped low, a throaty, almost inaudible whisper. She chewed on her bottom lip, searching my gaze. "Jesse—"

"Could we start reading now?"

I shut my eyes as Maddie shuffled in behind me.

"I think the soccer game made me tired, so if we don't start now, I may get too sleepy to read a whole book, and I don't want to waste Emily being here."

"Sure." Emily let go of my shirt and patted my chest, her eyes still pleading with mine, but I had no idea what she wanted or what she was about to say.

"Emily may be sleepy too, so just start with a couple of chapters tonight, okay?"

"Come on," Maddie said, dragging Emily by her hand toward the stairs and most likely not hearing anything I'd just said.

I'd give Emily anything. All she had to do was say the word.

I had to figure out how to not lose my mind until then.

I GAVE THEM A GOOD TWENTY MINUTES BEFORE I HEADED upstairs and lingered by Maddie's door, laughing to myself as the last line of whatever she read was cut off by her loud yawn.

"Okay, kiddo," I said, padding to where she lounged next to Emily on the bed and slipping the book out of her hands. "I think it's time to give up and go to sleep."

"But we only have one more chapter," she groaned, her eyelids already shrinking to tiny slits.

"But I think you'll enjoy it more if you can remember it," Emily said, patting her arm. "Maybe we can finish over breakfast."

Maddie rolled over, peering up at Emily with a deep frown before she hugged her waist. Emily bent to wrap an arm around her, sneaking me a smile over Maddie's head.

I wished I could find Emily's ex-fiancé and punch his lights out for calling her a cold bitch and making her think she wouldn't be a good mother. She'd be amazing, just like she was at everything else.

What would it be like if life was just like this? Emily here to stay, reading with Maddie, eating diner cake with us, and sleeping in my bed next to me.

I was getting entirely too ahead of myself, wishing for things so out of my reach, despite how clearly I could see them all.

Emily sat up gingerly as I pressed a kiss to Maddie's head. She mumbled a defeated goodnight before she buried her face into her pillow and pulled her comforter up over her head.

"Thank you," I mouthed to Emily as we stepped out of Maddie's room and I shut the door. "I thought she'd be too excited to sleep with you here."

"It was a longer book than I thought she'd get through. I know that just-one-more-chapter feeling." Emily glanced back at Maddie's door. "She's a kid after my own heart." Her grin shrank when she met my gaze. "Honestly, I can sleep anywhere—"

"But you won't. You had a long day too." I eased closer, fighting with all I had not to grab the back of her neck and cover that beautiful mouth with mine. I kissed her cheek instead, running my nose along her jaw before I realized it and stepped back.

"Let me know if you need anything. Sweet dreams, Em."

I shifted toward my spare room, keeping my gaze and my feet straight ahead to avoid any more temptation.

When it came to women, I'd never really planned for any kind of future. I'd tried, coming close with a few, but something always didn't work out. Sometimes it was me. Sometimes it was her. I'd never given it too much thought.

Maybe it was because my future was meant for a girl from my past.

22

EMILY

JESSE'S BED WAS AS COMFORTABLE AS I'D REMEMBERED, BUT I had a better chance of sleeping on a slab of concrete than anywhere in this room.

I couldn't escape him here. He was in every single nook and crevice. It smelled like him, it felt like him, and all the memories that I had from the last time I'd been in this bed barreled over me every time I tossed and turned, and my weary eyes wouldn't shut.

Did I really think I'd be able to relax at Jesse's house?

I was exhausted in every way and all I wanted to do was sleep, but sleep was not coming to me anytime soon. It had nothing to do with the softness of his sheets or how firm his pillows were. Every time I'd try to close my eyes and pretend I was somewhere else, the faint scent of his cologne would float up my nostrils and remind me of where I was and how Jesse was only a few feet away.

I'd get no rest tonight. I had a pesky thing called clarity to thank for that.

I'd had enough of the turmoil rolling around in my head. We couldn't stay in this limbo I'd forced us into. It wasn't fair to either of us—and especially not fair to keep Jesse on a hanging thread until I figured out what I wanted.

I was taking advantage of his guilt over what had happened to us all that time ago as an excuse for him to wait around until I was ready to make a move, whether I realized I was doing it or not. Now that I had, I was disgusted enough with myself to sit up in Jesse's bed and stop fooling myself that this sleeping arrangement would ever work.

That wasn't fair on so many levels. What he'd done back then, how he'd broken up with me, hadn't been intentional. In fact, it was a lot kinder than what I was doing to him right now. He'd made a clean break because he hadn't wanted to drag it out and hurt me even more.

Either I gave us a chance, or I cut him off. And cutting him off meant cutting Maddie off. The thought of doing that made my chest pull so hard, I rubbed at the sudden and sharp ache. At the beginning, I was drawn to her because of who her uncle was and the strong resemblance to her mother. But if I was honest with myself, I looked for her more than my other kids on the field every week for a lot of reasons.

I'd grown to love all the kids on my team and had even told Penny that I'd enjoyed coaching so much that I'd do it again next season, but coaching Maddie was different. I couldn't imagine living without her boisterous hugs or watching her eyes light up whenever she saw me.

I'd originally thought it was because I felt so badly for her since she'd lost her mom. And after Jesse's mother had pointed out that Maddie needed someone like me, I'd figured that was the reason why I connected with her so easily.

But maybe I needed her too.

Along with all of that, my mind kept drifting to the book

Maddie had found and how Tessa could have known it was my book. Was it a random discovery, or had she searched for it?

I'd played it off to Jesse, but it was a little spooky.

After I officially gave up trying to sleep, I grabbed my phone and opened Facebook. When I found her still-live page, my heart seized as I scrolled through photos of Maddie as a baby, Tessa holding her as she beamed at the camera with so much joy.

I rubbed my bleary eyes after finding nothing but more sadness and regret. The messages of condolence posted on her wall hit me hard enough to close the app, not wanting to see anything else.

I'd never find a real answer since Tessa wasn't here to explain.

But what if Tessa really was wishing us back together like Jesse's mother had said she'd done the summer after we'd broken up—and as she'd insinuated that she was doing now. It seemed like such a silly notion, yet not really.

He'd been in town for the reunion because of Maddie. I saw him again because Maddie joined my soccer team, and we'd connected as friends for her sake. I wasn't big on signs or miracles because you could always write those things off as coincidence if you looked hard enough.

Maybe this was the exception.

His room was pitch black, other than a few slivers of light filtering through the blinds from the streetlamp outside. I could make out his dresser and wondered if my picture was still in his drawer or if he had shared it with Maddie. I was tempted to check, but even if he'd given me his room tonight, that didn't give me the right to rummage through it.

Besides, Jesse wasn't the one keeping secrets or being

coy about what he wanted. He'd told me he loved me, and I'd taken that as a reason to run out of his house and away from him.

I was sick of running. Maybe I could sleep if I stopped.

I turned on my phone's flashlight and headed into the hallway, not wanting to turn on the hallway light and wake up Maddie, not that I could find it. A small night-light illuminated the top of the stairs, but it faded when I made my way to the spare bedroom door. I stilled, shining the light onto the doorknob for so long I saw spots in my vision.

Before I lost my nerve, I wrapped my hand around the silver knob and turned it slowly, cringing at the soft creak of the door.

The room was even darker than Jesse's bedroom, but I heard a grunt as he stirred on the futon. I felt around for a light switch and flicked it as I softly shut the door behind me.

I watched as it took him a minute to register the light in the room, his chiseled arms lifting out from under the comforter to rub his eyes. When I spotted his bare shoulder, I realized he was shirtless. I guessed that was how he slept both drunk and sober.

I set my phone down on the table by the bed and climbed in behind him, snaking my arm around his waist while I painted soft kisses between his shoulder blades.

"Am I dreaming?" Jesse's voice was groggy and full of sleep, but I could still note the hope in his tone.

"No, I don't think so."

He turned over, blinking at me with hooded eyes.

"Are you okay?"

"Fine," I croaked out, brushing the hair off his forehead. "You need a haircut, I think."

A sleepy smile stretched his lips.

"I'll put that on my list. Why are you here, Em?"

He opened his eyes, wide enough to scrutinize me as he waited for my answer.

"Why do you think I'm here?"

He caught my hand when I drifted it down his cheek.

"I'm not assuming anything, for both our sakes." He turned his head to kiss my palm. "I don't want to push you or get my hopes up. So, I'll ask you again. Why are you here?"

"I couldn't sleep."

"Is that it? You couldn't sleep?" he rasped, studying me without moving an inch. "Are you feeling okay?"

I shook my head, my throat too tight to form any words.

"What's wrong?" He dipped his head closer but still wouldn't come all the way. It was up to me to close that distance. My heart thudded in my ears as I inched toward him.

"I didn't want to be in your bed without you." I cradled his cheek and scraped my nails along the extra layer of scruff on his jaw.

"Did you walk all this way for a booty call? Do the kids still say that?" The corner of his mouth tipped up.

I shook my head and hooked my leg around his hip to draw him closer. He stared at me for a long moment before pulling me under him and rolling on top of me.

"I need you to be sure this time. *So* fucking sure." He settled in between my legs, his body quivering against me. "Because once we do this, that's it. I can't go back."

"I love you."

He stilled on top of me, eyes wide and jaw slack.

"Yeah?" I didn't know whether to laugh or cry at the tentative hope in his gaze.

"Yeah." I nodded and wrapped my legs around his waist.

"Say it again. I don't think I heard you."

I pushed against his shoulder to flip us over, curling my fingers into his hair as he narrowed his eyes at me, as if he was waiting for me to take it back.

"I..." I whispered, brushing my lips against his cheek and running them down his neck. "Love." I licked his Adam's apple as it rolled up and down his throat, his groan vibrating against my tongue. "You." I pressed my hands into the mattress on either side of him, trying to hold steady when the frame wobbled beneath us.

"Since that first day. And even when I tried to forget about it, I never stopped." I traced his lips as the rise and fall of his chest pressed against mine.

Jesse dove his hand into my hair, weaving his fingers around a fistful before he yanked my head back.

"Emily, please." His voice was low and husky. "Don't do this to me if you don't mean it."

"I mean it, Jess. I love you." My voice cracked, panic and dread soaking in with all the adrenaline it had taken to come in here. "But if you want me to go—"

Before I knew it, I was on my back again as a wicked grin spread across Jesse's mouth.

"I'm never letting you go again. Give me that mouth," he growled before he crashed his lips into mine. I whimpered into his mouth as he cupped my ass and pulled me closer, his erection hard and heavy between my legs as he pressed into me.

"I'm about to break this cheap fucking futon. Get in my bedroom and take your clothes off."

His hand slapped my ass with a loud smack as he popped off the bed.

I stood and let out a gasp when he lifted me by the waist and hoisted me over his shoulder.

"You don't need to do this every time."

"Yes, I do." He opened his bedroom door and shut it behind him before dropping me onto the mattress. "Especially since I'm still not convinced this isn't a dream yet. I had to move fast."

He climbed on top of me, roaming his gaze over my body as he grasped the waistband of my shorts.

"I said, take off your clothes."

Jesse yanked down my sleep shorts and threw them behind him. I was so wet, I felt a chill between my legs until he swirled his tongue over my clit, digging his fingers into my hips when I squirmed on the bed.

I sat up, grabbing the back of his head as I bucked my hips against his mouth. I let my head fall back, digging my heels into his shoulders as I rode his face. Jesse dove in harder, moaning as he sucked my clit into his mouth and slipped two fingers inside me.

This was already on another level than I'd ever had with Jesse. I had been too afraid of losing myself the last time I was here and about what would happen to us after. Now that I was all in, I could let myself go in ways I hadn't before because I trusted us both enough not to go anywhere.

I was finally able to choose him—and choose us.

I arched my back as my climax hit me, grabbing a pillow to grunt into as the spasms took over my body from the waist down.

"That was the hottest fucking thing. Those legs," Jesse panted, dragging his lips along the inside of my damp thigh.

I was a puddle on his sheets, but I managed to pull myself up.

"Lose the shorts, Evans." I held his eyes as I pulled his boxers down, letting them fall with a soft swoosh against his carpet.

"I need a— Shit, Em," Jesse groaned as I licked up his length and wrapped my lips around his cock. I swirled my tongue over the tip before I took him to the back of my throat. I'd done this to Jesse so many times as it was the only thing we could get away with most days, but he wasn't the only one who wanted to show off a little skill.

"Em, please stop," he begged as he grabbed my hair to pull me back. I dug my nails into his ass, shaking my head as I sucked him harder.

"Fuck, baby..." He gave me a slight push back until he fell out of my mouth with a wet pop.

"I wasn't done," I whispered.

"But I almost was," he said, sliding his hands under my arms to pick me up and move me back on the bed. "I don't want to know where you learned to do that, but holy shit."

"Good?" I teased, peeling off my shirt as Jesse searched through his nightstand drawer.

"Too fucking good." He rolled on the condom and climbed on top of me. "And from now on, you're only ever doing that to me."

"Is that so?" I spotted his cheeks lift in the dark.

"Oh, this is it. I told you," he said, teasing my entrance with the tip of his erection. "Never letting you go again."

He plunged inside with one thrust, easily sliding all the way in. We both exhaled a long breath but didn't move, as if both of us wanted to feel every inch of each other first to make sure this was really happening.

"You're not dreaming, Jess," I whispered. "I'm not going anywhere. You can move."

His chuckle rumbled against my chest as he glided in and out of me, tears pricking my eyes as he inched back and forth.

"Still heaven," he whispered, dropping his head into the

crook of my neck as he picked up the pace. Sweat beaded on my temple and dripped down my cheek as Jesse's mouth found mine in a sloppy kiss. I lifted my hips, meeting him thrust for thrust while trying to muffle the creak of the mattress.

"Are you with me? I can't hold back, Em."

Jesse shook in my arms, slipping a hand between us to thumb my soaked clit. I came hard, digging my nails into Jesse's back as he spilled into me.

He collapsed on top of me, chasing his breath as he held up a finger.

"Give me a minute."

"Take your time," I said, dropping my head against his shoulder as I tried to slow my racing pulse. My body was wrung out and spent in every way.

"For the record, this is not why I asked you to stay with me tonight. I didn't expect this." He propped an elbow onto the pillow. "I sure as hell hoped for it, but I didn't think it would happen again for a long time."

"I know that. I didn't expect it either."

"I'll be right back. Just stay here, okay?"

"Jesse, I told you." I scraped my nails up and down the trails of sweat on his back. "I'm not going anywhere."

"You did. And I believe you. Just need to get used to it." He kissed my forehead and stood.

I turned onto my side, my eyelids already growing heavy as all the uncertainty and trepidation that had kept me awake began to dissipate. I started to drift off when the bed dipped behind me.

"So, can you sleep now?" Jesse kissed the top of my head and pulled me back.

I turned to face him, smiling at his tousled hair and sleepy grin.

"I think so."

He wrapped his arms around me and brought me into his chest.

"I said I was staying. You don't have to keep me in a death grip," I joked as I cuddled into him.

"I know." He dipped his head to meet my gaze. "I've waited a long time to be back here, so like I said..." He smoothed my hair away from my eyes. "I'm getting used to it."

23

JESSE

"Ready for your last game?" I asked Maddie as she scarfed down a waffle.

"Yep," she murmured as she swallowed the last bite. "Emily said that we get trophies today. Even though we didn't win anything since there's no champion." She shrugged and gulped down the rest of her orange juice.

"You finished your first season of soccer. That's still something. And your first sports trophy." I scooped up my empty cup of coffee and set it in the sink. "Your uncle had to wait until senior year to get one of those."

"You have a trophy. Where is it?" She peered up at me with a scrunched nose.

"Grams wanted to hold on to it. And I think Grandpa liked having one kid sort of win a sports award, so I let them keep it."

She giggled at my wink.

"I bet Emily has a lot of trophies."

"*So* many." Maddie's jaw went slack as her eyes widened. "Medals too. Her room was nothing but a sea of silver and gold." I bent down to kiss the top of her head. "I wish I could get you up for school two hours earlier than you're supposed to be like you are before a game."

"Soccer is fun. Easier to get up."

"I'm sure." I nodded, letting go of a yawn.

"Why are you so tired lately?" Maddie stood and examined my face. "Are you feeling okay?

"Fine, kiddo. Just a long couple of weeks at work."

"Are you sure?" She pressed her hands against my cheeks and pulled my face closer to hers.

"I am fine." I kissed her forehead. "I just need some sleep, that's all." I motioned to the living room. "You can play a little *Super Mario* before you have to get ready."

Maddie scrutinized me for a minute before she scurried away from the table and settled in front of the TV. I really was exhausted, but not from work. I wasn't used to long nights of amazing sex with the girl of my dreams. It had been a long buildup, and every night, we'd say we'd give it a rest, and we'd still end up not getting to sleep until two a.m. or later.

It was a great problem to have, except when I trudged through the first few hours of my day like a zombie.

I headed upstairs while Maddie was engrossed to get an extra hour of sleep. The soccer field wasn't the place to show up tired, even if it was the last game. Emily had stayed over almost every night for the past two weeks, only stopping at her place to work and pick up more clothes to bring here.

I should have been more worried about Maddie becoming too used to Emily being here, but I didn't want to waste any more time now that I finally had her back. As her therapist had once suggested, I wouldn't bring anyone around my niece whom I didn't plan on keeping in my life, and there was no way I'd let Emily go again.

When the shower squeaked on as I made my way up the

stairs, an idea came to me. I descended back a couple of steps to make sure the *Super Mario* theme was still playing and raced toward the bathroom, locking the door behind me once I slipped inside.

"Jesse?" Emily peeked her head out from the shower curtain, wiping her face. "What's wrong?"

"I figured we'd save time and shower together." I peeled off my T-shirt and shorts and stepped inside.

"You think that's going to save time?" She crossed her arms over her full, wet breasts and tried to glare at me as her eyes traveled down my body.

"That's why we have to be efficient."

My shower was regular size but not big enough for two people. I pinned her against the wall, running my nose up and down her neck. Her lean curves were already slick with soap as I skimmed my hand down her thigh.

"These fucking legs," I growled as I grabbed her calf and hooked her leg over my hip.

"Your niece is awake." Her low whimper echoed off the steamy walls as I dragged openmouthed kisses along her collarbone.

"She's playing video games, and the door is locked." I cupped the nape of her neck. "I think you're wasting too much time talking when you could use that gorgeous mouth for better things."

Our mouths fused together, our moans drowned out by the running water as Emily grabbed my hand and brought it between her legs.

"That's a good girl. Always so wet." There was just enough room for me to drop to my knees and bury my head in her pussy. I sucked her clit right into my mouth, twisting my fingers inside her to hit all the right spots for her to come fast and hard on my tongue. We were ravenous for each other, even worse than our teenage days—or better, depending on how you looked at it.

Because there was no end. No curfew, no impending departure. I finally had my girl back for good. Life was sweet as hell, and I couldn't get enough of it.

I gazed up at Emily, grasping on to the towel bar with her hand over her eyes.

"Hey." I swatted her hip. "Eyes on me when I'm making you come."

She bent forward, digging her nails into my shoulders as her legs shook against my face.

"That's my girl," I rasped as I kissed up her leg.

"You're crazy," she whispered, taking my dick in her hand when I stood, holding my gaze as she pumped up and down. The corner of her mouth turned up when she stopped, squirting body wash into her palm, and glided her hand along my length.

"Eyes on me," she whispered as she sucked on my bottom lip, letting it go with a nibble as she pumped faster.

"That's it," I breathed out, clenching my jaw so I wouldn't scream as she worked me over from root to tip. She cupped my balls, clasping a hand over my mouth when I let go of a loud groan. I came in long spurts against the tile, pressing my hand against the wall as I buried my head in the crook of Emily's neck.

"I came in here on a whim," I panted out. "I don't have any condoms in here, but I don't know a good place to keep them."

Emily laughed as she grabbed the showerhead and rinsed both of us off.

"Anyone ever tell you that you're an animal?" She shook her head as she hung the showerhead back on the hook.

"I've never really been an animal until now." I kissed her

cheek. "Sorry if I want to enjoy it. Ready for your last game?"

"Well, last game of the season. I'm excited to give the kids their trophies."

I stepped out of the shower and held out a hand.

"Such a gentleman." She smiled and slid her wet palm against mine.

"I figured your legs might still be a little shaky." I grabbed the towel off the rack behind me and wrapped it around her, pulling her in for a quick kiss. "Do you really want to do this again? Deal with other people's kids for two days a week?"

"Why not? The kids are cute, most of the time. I get to enjoy soccer, get out on a weekend." She took the towel from my hands and turned away from me. "It's fun for me, believe it or not."

Her smile faded as something flashed across her face.

"What's wrong?" I asked as I plucked the other towel from the lower rack and wrapped it around my waist.

She shook her head. "Did it seem like anything was wrong before?" She batted her eyelashes as she cinched the towel around her.

"No, everything seemed very right then." I jutted my chin to the empty shower and leaned on the inside of the door. "But I thought I saw something on your face." I reached out to cup her cheek. "Maybe I'm just staring at you too much."

She slipped the clip out of her hair and let the brown waves billow around her shoulders.

"Do you remember when I said I broke my engagement because he didn't want kids?"

"I do. Why is that bothering you now?"

Her shoulders drooped as she adjusted the towel.

"I'd been thinking of having kids on my own. I finally went to a fertility clinic for some tests just to see what my options were." She fixed her gaze on the porcelain of the sink. "Long story short, they didn't tell me it was impossible, but they gave me the impression from what the tests showed that it wouldn't be easy for me. I don't know if that was always the case or if the potential complications were because I waited too long."

She brought her gaze back to mine and lifted a shoulder.

"I didn't tell anyone I was going or even thinking about it, so no one knows what the results were. Well, now, no one but you. I was a little disappointed, of course, but that's life, right?"

I nodded, smoothing my hand up her back and squeezing the nape of her neck.

"I wasn't sure if I wanted to coach or even how when Penny asked me, but I was a little excited for it. Once I started doing it, I found that I liked being with kids. Even if they aren't mine, like the ones on my team and Maddie. It's soothing in a way I can't explain. Plus, soccer without the intense competition takes me back to a simpler time, which is nice too." Her chest deflated on a long sigh. "It sounds silly, and I don't know why I'm telling you all of this."

"It doesn't sound silly at all. Do I have to bring up how Tessa and I used to fight over you? Kids love you. And most adults too."

"Oh yeah, everyone loves me." Her shoulders jerked with a chuckle. "I think you're just biased." She glowered at me before she opened the medicine cabinet.

"Because *I* love you? Definitely." I came up behind her, wrapping my arms around her waist and holding her gaze in the mirror. "But people of all ages adore you. And maybe it's too soon to bring something like that up, but I've recently learned that the almost impossible sometimes happens. If that's a dream you still have, you, or we, can cross that bridge when you're ready to get to it."

"I didn't know you were so philosophical in your old age," Her eyes were glossy as her mouth curved.

"That's mostly because the dream I've had for a couple of decades recently came true." I kissed her shoulder. "Makes an *older* guy very optimistic."

I cupped her chin when I noticed it quiver in the mirror.

"Why are you both in the bathroom?"

Emily's head whipped to mine at the sound of Maddie's voice coming through the door.

"I told you," she mouthed to me.

I held up a hand.

"I had to fix the showerhead for Emily. It was leaking again."

"The showerhead leaks? I thought it just dripped from using it." I cringed when she jiggled the doorknob.

"That too." I cupped my forehead as a familiar headache came on. My niece was so much like her mother, catching me at all the wrong times and asking questions too smart for me to be able to explain with my pants down—or off, as they were in this case.

"We'll be right out, Mad. Use the bathroom downstairs if you need it."

"Okay." Emily and I shared a silent laugh at her slow reply. I imagined her face twisted up in confusion on the other side of the door.

"It's like déjà vu, right?"

"It is." I let my head fall against the door with a soft thump. "The only difference is that I'm not as worried she's going to run to tell my parents about my locked door."

Emily laughed, inching closer to me. She drifted her

hand down my damp chest and pressed a slow, sensual kiss to my lips.

"Now, get out so I can get ready."

"Anything you say, Coach," I said, skating my hand up her thigh to squeeze her bare ass.

I gave her one last glance before I left the bathroom, rushing to my bedroom to hide the towel tent rising below my waist from that last kiss.

Maybe it was too soon to think of a future with Emily, but as far as I was concerned, too soon didn't count when it came to something I'd wanted for most of my life.

24

EMILY

"Did you meet any celebrities?" Mikayla asked me with a mouthful of pizza.

After the game ended and the trophies had been distributed to all the players, I'd invited the team and their parents for a little end-of-season party at the pizzeria near the field. Mr. and Mrs. Evans and a few other grandparents had joined us as well, and we took over almost half of the space. The kids seemed too tired and full to cause much mayhem inside, and I was hopeful it would stay that way until we left.

"Any celebrities?" I tried to clarify.

"When you were a soccer star, did you meet anyone? Like how celebrities go to football and basketball games?"

Jesse smiled and squeezed my leg under the table.

"I only played in college. They had a press box at some schools, but no celebrity suites like you're probably thinking. Some could have been in the stands, but I don't remember seeing any."

The sad truth was my only real celebrity encounter had been when Raina Nello had liked Sharon's post about me on social media. I'd been working with best-selling authors for so long, I really didn't see them as celebrities, even though a fan or two would always find Mary when we were out to gush over her latest book.

"Oh." Her black brows pulled together as her expression deflated.

"Sorry to disappoint you, and I wasn't a superstar."

"Yes, she was." Jesse stretched his arm across the back of my chair. "She's modest," he told Mikayla.

Maddie was on my other side, chatting with most of the kids, but something was off with her today. She'd looked like she had fun at the game, but even then, it was muted, as if something had been weighing on her since this morning.

I worried that finding her uncle and me in the bathroom or hearing us, thank God not seeing us, might have confused her a little bit. Even though we were behind a locked door, Maddie was old enough to pick up on things, and we needed to be more careful.

Since Jesse and I had made it official, we often became a little too lost in each other to worry about the world around us. This morning really had been reminiscent of when Tessa used to run to Jesse's parents when she'd find his door locked and ask why. We'd gotten into trouble a few times, and while there were no parents to answer to anymore, we needed to be more mindful while Maddie was awake and aware.

I glanced down the table at the sea of silver, the hardware courtesy of Penny's league. The trophies were for making it through the season and had nothing to do with who kicked the most goals or ran the farthest during every game.

While one could argue that too many trophies were given out for simply showing up these days, I loved watching their eyes light up when their names were called. Some of these kids had never played soccer before, and so many of them had played their hearts out.

That was the great thing about playing in a youth recreation league. It was a successful season as long as the kids had fun and managed to make it through in one piece.

I gave Jesse a look when his hand wandered up my thigh. He lifted a shoulder, a sexy smirk curling his lips. I hadn't known what I'd been in for when I'd let Penny convince me to become a coach, but I'd never expected such a life-altering few months.

Coaches didn't receive trophies, but having Jesse and Maddie in my life was the best kind of prize.

"Did you get any parting casseroles?" I whispered to Jesse.

All the single moms who had taken such a big interest in Jesse congregated at the far end of the table, watching us until they'd accidentally make eye contact and look away.

"No." He chuckled and shook his head. "Janie keeps pushing for a playdate, though."

"For Aubrey or her?" I waggled my eyebrows.

"I'm guessing Aubrey since I'm *very* taken." He leaned in and kissed my cheek. My neck heated when a few swoony sighs drifted across the table.

"I think Maddie's uncle makes a much better boyfriend than the ref, if you want my opinion," Mikayla said before slurping the rest of her soda out of the plastic cup.

"Thanks, Mikayla. I completely agree."

Jesse met her gaze with a big smile, and I swore I spotted a little blush staining her cheeks. I couldn't blame her.

"If your uncle is Coach Emily's boyfriend, does that make her your aunt?" Candie asked Maddie from across the table as she moved her finger back and forth between Maddie and me.

"I...I don't know," Maddie stammered and turned toward me, a big crease denting her forehead.

"Not yet," Jesse answered before I could think of what to say.

Candie had forgotten the question, but Maddie's brow still pinched in confusion.

We'd been going so fast, we hadn't taken the time to really understand what Maddie thought about a new person in her uncle's life, even if it was someone she already knew. I also had to talk to Jesse about his "not yet." I was all in and not going anywhere, but we'd only been back together, in the literal sense, for a couple of weeks. I loved them both fiercely, but she had to get used to me as her uncle's close *friend* before she entertained the notion of having a new relative.

It was hard to consider what Jesse and I had as new since we had so much history, but to this poor kid, too much in her life over the past year had been new, both bad and good. The three of us, and then the two of us, had a lot to discuss tonight after we went home.

Or when *they* went home, and I accompanied them to their house.

I guessed I was jumping ahead too.

"What a great season," Mr. Evans said as he scooped me into a hug on their way out. "With a great coach."

"Yes. Before you argue with us, you were a great coach." Mrs. Evans swept her gaze along the tables as the kids and parents started to pack up to leave. "They were happy to have you," she said, pulling me in for a hug. "And I'm so happy to have you back."

"Please don't make me more emotional," I sniffled as I gently pushed her back.

"Your mother will be happy to hear you won the last game," Mrs. Evans said, squeezing my shoulder.

Mom was recovering from surgery in a rehab facility, and I tried to visit her as much as I could. Jesse's parents went twice per week, bringing my mother a tin of the butter cookies she loved every time.

"Thank you for visiting her. I know she appreciates the company."

"We always loved her company too," Mrs. Evans said with a chuckle. "She cracks us up."

I nodded, knowing that Jesse and I were most likely what they all joked about.

Maddie hugged her grandparents goodbye, and while they didn't appear to notice anything wrong, something about the vacant look in Maddie's eyes concerned me.

"Thank you for coaching this season." Janie Cooper snuck up on me as I fixated on Maddie.

"And the pizza party," Aubrey chirped and rushed over to me, wrapping her arms around my waist.

After all I'd shared with Jesse today, and watching all the excited faces at the table as they admired their trophies, I'd had to pull myself back from getting choked up more than once. If these were the only kids I was meant to have, I still felt incredibly lucky, even if I would only know them for a little while. I still remembered my youth league coach, and if these kids didn't come back for another season, I hoped they'd remember me a little too.

"You are very welcome, Aubrey." I bent to hug her back. "I hope I see you next season."

"There's a division league out east. We may check that

out first," Janie said, her nose turned up as she shot me what seemed like a dirty look.

I nodded as Aubrey still squeezed her arms around me.

"I think I know that league. Definitely a great place to play."

"As you saw Aubrey's talent, I think it's good if she's pushed a bit."

I held in a cringe. My mother had pushed too, but for different reasons. She hadn't been as callous about it, but I recalled with too much clarity that first taste of pressure. But I'd made friends and loved the game, and I wished the same for Aubrey.

"I don't think I have your number," Janie said, strolling up to Jesse and pulling out her phone. "For when the girls want to get together."

I fought an eye roll as her voice dropped to a much more inviting and friendly octave.

"You can text Em. I know you have her number, and she's with us most of the time. Aubrey is welcome over at our house anytime. You don't mind if she reaches out to you, right, babe?"

"I don't at all," I said, fighting the smile that wanted to break out across my face. "Text me, and we can set something up."

"Right. We should be going." Janie grabbed Aubrey's elbow and pulled her away from me. "Thanks again, Coach Emily."

Aubrey waved as her mother dragged her out of the pizzeria.

"That should take care of it, right?" Jesse snickered as Janie and Aubrey made their way out.

"I guess so, *babe*. Unless you get slipped any casseroles on the way out."

"Like I said, none so far. I guess after watching me drool over the coach every week, they got the hint." He pecked my lips. "Shame. One of them made a *killer* baked ziti."

I jabbed his arm. "*I* make a damn good baked ziti, but if you want to catch up with that one—" I pointed to the door "—she may still be in the parking lot."

Maddie chatted with a couple of the girls lingering by the table as we packed everything up. When she came over to us, I still spied something in her face.

"Ready to go, kiddo?" Jesse looped an arm around Maddie's shoulders. "Congratulations on your first completed soccer season."

She peered up at him with a tiny smile. "Can I play again next season?"

"If you want, absolutely." He tucked a loose hair falling out of her ponytail behind her ear.

"And Emily could be my coach?"

"I am sure Penny would let me keep you on my team," I said, hooking my purse strap over my shoulder. "And we can practice together whenever you'd like. I made your uncle practice with me all the time."

"But he can't play soccer."

"Thanks," he said, tugging on her ponytail. "Let's go home." Jesse let out a yawn. "All that time watching you run back and forth has me ready for a nap."

He took her hand and led her out the door into the parking lot. I noticed a frown pulling at her lips as she followed Jesse, her steps slow as she leaned into him.

The drive home was more of the same. Jesse and I would make a joke and try to get a laugh out of her, but all we'd managed to get was a weak smile.

"Feel like some ice cream, or are you still full on pizza?"

"I can have ice cream now?" Her brows shot up at Jesse's question. "I don't have to wait until tonight?"

Jesse's gaze caught mine for a minute as he leaned into the back seat.

"It's a special day." He stepped out of the car and opened Maddie's door. She seemed to perk up a little bit at the mention of ice cream, so maybe whatever was bothering her wasn't that bad. I followed them into the house, watching as Maddie stayed close to Jesse, her eyes lingering on him while he unlocked the front door as if she was holding back something she wanted to say.

"Have a seat, ladies," Jesse said, motioning to the kitchen table as we dropped all the soccer gear by the door. I sat next to Maddie at the table, my stomach knotting as she wrung her hands.

"Are you about to tell me something bad?"

Jesse froze as he scooped a mound of chocolate ice cream into a bowl.

"No. Why would you think that?"

Jesse left the bowl on the counter and rushed over to his niece.

"When Mom told me she was sick, I had ice cream in the afternoon too." Her eyes went to Jesse before she dropped her gaze to the table.

"Hey, look at me." He crouched in front of her. "I'm not going to tell you anything bad. I just thought it would be good to talk. Emily is here a lot now, and I know that while you love her, you must have some questions."

She shook her head. "No, I love having Emily here. I didn't think that made her my aunt, but I guess that makes sense."

"I'm your uncle Jesse's girlfriend and your friend." I scooted my chair closer to her.

"Grams said you were Uncle Jesse's girlfriend when you were in school, and you probably would be again soon."

"Of course she did," Jesse sighed, cutting a look to me.

"I wouldn't mind if you were my aunt." She shrugged at me with a tiny smile playing on her lips. "I love having you here. Reading at night is more fun with you. Uncle Jesse tries, but it's not the same."

"I'm sure it's not, and I understand why. Your mother and I used to argue about who got to spend more time with Emily, so I get it." He grinned at me and squeezed Maddie's shoulder. "Are you sure you don't have any questions? You can ask us anything."

"No. Everything is better when Emily is here. I always wondered what having two parents would be like."

Jesse winced at me, and I nodded back. As a child of a single mother with no recollection of my own father, I was sure I felt Maddie's observation deeper than Jesse did. While that was heartbreaking to hear, to Maddie, it seemed to be just a fact. I didn't believe getting used to our new dynamic was the root of her sullen mood today.

"So why the long face?" Jesse asked. "You looked like something was bothering you today."

"I guess I'm sad soccer is over," she mumbled into her hand.

I wasn't convinced, but I didn't want to press.

"It's never really over. Maybe the season is, but remember, you and I can play whenever you'd like."

She nodded and pushed away from the table.

"I'm kind of full. Can I play my game now and have ice cream later?"

"Sure." Jesse studied her face. "Come down if you change your mind."

We both watched her trudge up the stairs, not looking back at either of us.

"I don't think that's about soccer," he said, his gaze still lingering on her departure. "I try not to think about it, but she's still just a little girl who lost her mother."

"I don't think it's about soccer, but it could be. I'm sure missing her mother is harder on some days. As long as she knows she can talk to us, we just have to wait until she's ready."

"Every time I catch her like that, I bring in something else that's purple. That's how she has that beanbag thing."

I laughed and wrapped my arms around his waist.

"It's not the worst coping mechanism. And she knows she can talk to you. I think she will when she's ready." I kissed his cheek. "Now that we're not going to have ice cream, I'll head upstairs and change. Hopefully I have enough clothes here before I do laundry at my apartment tomorrow."

Jesse grabbed my hand when I shifted to leave.

"You know my closet is half empty. Why don't you just keep your clothes here?"

I arched a brow. "Like, all of them?"

"Why not?" He shrugged. "And the living room needs something, right?" He ambled across the carpet, sweeping his gaze over the walls. "The bookcases in your hallway would be good right here, don't you think?"

"Really?" I crossed my arms and leaned against the wall.

"And the spare room upstairs, you could use that as an office. I work out of the basement."

I let my eyes sink shut for a moment before I padded across the carpet over to Jesse.

"I know I've been here more than at my own place lately, but it's too soon to be here permanently." I held up my hand.

"Before you panic, I love you. I love Maddie. And I love being here with both of you. But it's not the time to talk about aunts or closet space or where bookcases will go yet. I love the enthusiasm." I clutched the back of his head. "But we need to dial it down a notch. Yes, we were together twenty years ago, but not really again until a couple of weeks ago."

"I count when you kissed me the night you took me home as being back together. Or the start of it."

I groaned at his raised brow.

"If you want to start the clock then, fine. But that's only weeks ago. Still too soon."

He gave me a reluctant nod.

"I guess since we wasted all that time apart, I didn't want to waste anymore."

"We aren't wasting anything. I'm here. You're here. We'll both be naked again in a few hours. Most likely."

"Most definitely." He cupped my ass and yanked me flush to his body.

"But we need to get to sleep earlier. I promised my mother I'd spend the morning with her, and I have a manuscript to work on in the afternoon. I need to be alert enough to read the words."

"So, you're not going home tonight?"

"No. I'm going home tomorrow. But I'll come back. How's that?"

He lifted a shoulder, running his bottom lip across my cheek. "As long as you always come back, I'll take it."

Maddie came back down for ice cream, but she didn't say much to either of us before she went to bed. She'd eyed Jesse as he left her room as if she wanted to tell him something, but she still insisted she was fine when he asked what was wrong.

We'd managed to fall asleep earlier but woke up to Maddie's loud sobs. We both shot out of bed, Jesse jogging ahead of me into her room.

"Maddie? What's wrong?" Jesse asked as he flicked on the light and raced to her bed.

"I had a bad dream," she said through sniffles. I lingered by the door, not wanting to intrude. Yes, I'd gotten much closer to her since becoming her coach, but Jesse was still her parent.

"What was the dream? Don't cry, baby. You can tell me."

"You were sick. Just like Mom. You're always tired like she was."

He flinched back. "I'm not always tired."

"Yes, you are. You yawn all day, just like Mom did at first. I've never seen you that tired. And she was never tired either, until one day, that's all she was." She dropped her head into her hands, hiccupping as her shoulders shook.

"Maddie, no. Come here." He drew her into his arms, his eyes wet as if he was about to sob himself. "I'm not sick, sweetheart. I was just staying up too late every night, and it made me sleepy. I'm fine." He eased her back, swiping his thumbs along her cheeks. "I know it must've been scary to see your mom get sick. It was scary for me too. But when you're afraid of something, you have to tell me."

She nodded, the tears dripping down her face slowing as she lay back down.

"Want me to stay here until you go back to sleep?"

She whispered a "Yes." Jesse shot me a sad smile as he climbed in next to her.

"I'm sorry you had a bad dream." I crept over to her side of the bed and kissed her forehead. After a soccer season of watching Maddie being a regular kid, it was easy to almost forget how much she'd gone through in her eight years.

"Can you stay too?" she asked, her red and swollen eyes fixed on mine.

"I don't think I can fit, but I'll tell you what." I pulled the beanbag next to the bed. "I'll hang out here. Hopefully one of you can scoop me out if I get stuck."

Jesse smiled when I pulled a giggle out of her.

"You can make it out, Legs. I believe in you," Jesse teased, his croaky whisper breaking my heart as much as his niece's tears.

I sank into the surprisingly comfortable softness and rested my head on the bump at the edge I guessed was supposed to be the pillow.

I found Jesse's gaze as he reached over Maddie, flexing his fingers when he stretched out his hand.

I took it, lacing our fingers together as he nodded at me and rested his chin on top of Maddie's head.

It was still too soon to be here for good, but tomorrow, it would be next to impossible to leave either of them.

25

___

EMILY

"Did we ever really do this back then?" Jesse asked me as we strode to the restaurant entrance.

"Do what? Have dinner together? Yes, lots of times," I said. "I couldn't have the pizza burger I always ordered with you at the diner for at least five years, because the thought of it made me pissed at you all over again."

"I mean a date. Diner dates don't count, even if my niece disagrees." He pulled the glass door open and stepped to the side for me to walk through. "We never did any...I don't know...adult couple stuff."

"Um, I remember plenty of adult couple stuff. Especially that last month," I whispered as we stepped into the restaurant.

Jesse had made reservations at a steakhouse and arranged a sleepover for Maddie with Jesse's parents. We'd been officially together for two months, celebrating the holidays with our families like we used to, although watching my mother so happy to see Jesse would always be an adjustment. Despite my attempt to slow things down and create boundaries, I'd gone back on almost everything I'd said.

My furniture wasn't in Jesse's house, but everything else of mine had piled up as I spent more nights there than in my own apartment. Rent was becoming a needless expense for a place just to pick up my mail.

"The best I was able to do was that clam bar in Seaford when I worked with Caden that summer. I always felt like I never took you out on a real date. And after all this time back together, I should have done this sooner."

I stepped in front of him and smoothed my hand down the front of his jacket.

"I love that you planned a night like this for us, but I'm very happy eating cheeseburgers with my two favorite people. And back then, you know I never cared about that."

"But I did. I always pictured some asshole jock buying you lobsters in Maine," he muttered as we approached the hostess.

"I was too busy in Maine to eat any lobster. And again, I'm very happy to eat anywhere as long as I'm with you. But if you want to date me, I won't fight you."

"Thank you." He cracked a grin and gave his name to the hostess.

"Come to think of it," he said, glancing back at me as we made our way to the table, "I don't remember us going to an actual restaurant for dinner, other than the night I followed you on your date."

I groaned and shook my head as he held out my chair.

"I guess I technically went on two dates that night."

I fought a laugh when Jesse's eyes narrowed in a glare.

"I wasn't sharing you then, and I'm sure as hell not sharing you now," he whispered, his breath fanning hot on my neck, sending goose bumps across my shoulder.

"You know, I have to say, I don't hate your alpha side."

"Which part?" He squeezed my knee after he settled

next to me. "When I get jealous or when I tell you to crawl to me in bed so I can—"

"Stop it," I gritted out, pushing his hand away and raising my menu to block his face.

"I think it's both. Look at those cheeks. I bet I know where else you're flush—"

"I said, stop." I kicked his foot under the table.

"You are so damn sexy when you're flustered." He pulled the menu down and leaned in to brush my lips. "Dating you is fun."

"Emily? I thought that was you."

I turned to find Sharon standing next to our table, a squeamish look on her face as she glanced between us.

"Hey, Sharon. You remember Jesse."

"Yes, hi." She nodded at Jesse. "I didn't realize you were back together."

"It happened after the article. How are you?"

It had been just as awkward on the video call with her. For someone so well-versed in public speaking, small talk was not her forte. But that could have been due to lack of interest. At the end of our discussion, I'd asked if she wanted to get lunch sometime or schedule a follow-up call if she needed more info, but she'd ended the call quickly and I'd never heard from her again until she'd tagged me in the post.

Once she'd gotten the information she'd needed from me to pump our connection, she'd had no interest in *connecting* with me since I'd served my purpose. I'd already more than suspected her sweet new persona was a mask, so I was more amused than insulted.

"I was going to reach out to you in the morning. Someone wanted to contact you after seeing the article, and

I wanted your permission first before I passed along your information."

I hadn't had many inquiries for new clients, just a few offers to be a sports influencer on social media because of the college shots of me Sharon had included with the post. I'd been relieved that was all it had been since the article's circulation.

"Who wanted my information?"

"Raina Nello."

"Are you serious?" I blurted out, my eyes bugging out of my head before I could help it.

"Who's Raina Nello?" Jesse asked.

"She played on the last US women's soccer team to win consecutive World Cups. My grandfather made me a fan because she was an Italian American soccer player." I turned back to Sharon. "I saw that she liked the post, but I don't understand why she'd want to contact me."

"Rumor has it she's writing a memoir. Maybe she's looking for an editor?" Sharon grinned, her eyes a little feral. "I'd be happy to help promote if I'm right. She's a huge advocate for women in sports and female entrepreneurship. I could almost see a whole exclusive series. I'd love to support you."

Support *me. Right*, I wanted to say. An exclusive post about Raina Nello's memoir would draw in all the big health and fitness sponsors that Sharon loved to feature. I laughed, thinking of our video call and how she kept trying to change the subject of how I'd played soccer on a full scholarship in college while earning my communications degree to shift focus to the famous-to-her authors I worked with instead.

I was surprised she'd included the soccer photos, but I had no doubt she'd push the fact that it was *her* article about me responsible for connecting us and celebrate herself as she pretended to celebrate me.

"I'm so glad that I could make this happen for you."

"Well," Jesse began, stretching his arm along the back of my chair. "I read the post. And it was a great piece about Emily, but that's because Emily herself is pretty amazing. She's had a successful career and was an incredible athlete, whether or not she went pro. It's great that you were able to make the connection, but my girl gave you the tools to do it. So I'm glad she was able to do this for *you*."

At thirty-nine years old, hearing Jesse call me his girl shouldn't have given me the same rush as when I was eighteen. I didn't need him to put Sharon in her place for me, and I was very grateful, no matter what her intentions were, that she'd given me a chance to possibly work with a childhood hero of mine.

But watching Jesse get insulted on my behalf was a huge turn-on.

"Yes, it's all wonderful," I told Sharon as she glared at Jesse. "Tell Raina I'd be happy to connect."

"Great." She straightened, pushing a tight smile across her mouth. "I will let her know tonight and get back to you if anyone else reaches out. Have a great dinner."

"Thanks," Jesse called after her, looping an arm across my shoulder.

"That was kinda hot." I ran the tip of my knee-high boot up and down over Jesse's shin. "Unnecessary, but hot."

I put down my menu and slid my hand to the back of Jesse's neck and pressed my lips against his.

"Still my biggest fan?" I teased.

He smiled into the kiss and cupped my jaw.

"Always."

By the time we got back to Jesse's house after dinner, I

already had an email from Raina. I waited until he'd gone upstairs to change before opening it, not wanting to squeal like a fangirl, even in front of him.

Hi Emily,

I'm sorry for the random message, but I think finding Sharon's post about you was a sign. I'm writing a memoir and have no idea where to start or how to write, to be honest. Unlike you, my strengths in school were only in soccer and not words.

I don't know if you'd be interested, but I'd love to work with you to bring my story to life. Not only do you come highly recommended as an editor (I contacted a few of your clients before reaching out to Sharon), but you obviously know soccer too. I've seen some videos of you playing in college, and I was really impressed. From what I saw, you absolutely could have made it a career, but I completely get why you didn't.

There are a few events I'm supposed to attend in the next couple of months that I want to mention in the book, and I was curious if you'd be interested in coming to California for the next few months to both attend the events and work with me on the book. It could be two months or as many as six. I won't be able to give you an answer until we get started.

Please email me or call me at the number below if you're interested. Either way, I loved reading about your journey and success.

"What's wrong?"

I jumped when I found Jesse next to me on the couch, his body rigid with panic as he searched my face.

"Shit, you scared me."

"Well, you scared me too. You look like you just saw a ghost." He squeezed my knee. "What's going on?"

"Sharon must have given Raina my information as soon as she saw us tonight. I already have an email from her." I kept my gaze on the carpet as Jesse squinted at me in my periphery.

"Okay, so I thought that would be a good thing." He scooted over and glanced at my phone screen. "What did she say?"

"Sharon was right. She's writing a memoir, and she wants me to help her write it, not just edit it."

"Is that something you've done before? Is that why you look so nervous?"

"Yes. I haven't in a while, but I've ghostwritten in the past." I rubbed at my temple. "She thinks I know enough about soccer that I can help her craft the story, and although I prefer editing, actually helping to write her story would be an amazing privilege."

"That's great. You're going to do it, right?"

"I want to. Grandpa would flip if he were still alive. He thought for sure I'd be on a World Cup team someday."

"You could have been if you'd wanted to." He rested his head on my shoulder and kissed my cheek. "What's stopping you?"

"I'd have to go over the details with her, but she'd want me to come to California for a few months so I could attend a few events with her that she wants included in the book. And work with her during the day to write it."

Jesse's grin faded in almost slow motion. Maybe it wasn't the same, but that identical dread from twenty years ago spread in the pit of my stomach.

I loved being here with Jesse and Maddie, and although we hadn't discussed it again, I was seriously considering giving up the apartment I hardly used and taking Jesse up on his offer to move in. This was a curve ball I'd never expected, but as much as I wanted to stay, I couldn't ignore it.

"Can you do that with the clients you already have?"

"I don't know. Maybe. I'd have to see what my downtime would be like. I have a lighter schedule over the next two months and could probably handle a big project like this. Beyond that, I'd have to see if I'd have the time to work on what I have scheduled." I dragged a hand through my hair and dropped my chin to my chest. "Please don't look at me like that."

"Like what? I'm sorry, I'm just a little surprised. I didn't think she'd want you to travel to her. You have clients all over the country, and they don't make you come to them, right?"

"No. I'll probably decline, but—"

"But you want to do it?"

"I at least want to reply and look into it."

Jesse gave me a slow nod when I met his gaze. How could I leave him again? And Maddie. Mom was doing well, already up and walking with a cane. She had daily therapy and liked the rehab facility she was recovering in, but across the country was a lot of miles away from the people I loved.

"I'm just going to tell her no. I'll say thank you for contacting me, but I can't make this work."

I pushed off the couch, grabbing my phone to head upstairs.

"Wait." Jesse caught me by the crook of my elbow. "If I wasn't in the picture, would you say no just like that?"

"I don't know. It's a big ask, and there's my mother to think about. It's a lot, like I said. A big opportunity—"

"A huge opportunity. Don't make me that guy, Em."

"What guy?" I finally turned around, afraid to look Jesse in the eye and darting my eyes everywhere but at him.

"The one who holds you back. The one I never wanted to be. Do I want you to go when it feels like I just got you back? No. I don't."

He brought me into his arms, his hand in my hair as he pulled me to him.

"But do I want you to just say no and regret it someday? Absolutely not."

"How do you know I'd regret it?"

His chest jerked with a chuckle.

"When Sharon said her name, your face lit up like the most beautiful Christmas tree." He ran his knuckle across my jaw. "Plus, your grandfather liked her too. He always did right by me, so I don't want you to let him down."

"Are you kidding? He'd love this." I rubbed my eyes, my nose burning at how he really would have loved it and would have wanted an introduction. "I'll deal with this tomorrow. Now that Maddie is at your parents' house for the night, let's head to bed early." I slipped out of his arms, not looking back as I walked upstairs.

The epic night of loud sex we'd had planned seemed doubtful, so I grabbed one of Jesse's T-shirts and headed to the bathroom. I took extra time getting ready for bed, Jesse's scent along the cotton collar making me feel even worse.

I burrowed onto my side after I climbed into Jesse's bed, not hopeful for any kind of sleep. We weren't the kids we used to be, but I couldn't help thinking back to the night he'd broken up with me. He'd seemed fine the day before, and then, all of a sudden, he'd decided having me so far away was too much for him.

Teenagers were known for not thinking clearly and living by impulse, but while Jesse had matured since then, he had other things on his plate now to alter his judgment. We were insanely happy, but it still felt like we were maintaining a delicate balance sometimes. He was in therapy, his niece still had the occasional nightmare, and some days, I knew he was trying his best to appear like he was holding it together when he was just exhausted.

How could I leave him? Or her? What if Jesse didn't want me to hurt Maddie, so he cut me off? Two hours ago, I never would have believed it was possible, and now I was terrified of it.

"Hey," Jesse whispered as the bed dipped behind me. "I've never heard you breathe so hard while you were lying this still."

"I guess my body is still, but my head is racing." I tried to joke, the dull tone in my voice making it fall flat.

"If I had to guess—" he looped his arm around my waist and rolled me onto my back "—you're probably thinking I'm going to freak out again and run." He raised a brow when I didn't answer.

"It may have crossed my mind a little." I turned my head, sinking my cheek into the pillow when a lump scratched at the back of my throat. Losing Jesse now would be so much worse than when I'd lost him back then. I both couldn't fathom it and couldn't stop thinking about it.

He draped his hand over my throat, pressing his finger into my cheek to turn my gaze to his. Inching down and holding my eyes, he pressed his lips to mine, slow and sensual, his tongue swirling with mine in lazy strokes as if he was trying to savor the taste of us.

"You're the love of my life. I knew that back when I was fourteen, even if it scared the shit out of me."

"I knew it too." My voice cracked, already laced with tears.

"So." He rolled on top of me, sliding his arm under my

waist, and pulled me closer. "My only question is, are you going to come back to me?"

"Of course."

I blinked away tears at his slow grin.

"Then that's all I need."

26

JESSE

Maddie rested her head on Emily's shoulder, her sad face matching the ache in my chest as I came inside for Emily's last suitcase.

From the beginning, the hardest thing I'd ever found about being a parent was hiding my emotions. Not only hiding the grief over my sister, but about life in general. I was blessed with a smart and all-too-perceptive kid who could tell simply by the way I was standing if something was bothering me.

Emily would be back. This wasn't college, where she'd be gone for long months at a time for four years. And what we had now was so much more solid than it was back then. We had a real life together, not just a hot and heavy love. When she was here with us, everything fit and fell into place. Something told me not to get used to it, but I figured that was just my childhood insecurities that I'd never be good enough for Emily creeping in.

I'd always thought that because I'd never been able to believe how lucky I was to have her for myself. While I

292

trusted her to come back, that scared kid in me was still there, expecting the worst and wondering if he'd ever be good enough for someone as amazing as she was.

"I think it's a couple of hours away, but I wouldn't have the time to go there anyway. I'm going to be super busy, at least for the first few weeks."

"When do you come back again?"

Her question made both Emily and me flinch.

"I'm not sure. I may be able to come home a weekend or two in between, but I'll be there for at least a couple of months."

"Don't be so sad, kiddo." Caden sat on the other side of Maddie on the couch, his eyes full of maddening sympathy as they flicked to mine. "There's FaceTime and text, and before you know it, Emily will be back."

"That's right," Sabrina said, holding a large bowl of popcorn. "I know everyone is sad, but I'm sure it's going to fly by."

"Exactly. And while Emily's away, Sabrina and I will make sure to distract you both."

"And I will be the best subletting tenant and keep Emily's apartment nice and pristine for when she gets back."

The owner of the private house Sabrina had been renting her apartment from had sold it, giving her only a few weeks to find a place to live. She'd said she was grateful that Emily's departure had given her a place to stay *indefinitely*, and the word had echoed around in my troubled mind ever since.

"If you keep it nice and pristine, I probably won't recognize it when I come back." Emily stood from the couch and cradled Maddie's cheek. "But your uncle Jesse and I need to go if I'm going to make my flight. I need one more huge hug."

Maddie almost leaped into Emily's arms, and I had to look away, pretending I was checking for my keys. She'd taken to Emily so quickly, and with all the fears that played in the back of my mind, the thought of my niece losing someone else she loved made my stomach roll.

But she wasn't losing Emily, and neither was I. She'd go and do this amazing thing and be home before we knew it, although I didn't believe Caden or Sabrina when they suggested that time would just fly by. Sleeping without Emily would make every night seem endless.

Caden gave Emily a quick hug before Sabrina whispered something in Emily's ear. She nodded, meeting my gaze with a sad smile.

We were silent as we climbed into my truck and headed onto the highway. We had plenty of time to get to the airport, and I almost welcomed the traffic. Even if we didn't know what to say to each other, she was here and with me. It was a luxury I'd miss the second I dropped her off.

"I think Sabrina was going to play the movie *Clueless* for Maddie when we left. I was about her age when I watched it, so it's more or less appropriate and should distract her for today."

"Em, nothing is going to distract either of us from missing you. Caden and Sabrina are trying, though. I'll give them that."

Emily nodded and drifted her gaze out the window.

"Hey." I squeezed her knee. "I'm sorry. I'm thrilled that you get to do this. Missing you is an us problem. I swear I'm not trying to make you feel bad."

"I know that. I already feel bad. I told her we had to head to the airport because her sad face made me want to cry."

"Oh, me too." I locked eyes with her as traffic started to inch forward. "We just love you. A lot."

"I love you both. A lot."

I smiled, reaching for her hand and bringing it to my lips. When my mouth touched something metal, I turned her wrist around.

"Remember this?" Emily twisted her wrist back and forth.

Out of the corner of my eye, I spotted a tiny soccer ball with black and white rhinestones. It was the bracelet I'd bought her for her sixteenth birthday. I'd given it to her at the small party I'd convinced my parents to have for her at their house.

"I figured it would be a perfect piece of jewelry to wear while helping to write a soccer legend's memoir."

"You kept this? You didn't donate it with the rest of my stuff?"

"I didn't donate *everything*. Yes, your hoodies were gifted to the local clothing drive when I got back from school the first year, but no matter how mad at you I was, I could never get rid of this. To this day, that was the best birthday I ever had. And it was all because of you."

"That was the first time I told you I loved you."

"Well, it was the first time I told you that I loved you, and you said it back. I was the jock, remember? We're aggressive."

I laughed, holding her hand as I steered toward the terminal with the other.

I plucked her suitcases out of the back of my truck and set them on the curb. I had about two minutes before I'd be honked at to keep moving, so I grabbed Emily and pulled her close for a deep but quick passionate kiss. It was intense enough for both of us to chase our breath once we broke apart.

"There is no such thing as too much texting or calling. FaceTime, phone calls. I don't care when or what time zones we're in. I always want to hear from you, okay?"

"You sound like you got it bad, Evans."

"I do." I took her face in my hands. "So, so bad, you have no fucking idea." I kissed her again until we both flinched at the blaring of horns behind us.

"I love you. Have a safe trip."

"I love you too," she said, cracking a smile as I spotted a lone tear trickling down her cheek. I stepped into my truck and watched her head through the automatic glass doors until I lost her inside.

I tried to reason away the ache from what felt like the same empty hole in my chest from twenty years ago. I wasn't losing her again. I hadn't thrown her out of my life and peeled away from her curb as fast as my tires could take me. When she came home, she'd be home.

I just had to figure out how not to lose it until then.

"Wait, which way am I supposed to hold this?"

I laughed as my mother tried to angle the phone the right way for a FaceTime call, giving me a scan of her room at the rehab facility she was staying in instead, followed by a wisp of white hair on the top of her head. The recovery from my mother's surgery had taken longer than we all had anticipated and her stay in rehab had been extended, but she was getting daily therapy and was still heading in the right direction. I hated that she'd been away from her home for so long while I'd been across the country, but Jesse and his family had made sure she had almost daily company since I'd left for California.

"This way," I heard Jesse tell her as her face finally came into view.

"I can never figure this out. Thanks, honey."

"Honey?" My brows shot up. "I know it's been a couple of months since I saw you in person, but when did this start?"

Mom scowled at me. "Jesse has been a good kid since

you've been gone. He comes to see me when he can and his parents still come by. I even have an extra visitor today."

"Hi, Emily!"

My heart swelled at the sight of Maddie leaning on my mother's shoulder to get her face on the screen. The three most important people in my life were on the other end of this phone call, and I had to swallow back the rush of emotion.

It was hard not to miss them so much and think of what Maddie was doing, how my mother was feeling, or what Jesse's headspace was like that day. I had no regrets about coming to California to take on this project, but the need to get home was weighing on me.

"Hey, Maddie. I miss you guys so much."

"We miss you too. Are you almost done?"

"Soon, I think. I'm having dinner with Raina at her house tonight to go over our progress. I should know more then."

"I never asked you what her house is like." my mother asked. "I bet it's a mansion."

"I wouldn't call it a mansion." I lay back on the soft cushion of the chaise longue in my hotel room. The room was more like a swanky apartment with plenty of room to work on my regular clients' manuscripts during my down-time at night and on the weekends. It was nice, but again, it wasn't home. And the more I stayed here, the more the walls felt like they were closing in on me.

"But it's nice. She has a big house on a lot of property and a huge pool."

Maddie's eyes grew wide. "She does? I wish our house had a pool."

I smiled when she pursed her lips at her uncle offscreen.

"I didn't get to swim in it, though. On nice days, we work

outside. March is a little warmer in California than it is in New York."

"I would think that someone like her would have a mansion." My mother huffed.

By working on this book with Raina, I had a glimpse into the world of professional sports they'd never told us about in college. Going pro was the ultimate goal and prize, why you had to give it your all plus a little more to get there. I'd never had regrets about tapping out, but I'd never truly known what being a professional athlete entailed until I'd learned about Raina's experiences off the field.

Female athletes weren't as revered as men were—or paid the same wage. While Raina had had a very successful career in professional soccer, and she'd stayed relevant through various organizations within women's sports and entrepreneurship—how she'd found me on Sharon's page—she'd given me a candid look at how she'd struggled compared to male athletes in the same sport.

I hadn't planned on being away for so long without a trip home, but the days were longer than I'd anticipated, and in order to keep the projects with my other clients on schedule, I had to work for half the weekend. I didn't want to make the long trip home, just for my loved ones to watch the back of my neck as I sat in front of a computer screen.

Raina's story was fascinating, but I was burning out and needed to speak to her about it tonight. If we still didn't have a time frame on when the book would be finished, I needed some time off to go home.

"I hope you're finding some time to rest. I don't like this working around the clock seven days a week for so long."

"I'm not a fan of it either, Mom. But it's over soon."

"I hope so," she said as she frowned at me. "You're too old to be working all hours without a break."

Jesse snickered off-camera.

"Please remind your *honey* over there that we are the same age."

"Actually"—Jesse's handsome face came into view—"your birthday is four months before mine. So I agree with Carmela. You're not so young." He winked and leaned back out of view.

"I better finish working so I can get ready for dinner later. I love you guys, and I'll see you soon."

"I love you too, cookie," Mom said as she wrapped her arm around Maddie. I loved watching them getting to know each other, and as tough as my mother was, I was sure she found ways to spoil Maddie when she'd come to visit. No matter where Mom stayed, either the hospital or rehab or back at her apartment, my mother always made sure to have treats on hand for potential visitors.

"Call me when you get back. I want to know what she says." Jesse's brow furrowed as he took the phone and stepped away from Mom and Maddie.

"It would be really late."

"And I couldn't care less. I fucking miss you, Em," he whispered into the phone, husky and low and causing a different kind of ache.

"I miss you too. I'm sorry this is taking up more of my time than I thought."

"It's okay. I just want you home. For a lot of reasons."

I laughed when his brows popped.

"Trust me, I want to be home for all those reasons. Until then, you finally got my mother to like you enough to call you pet names. Congratulations."

"Didn't take much. I come by and move things around wherever she tells me."

"So, she owns you now."

Jesse shook his head.

"*You* own me. I'll talk to you later."

He blew a quick and quiet kiss at the screen before disconnecting the call.

He owned me right back, and I feared what all this time apart was doing to us.

"EMILY, YOU'RE EARLY." RAINA SMILED AS SHE HELD HER front door open for me to step inside. The ceilings were so high, any shoes I wore clicked with an echo as I made my way down her hallway.

"I hope that's okay. I should have called you first, but I wanted to speak to you before Ashley arrived."

Ashley was Raina's personal assistant and kept notes on our progress, and while I liked her, I'd wanted to speak to Raina alone.

"Of course," she said. "We can chat in my living room until Ashley gets here." She motioned for me to follow, her fancy white flip-flops that probably cost more than one of my car payments shuffling on her shiny wooden floor. She was a stunning woman in her midfifties. Her shoulder-length black hair, dark eyes, and olive skin reminded me of one of my cousins. Thanks to my Irish/Scottish father, I burned more than I tanned and was always jealous of the sun-kissed glow most of my family enjoyed year-round.

Raina was classy and intelligent, but humble and down-to-earth. She hadn't pulled any punches in the stories she'd told me, and I hadn't picked up on a shred of arrogance despite her record-breaking stats—stats that *still* hadn't been broken—throughout her soccer career.

It was such an honor to work with her, but my mother

had been right. I was burning out and so homesick it seeped into my bones. I was trying to find a professional way to articulate that I wanted to cut my trip short because I missed my mother, boyfriend, and my boyfriend's niece terribly and just wanted to go home—or at the very least, be able to ask for a few days off.

"Anything wrong?"

"No. Well, not wrong. Depending on what we decide tonight, I'd like to have some time off. I'd planned to go home a weekend here and there, but between the hours we've been putting in, plus the manuscripts I'd already committed to working on, I haven't had the chance to step away. I know this is an open-ended type of assignment, but either way, I'd like to take a long weekend to go back to New York as soon as it's feasible."

Raina leaned back in her chair.

"Why didn't you bring this up before? I'm surprised you haven't asked for time off earlier."

"We were in the thick of everything, and I didn't want to go home when I'd have work to catch up on anyway and couldn't spend time with anyone."

A smile curved her lips. "Spending time with the people you love is important. We never really chatted about your personal life. The article mentioned that you were single, but I should have asked."

"It's fine. I've been immersed in your fascinating life story and didn't offer anything about my personal life."

"I see." She smiled. "So, there's someone special waiting for you to head back home?"

"There is."

She arched a brow. "They must be very special to make you smile like that. Have you been together for long?"

"He was my high school boyfriend. We broke up—well,

he broke up with me before I left to attend school in Maine. We reconnected at our high school reunion."

"You had one of those too," she said, a wistful smile playing on her lips.

"One of those?"

"I had a boyfriend I was madly in love with before I earned a soccer scholarship for college. Playing professionally had been my dream since I'd first kicked a soccer ball, so I'd been laser-focused on it since I was a kid. Boyfriends didn't factor into it. I broke up with him before I left, making sure I cut all ties so I wouldn't be tempted to change my mind."

"I'm guessing you never saw him again?"

Raina had gotten personal in her memoir, but the timeline started the first year she'd played pro. We hadn't included anything about her past before that, other than her being the daughter of immigrants and the first in her family to earn a college degree.

"I did. I ran into him one evening with his wife and children. Our hellos were more sad than awkward. It was strange. I'd written off any feelings I'd had back then as teenage infatuation, but it all came back again when I saw him. I think I felt a little spark from him too, but it was too late." Her gaze drifted outside to the beach and waves of the Pacific Ocean in the distance.

"I'm sorry."

She shrugged. "I'm glad he's happy with his family. Life happens how it happens. Even with all the struggles, I knew I was meant for this. Similar to how you figured out early on that you weren't."

"Makes sense." I relaxed at her warm smile.

"When Ashley gets here, we'll sort everything out for you to work remotely from now on. I can't promise I won't ask you to come back once or twice, but I don't see why you can't work on what we have from home."

I jerked back against the cushion. "Are you sure? I'm committed to this project and want to see it through—"

"You have." She reached over to pat my hand. "You've been wonderful. I've shared all I planned to, and now we just need to make it readable. I'm sure that's very doable via email, like how you handle your other clients. We'll discuss how to set everything up tonight, and you can head home this weekend."

"Thank you. As long as you're sure—"

I was cut off by the musical chime of the doorbell.

"It sounds like when you decided not to make soccer your career, you didn't waste any time with next steps. Don't do that now. It's a blessing to know what you want at the same time you're able to grab it."

I nodded as she made her way to the door.

I did know what I wanted. Not only was I going home to Jesse, I thought of a way to make it even better.

After our meeting, I headed back to the hotel and called Sabrina as soon as I shut the room door behind me.

"Hello?"

I glanced at my watch, forgetting once again that I was three hours behind her, but she sounded more breathless than sleepy.

"Hey, sorry to bother you this late. But I'm coming home."

"You are? When?"

"As soon as I can wrap things up here and get a flight to New York. And I had an idea for a surprise homecoming if you'll help me."

"I'd love to." I heard a loud thump, as if the phone dropped, followed by muffled whispers.

"Is someone there?"

"What? No?" Sabrina's shriek pierced my ears.

"I'd be so grossed out about what you're probably doing on my sheets if I weren't going to let you keep the apartment."

"You're letting me keep the apartment? Does that mean what I think it means?"

"She's letting you keep the apartment? Where is she going?"

I shut my eyes, covering my mouth to stifle a laugh as I recognized the low whisper.

"Tell Caden I'm coming home, and I'm going to need his help."

28

JESSE

"Will you perk up, for fuck's sake?"

I didn't look at Caden as I wiped the glitter off my kitchen counter. Maddie had made me an early birthday card and was so excited to give it to me, I had to accept that our kitchen would sparkle from every angle for a very long time since she'd managed to get glitter everywhere.

"I'm fine. I'm not sure why you all wanted to celebrate my birthday a week early, but I'm going along with it."

"Going along with it?" He lifted Maddie's masterpiece from where I'd hung it on the fridge. "Look at the effort your niece put into this."

I grabbed it from his hands and clipped it back on the fridge.

"I see the effort and the trail of glitter it leaves whenever it's touched. It's great and I love her for it, I'm just not into celebrating anything."

"I know. That's why we're all here trying to cheer your grumpy ass up."

I ignored him as I grabbed the hand vacuum and attempted to suck up the green and white sparkles along the floor. I hadn't heard from Emily other than short texts for the past couple of days. Despite my attempts to have a good attitude about my girlfriend on the opposite coast, it was wearing on me. Maybe she hadn't called because she had to be there longer and didn't know how to tell me. She had said it could be up to six months, so I had to find a way not to lose it after two.

I'd gone twenty years without Emily. I should've been able to handle a few months.

But I wasn't. At least, not well.

"Can't have a party without streamers," Sabrina said as she came into the living room. "Maddie, can you help me put these on the wall behind the couch?"

"Sure!" My niece paused the video game on the TV and popped off the floor.

"See how excited she is?" Caden whispered behind me. "Stop being an old grump and loosen up."

"Yeah, you have enough lines already." Sabrina pointed at my face.

"Have you heard from Emily?"

"Yeah, I think this morning. She's busy."

She shot a weird look to Caden as she twisted a streamer across the frames on the wall.

"What was that look for?"

"I didn't look at anything. I'm focused on decorations." Sabrina didn't look back at me as she spent entirely too much time attaching crepe paper to my wall.

Caden and Sabrina were up to something, but while I had my suspicions, I didn't have the energy to ask.

I turned to head back into the kitchen when my doorbell rang.

"Ah, that must be the cake," Caden said. "Could you get that? I have to help Sabrina."

"There are four people at this party. I don't think you need to put so much effort into streamers on a wall."

"Whatever is worth doing is worth doing right, Jesse," Sabrina said, glowering at me from my couch. "Wow, your uncle Jesse is really in his grumpy old man era this birthday."

I rolled my eyes and headed for the door, not in the mood for whatever silly cake Caden and Sabrina had ordered to pull me out of this funk. Underneath my nasty mood, I appreciated what they were trying to do and I knew they meant well, but I couldn't find it in me to fake having even a little fun.

If Emily and I had stayed together after high school, I probably would have spent four years clutching my phone, awaiting the next call or text, wondering what she was doing. I'd broken up with her to avoid becoming that pathetic and needy, but here I was all the same.

I peeked through my side window and couldn't tell who was there behind the bundle of balloons. My party planners were exhausting me with all this forced joy.

"Again, you do know that this party is just the four of us." I glanced back as I opened the door.

"Actually, there're five."

My jaw dropped when Emily pulled the balloons to the side and peeked her head through.

"Thank God," Caden said behind me. "I almost told you when it looked like you were about to cry into the glitter."

"Hold on a minute." I stepped outside and closed the door behind me, stalking toward Emily. *My God, she was gorgeous.* Wrapped up in a bubble coat and furry boots, a smile lifting her rosy cheeks, she was the most beautiful woman I'd ever seen.

"I thought I'd get a happier reaction than this after two

months." She propped her hands on her hips, backing up as I stepped closer until her back was to the railing.

I snaked an arm around her waist and yanked her closer, reaching under her coat to graze my hand over her glorious legging-covered ass and pinched her.

"Ouch, what was that for?"

"To make sure I wasn't dreaming." I let a smirk curl my lips as I sifted my hand into her hair.

"You're supposed to pinch *yourself*." She glared at me, her eyes dancing as they bored into mine.

"I'll remember that for next time." I leaned over to grab the balloons and set them in front of the window to block our view. "Now, give me that fucking mouth."

I crashed my lips against hers and kissed her, deep and wet and far too obscene for my front porch. Hopefully Caden and Sabrina would get the hint and distract Maddie from looking out the window, but despite the free show I was giving the neighbors, I wasn't ready to let Emily out of my arms yet.

Or ever again.

"Now that's better." She smiled, panting out white puffs of air as she chased her breath. "Happy early birthday."

"So, the three of you were in on this?"

"Four. I'm impressed Maddie didn't blab."

"That may be the one way she's not like her mother. My sister could've never kept a secret like this." I ran my thumb along her swollen lips. "How long do I have you for?"

She sank her teeth into her bottom lip as her eyes glossed over.

"Forever. If that's what you want."

"What...so, it's over?"

"Yes and no. I may have to go back for a couple of days at some point, but I'm working on the book remotely from now on. So, I'm back for good. And Sabrina really liked staying in my apartment, so I thought maybe I'd let her have it."

"Don't play with me, Em. Are you saying you want to—"

"Work out of the spare room, move my bookcases into your hallway, climb into bed with you every night for the rest of my life. Absolutely, yes," she breathed out. "If you'll still have me."

"If I'll— Are you kidding me?" I hauled her to me again, gripping the back of her head as I devoured her mouth, going in harder each time she'd try to pull back.

"I'm guessing that's a yes."

"I'll think about it and get back to you," I said, dipping my head to kiss her again when our heads whipped to knocking from the inside of my door.

"You know this is a family-friendly neighborhood," Caden called out from inside. "Don't get arrested on the first night Emily's back."

"I guess we have a birthday party to go to." I laced my fingers with hers and brought our joined hands to my mouth. "And I am suddenly in a very festive mood. You didn't cut anything short, right?"

"Why, are you sending me back?" She grinned, roping her arms around my neck.

"No way. I just... I never wanted you to miss out on anything because of me. I would have waited as long as I had to."

"I didn't want you to have to. I think both of us have waited long enough. But I need you to do something for me."

"I'd do anything for you."

A smile ghosted her mouth.

"Stop thinking I'm missing out on anything because of you. With you is the only place I've ever wanted to be."

"Then I want you to stop being afraid I'm going to take it all back again someday." I leaned my forehead against hers. "Since the moment we met, there hasn't been a second when you weren't all I've ever wanted."

A grin broke out on her face before she cuddled into my chest.

"So, we're good?"

"Better than good." I breathed out the biggest sigh of sweet relief. "We're finally home."

EPILOGUE

EMILY

Six months later

"TIME TO WAKE UP."

I squirmed out of Jesse's hold and shook his shoulder.

"It's early," he grumbled, pulling me back against his bare chest.

"We have a game, remember? And you're my new assistant, so we have to get there early to set up and check the kids in."

I pushed off the mattress and swung my legs over the side.

"Come on, Em. Five more minutes."

He wrapped his arms around me and pulled me back, burying his head into the crook of my neck.

"Jesse, you have to get up."

"But I am up," he rasped, pressing his hand against my stomach and pushing me flush to his body—and closer to the poke at my back.

"No more of that. That's why we went to bed too late when we had to be up early." I groaned into the pillow when he drifted his hand up my stomach and cupped my breast, tracing my now-rigid nipple with his thumb.

"I can't help it if the coach I'm working for is hot." He swiped the hair off my neck and dragged kisses over my nape. "I promise, I'm here to serve you. I'll be your good boy later if you'll be my good fucking girl now."

I fisted the sheets as he traced slow, torturous circles around my clit.

"Now, that's a *very* good girl. Spread a little more for me. That's it."

I whimpered as he slipped a finger inside, trying to watch the clock next to the bed as my boyfriend drove me out of my mind.

We'd moved in together right after I'd returned from California. I worked out of the spare room, loving the novelty of an office with a door, and lined the living room wall with new and old bookcases. Everything was so perfect, and it was hard to imagine a time I'd been terrified to move too fast with Jesse.

We'd all come a long way. Jesse had mostly reconciled with the grief he'd always have when it came to his sister, and Maddie was thriving, despite having the occasional sad day when we'd hit a new milestone without her mother. She'd grown almost a head taller since last season and couldn't wait to get back on the field.

I was excited too—if we ever made it there.

My mother adored Jesse now, and it was still so strange to watch. She hadn't even pushed marriage too much after we'd moved in together, other than the occasional comment on showing Maddie a good example "whenever you decide that's what you want."

I'd marry him in a heartbeat, but I would also be content

with just getting to keep him for the rest of my life. What we had transcended time and pieces of paper.

Jesse slid inside me with one thrust, moving back and forth in a slow rhythm before yanking me closer and picking up the pace, plowing into me so hard the mattress squeaked. He covered my mouth when I let go of a loud moan, muttering curses and dirty words of praise that almost made me forget my own name or where I had to be today.

"Come, baby. Let me feel you."

I buried my head into the pillow and let out a muffled whimper as my release crashed over me. Jesse grunted as he spilled into me, his breath slowing against my back as he gripped me tighter.

"I can help you in all sorts of ways, Coach Emily." He kissed my shoulder. "I told you. I'm here to serve you today."

I rolled over on my back and smoothed the hair off Jesse's damp forehead. I was about to bring him in for a kiss before we jumped at a knock on the door.

"Hey, I thought we had to get to the field early."

"She's like our own little alarm clock and stopwatch all at once," I whispered to Jesse.

"Just like her mother more and more every day." He groaned and stood from the bed. "I'll take a shower first. Alone, or we'll never go anywhere."

The game was the usual happy chaos. A handful of new kids who hadn't played soccer at all before had signed up this year. The other team seemed just as green, and the ball went everywhere but in a straight line to the goal for most of the game. We'd barely won, but the kids seemed too exhausted to care either way.

"This takes me back," my mother said. For some reason,

she'd insisted on coming to our first game and had arrived with Jesse's parents.

"I'm sure it does. You and Grandma and Grandpa came to every game."

"Of course we did." She gingerly stood from her folding chair. "You were our pride and joy."

"Grandpa died thinking I'd go pro." I shrugged as I packed up what I now called my coaching bag.

"They both died knowing you'd make them proud. And you have." My mother's eyes filled with tears as she clutched my biceps. I'd seen my mother cry exactly three times in my life. I'd been the sap, not her, so to hear her voice crack unnerved me.

I kissed her cheek. "Thanks, Mom."

"Looks like the start of another great season." Mr. Evans came up to me. "Which one of you is going to get my grand-daughter off the field?" He pointed to where Jeffrey and Maddie were practicing blocking and kicking goals on the mostly empty field with Candie and Mikayla.

"Hey, guys," I called out and blew my whistle. "Time to let the next team set up."

"Coach Emily, what was the longest goal you've ever kicked?" Jeffrey asked me as he came over to us.

"You know, I'm not sure. I think it was half a field length."

"Like that video we found?" Mikayla asked, her eyes lighting up.

"Maybe. I honestly don't remember."

"That's because it was a long time ago," Jesse said. "Coach Emily can't play like that anymore." He smirked at me as he shifted a soccer ball back and forth in his hands.

"Excuse me, I can still play if I want to."

"Do you think you could kick a goal from the other end

of the field?" Candie asked me, pointing to where the cones were still set up.

"Coach Emily is older," Jesse told her while smirking at me. "Probably not."

"Give me that ball," I said, snatching it out of Jesse's hands.

I stalked over to the end of the field, ignoring Jesse's snicker behind me. The kids stood at the sidelines, bouncing up and down as I set the ball in front of me.

"Wait. I'll play goalie." Jesse jogged to the front of the net. "Let's see what you got, Patterson."

"You better move out of the way, Evans." I tucked a loose hair behind my ear and focused on the ball. I'd made this shot a million times from a lot farther away, and even though I had been a lot younger the last time I'd done this, I wouldn't falter now as Jesse goaded me from across the field.

I took a running start and kicked, the ball shooting straight across the field and right into the net next to Jesse. He hadn't made a move to stop it as he watched me and laughed.

I reached my hands into the air and turned to the kids.

"I told you..." I trailed off when I noticed Maddie and two kids holding a large sign that read, "Please turn around." I swiveled my head and spotted Jesse, on one knee with what looked like a black box in his hand.

"What are you doing?" I asked, already too choked up to form any words as I made my way over to him.

"I knew you couldn't resist a challenge." He laughed and lifted his head. "I figured this was the best place to do it since I fell in love with you on a soccer field. I'd watch you run back and forth with so much grace and beauty, and I'd think, how the hel—heck is that my girl?"

I laughed when his gaze snapped to the kids behind me.

"Really, I fell in love with you on a high school classroom carpet when I was fourteen years old. I lost you for a little while…or a long while. But now that I have you back, I'm never letting you go. I've been yours for my entire life, and I want you to officially be mine. Emily." He opened the box, and I couldn't make out the ring through the blur of my tears. "Emily, will you marry me?"

"I mean, this is all so sudden." I coughed out a laugh through my tears and knelt on the fake grass in front of him to grab his face. "But yes. All I've ever wanted is to marry you."

I kissed him soft and slow, mindful of the little ears and eyes that were focused on us as he slid the ring on my finger.

I met Maddie's gaze as all the kids and parents cheered. I almost lost it when I spotted her wide smile, looking at Jesse and me with a mix of love and relief in her eyes. I could never replace Tessa, but I was thrilled to have the privilege of loving her as much as I'd loved her mother.

My eyes found my own mother. I laughed, now knowing the reason why she was here. She wasn't crying, but her eyes shone as they held mine. Jesse's mother was full-on sobbing against her husband's shoulder while trying to smile at us.

My heart was full, and my life, however unexpected, was complete.

"What do you want to do to celebrate, Mrs. Evans?"

I stood from the ground and held out a hand for my fiancé.

"Let's take our niece home."

BONUS EPILOGUE

Emily

Ten years later

"Glad to see the field improvements," Caden said, nodding in approval from where we sat in the stands.

"St. Kate's is still a big sports school. It's why out-of-town students like me traveled to attend. I would think keeping up with the facilities is still a top priority," I said, scanning the new turf and other upgrades I could spot as the girls' soccer team practiced along the edge of the field.

It had been a very long time since I'd been one of those girls, perfecting a kick or a move before a game, while trying not to think about who was watching me. Once the game started, adrenaline took over, and I never thought about who was or wasn't on the sidelines.

Other than Jesse, that is. My husband was always on my mind, even when my focus was elsewhere.

"Alumni donations help, I would think. Makes me feel

good that my contributions may have been put to good use." Caden grinned, resting his elbows on his knees.

"You donated?" I leaned forward to meet his gaze.

"Yeah. For Maddie's sake. Not that I gave thousands of dollars, but I hoped that maybe it would trickle to the girls' soccer team." He smiled and bumped my knee with his.

"You old softy." I bumped him back, searching the field for Maddie.

I found Maddie in the same corner to the right of the field I'd always practiced in, away from my team so I could nail some kind of shot or move. Her long brown ponytail bobbed behind her as she shifted the ball back and forth from one foot to the other. Most of the team was made up of tall, lean brunettes like she was, but I spotted the number twenty-three on the back of her jersey.

My old number when I was down on that grass.

"What did I miss?" Jesse said, sliding into the seat next to me.

"Just practicing." I pointed down to the field. "She's right in the corner." I smiled, noticing her furrowed brow as she lined up the ball.

"Ah, hovering in the corner to practice a move by herself, just like her aunt." Jesse looped his arm around my shoulders. "She even has the same pissed-off exhale." He chuckled, jutting his chin toward his niece as he handed me a water bottle.

"Where's my wife? Did she get lost on the way back?" Caden craned his neck to the concession stand behind us.

"Sabrina ran into someone she knew and said she'd meet us back here." Jesse snickered and shook his head. "So whipped."

"This is why I offered to go get us something to eat. She always runs into someone she knows and gets sidetracked."

I laughed at Caden's pursed lips. "I think he *is* a little whipped," I told Jesse in a loud whisper.

Caden and Sabrina had been together in the official sense since right before I'd moved in with Jesse. Caden had moved in with her into my old apartment right around the time Jesse and I were married, but they'd only been husband and wife for a couple of years.

They'd both insisted they were "just having fun" for a while, until it was obvious Caden had fallen hard. We'd felt bad for the poor guy as he'd waited for Sabrina to be on the same page. Her divorce had made her afraid to love anyone again, even a man she knew as well as Caden. Once he'd finally convinced her to take the leap, they'd become equally obsessed with each other.

They both deserved nothing less.

"I'm here, I'm here," Sabrina said, shaking her head at Caden as she took the seat next to him. "Here is your soft pretzel. Sorry I took more than five minutes."

"Thank you. These two think I'm whipped, and I tend to agree."

She stuffed a piece of pretzel into his mouth when he leaned closer, and she pressed a kiss to his cheek.

"Even with the renovations, our place under the bleachers is intact, babe," Sabrina mused as her gaze drifted toward the field.

My head whipped to Sabrina. "You had sex under the bleachers?" I whispered.

Caden and Sabrina glared at me as if I'd sprouted a second head.

"You didn't? Big soccer star with a longtime boyfriend." Sabrina's mouth twisted. "You really did miss out on a lot in high school."

I cut a look to Jesse, shaking his head as he rubbed his eyes.

"We didn't miss out on anything." He yanked me closer and brushed his lips against my cheek. "Sex in public was never possible for us since you tend to be a screamer."

I jabbed his shoulder, my cheeks heating at my husband's words and the wicked gleam in his eyes. We'd been married for almost ten years, and he always gave me that rush of butterflies when he looked at me like that. He was still gorgeous, even more so with the sparkle of gray at his temples and dotting his stubble. But he'd always be the boy I'd fallen in love with when I was fourteen.

"So, what happens when they win today?" Sabrina asked as the ref blew the whistle for the girls to line up.

"They go on to the play-offs," I answered as I kept my eye on Maddie. "Then we travel all over the place until they win state."

"Until, not if, huh?" Caden teased.

"This is the best team St. Kate's has had in five years. They're almost undefeated. They've got this," I said, a familiar stirring in my gut as the girls chased the ball. I still coached the rec league, but the urge to get on the field and play wasn't as intense as it was here.

Maddie loved soccer much more than I had at her age, for the simple fact that she was able to choose to do it. She'd played every year in the rec league until she'd aged out and then had played all through middle and high school. Her high school coach had told me she was in serious contention for a full scholarship, according to a few of the scouts who had come to the games during her junior year, and as fate seemed to be following our family, she'd earned a full ride to the same university I'd attended in Maine.

For our niece, the scholarship was a wonderful prize, not

a lifeline as it had been for me. We'd already prepared to finance whatever she wanted to do, wherever she wanted to go, and she chose her school freely without pressure or reservations.

Looking back, I had no regrets about the path I'd taken, regardless of how I'd gotten there. Playing soccer had given me wonderful friends and had helped me create amazing memories—and led me to Maddie and back to Jesse.

We might not have had any biological children together, but Maddie was ours in every way that mattered.

As the game progressed, I had the same nauseous wave in the pit of my stomach. St. Kate's was great, but the problem with any play-off or almost-play-off game was that the other team was just as good and harder to beat. Once the score was tied, we all didn't speak or move for fifteen minutes, other than gasps and muttered curses when the other team had the ball.

"Do you feel like you want to throw up too?" Jesse whispered. "Shit, I remember getting queasy watching you in play-off games, but not like this."

"You're getting old, Evans." I smiled and rubbed his back, laughing at his sexy scowl.

"I'll show you old later."

Our heads snapped to the field at the sound of a whistle, but it was only a time-out.

"It's because it's our kid down there. And she really wants this. That's why we're both a little sick."

Jesse nodded back at me with a wistful smile.

"I guess you're right."

I lost Maddie for a moment when the ball started moving again, but I found her as she moved it down the field, racing toward the goal. I could see the opening for the shot and clasped my hands under my chin so tightly my nails pierced my knuckles, wishing I could communicate it to her with my mind like a Jedi to make her see it.

I'd found that athletes were always superstitious and, if they believed in God, were at their most religious before and during a game. At moments like this, I used to pray to Jesus, my grandparents, and whatever saints I could think of to push me forward so I could land that ball in the net. I recited all those same prayers in my head, along with one extra.

Come on, Tessa. Push her through.

Once the ball sailed into the air, I grabbed Jesse's hand. I felt the ball go right into the net before it made contact and the whistle blew.

Caden and Sabrina were up on their feet as Jesse and I slumped with elated relief.

"I think you're right. My heart can't take this at my age," Jesse breathed out, clutching his chest. "I don't know how I'm going to handle college games or if she ever goes pro."

I nodded, watching the girls pile up onto one another in celebration. My eyes blurred when I met Maddie's gaze, her wisps of hair falling over her face as she smiled and pointed at me.

"Look, she sees us." My voice squeaked as I tapped Jesse's shoulder and jutted my chin toward the field.

"No, Em. She sees *you.*" He roped his arm around my shoulders and yanked me closer. "She just said, 'This is for you.'"

Maddie

Next fall

I eyed my uncle as he ambled around my dorm room, studying every corner and crevice before peering out the window as if he was looking for something.

"Uncle Jesse, what are you doing?" I asked as I glanced over his shoulder to the quad outside.

He craned his neck to me, his lips curving in a sheepish grin.

"I always wondered what this place was like when Emily went here."

"Because you broke up with her before she left."

He lifted a brow.

"I didn't realize you knew that."

"Well, I knew you broke up after high school." I lifted my ponytail off my sweaty neck. "Carmela filled in the rest."

"Of course she did." He dropped his chin to his chest. "I wondered about your aunt's life here. Like, what the field she played on looked like, what asshole jocks would hit on her." His mouth curled into a smirk when he turned around. "I'm more or less doing the same thing now, only it's about you."

I laughed and brought him in for a hug.

"You can see it all now and not have to worry so much about that last thing." I patted his cheek. "But maybe you both should get going. It's a long drive back."

"We booked an Airbnb halfway home. Not that long of a drive back. Throwing us out already?" Uncle Jesse dipped his head to meet my gaze. I was taller than Aunt Emily but came up to my uncle's nose. My mother's height, my grand-mother had said.

It was one of those things about her that became fuzzy with time. I had always been tall, but Mom had still towered over me until she couldn't stand anymore. I had no real idea of her adult height, but I'd caught plenty of spooky glimpses of her when I'd look in the mirror and make a certain face as I applied my makeup.

We were still twins, like Mom used to joke. She snuck into my thoughts almost every day, and for some reason, she was heavier on my mind today. Maybe because when my aunt and uncle left, I'd be on my own. I kept worrying if I'd let any of them down.

"We are so damn proud of you." He cupped my cheek. "And I know your mother is too."

"Thanks," I said, dropping my gaze to the beige carpet. "I've been thinking of her a lot today, and I'm not sure why."

"I am too. She was always so worried about giving you everything you wanted, so she worked her ass off to give both of you a good life. I hate that she didn't have the chance to enjoy it."

"Me too. I remember our apartment." I lifted my head. "And how cool it was when you'd sleep on the couch."

"I thought that was cool too." He smiled. "She was always so worried about you not knowing your father, but while she had the chance, she was awesome at both jobs. She'd get a kick out of you going to the same school as Emily." He raised his eyes to the ceiling. "She probably had a hand in that too."

"I'm sure." I nodded and kissed his stubbled cheek. "And I do have a father. The best father anyone could ever ask for. I'll do my best to make you proud while I'm here."

His eyes went glossy as his jaw quivered.

"Stop that," he whispered, pulling me into his chest. "You've made me proud every single day of your life. All I want is for you to be happy. And if you decide one day that you're not, I'll come right up here and bring you home." He angled me back, narrowing his eyes. "Understand?"

"What's going on? Why is everyone so weepy?" my aunt

joked as she padded over to us. "I wanted to see if the dorms were still the same, and they are, mostly. What I'm really excited about is your first game." She slid her arm around Uncle Jesse's waist. "It's going to be weird to see your uncle in the stands, after I used to picture him there all the time."

"You did?" I laughed and wiped my cheek with the back of my hand.

"I was sentimental." Her lips pursed at Uncle Jesse. "Even if I thought he was a big jerk."

"You both can have the whole experience now." I took in a shaky breath as I looked between them. They were the parents I'd never expected but the best ones I could've ever asked for after I'd lost Mom. More tears clouded my eyes as I dropped my head back onto my uncle's chest and reached for my aunt. I hadn't thought I'd cry today, but once I got choked up, I couldn't stop. This was exactly what I'd worked for, yet all I wanted to do now was go home. I had an early case of homesickness, and it would wear off.

I hoped.

"You're going to be fine." My aunt squeezed my shoulder. "After a day or two, you'll hardly miss us."

"Your aunt is trying to make me cry now instead, I guess," Uncle Jesse joked, swiping the back of his hand over his cheek to hide the tears I'd already noticed.

"I'm close to crying too, so we are going to go." Aunt Emily grabbed my hands, her voice cracking despite her wide grin. "I love you very much, and I'm so proud of you. Enjoy this. We are a text or phone call away if you need us."

I nodded as we all eased apart. I'd never forget my mother, but Aunt Emily was my idol and everything I'd ever wanted to be. Knowing she'd gone to this school and played on the very same soccer team gave me a smidge of comfort, like she'd be doing it all with me.

Each of them gave me one more hug and kiss goodbye as they headed out.

I trudged into the bathroom. My roommate wouldn't be here until tomorrow, so it was wise to get all the tears out now and not be an emotional weirdo when we met.

I slapped my hand down on the sink and glared at my reflection.

"You're Madison fucking Evans. Act like it."

I laughed, sliding the hair tie out of my hair, and sifted my hands through my tangles. I was about to unpack when my phone buzzed on my table.

J: *Guess who is here early?*

Me: *Where are you?*

J: *I just ran into your aunt and uncle, so I'm guessing I'm right outside your dorm.*

I grabbed my purse and key and ran downstairs, wiping my red eyes as I made my way outside.

"There she is!"

A smile bloomed across my face as I sprinted toward him, almost knocking him over when I jumped into his arms.

"Damn, you missed me that much." He chuckled and spun me around. "Wait, what's wrong?" He set me down and took my face into his hands. "Why do you look so upset?"

"It was hard to see my aunt and uncle leave. I'm a big baby today. A big, scared baby."

He quirked a blond brow, his blue eyes calming me and thrilling me like always.

"It's a little scary. But kind of exciting," he whispered,

pulling me closer. "I already met some of the guys on the team. Once you meet your teammates, I think you'll calm down a little." He dug a hand into my hair. "Until then, I can hold you like this without your uncle staring me down all the time."

"He doesn't stare you down." I rolled my eyes. "Dramatic much?"

"That is because you're not on the other end of his death glare. I never thought Mr. Evans could be so scary when we were kids."

"I guess you didn't give him a reason back then."

He glanced behind him. "Think they're out of the parking lot yet? Can I kiss you?"

"You can always kiss me. So, just do it already."

He shot me a crooked grin that I felt all the way to my toes, and he cupped my neck.

"Jeff!"

Our heads whipped around to a tall, ginger-haired boy bouncing a soccer ball on his knees.

"I guess this is your girl. I was going to ask if you wanted to head to the field and play for a bit."

"I'd love to," I said, smiling at the vibration of the groan from Jeff's chest against my palm.

"Oh, you play?"

"A little," I said, sneaking a smirk to Jeff.

"She's a superstar here on a full soccer scholarship. Be warned." Jeff pursed his lips as he peered down at me. "I'm saving you from being hustled by my beautiful girlfriend."

"I'm Liam," the boy said, chuckling as he stretched out his hand. "So we all know how to play. Let's take advantage of a mostly wide-open field."

"I'm Maddie. Nice to meet you." I followed Liam after I dropped his hand. "Ready?" I asked Jeff.

He pressed his lips to mine, closemouthed and quick, but hard enough to steal a little air from my lungs.

"I had no idea I was creating a monster when I asked you to play soccer with me when we were kids." He ran his thumb up and down along my jaw. "They're really never going to see you coming."

My mother had always said to believe in your worth enough to show it.

I'd celebrate her short life by making the most of mine.

AUTHOR'S NOTE

Story inspiration comes from many different places. This one came from a TikTok comment.

I wanted to write an emotional second chance romance that spanned over many years. I love writing all the history, the longing, and the idea of the one that got away. I don't remember the exact video, but the comment was "I just married my high school sweetheart after 30 years apart" and I was like bingo! That's what I want to do.

Second Time's the Charm wound up to be a lot more than that. It was about second chances, love of family and friends, and how the choices we make lead us to the life we're meant to have. Jesse and Emily had a soul-searing love that never truly went away, and I loved writing their journey back to each other.

I also had a hardworking single mother and grandparents who I still think of every day, wondering if I made them proud. It truly does take a village, and everyone who helped to raise me is still a part of me today.

I hope you loved this story as much as I loved writing it.

Much love,
Steph

ACKNOWLEDGMENTS

For once in my life, I'll try to keep this short.

For my husband and son, thank you for being my biggest fans even if I get cranky at the end of each manuscript. I love you both more than you'll ever know.

To my beta readers, Jodi, Lauren, Rachel, and Michelle, thank you for helping me make this a story I'm proud of and dealing with all my whining as you guided me through.

To Najla Qamber and her amazing team, thank you for a gorgeous and perfect cover. Your creative genius blows me away every time.

To my editor Lisa, thank you for polishing my books to make them the best they could be and making me laugh in the comments. One day I'll get tenses right the first time.

To Jodi, thank you for being my found family and all you do for me. I couldn't do this author life without you.

To my That's What She Said Publishing family. Thank you for all your support and all you've made possible.

To the Rose Garden, thank you for all your love and support and making this job so much fun.

To Lona, thank you for all the amazing reels of my books.

To Kathryn Nolan and LJ Evans, thank you for being the best hype friends and the use of each of your names in this story, and pushing me to never give up in the hardest moments.

To my readers, of all the books out there, thank you for choosing mine and sticking by me with every release. I'm blessed to be able to do this for a living and meet amazing people along the way.

ABOUT THE AUTHOR

Stephanie Rose is a badass New Yorker, a wife, a mother, a former blogger and lover of all things chocolate. Most days you'll find her trying to avoid standing on discarded LEGO or deciding which book to read next. Her debut novel, Always You, released in 2015 and since then she's written several more—some of which will never see completion—and has ideas for hundreds to come.

Stay in touch!
Join Stephanie's Rose Garden on Facebook and sign up for Stephanie Rose's newsletter at www. authorstephanierose.com

BOOKS BY STEPHANIE

Second Chances
Always You
Only You
After You
Always Us, A Second Chances Novella

Second Chances Spinoffs
Finding Me
Think Twice

Never Too Late
Rewrite
Simmer
Pining

Ocean Cove
No Vacancy
No Reservations

Kelly Lakes